BOSS LADY

Leanna,

Happy reading,

Sincerely,

Dorothy Mara

8/15/0

BOSS LADY

Dorothy O'Malia

3367-SHAW

To order additional copies of this book, contact:
Xlibris Corporation
1-888-7-XLIBRIS
www.Xlibris.com
Orders@Xlibris.com

CONTENTS

OTHER BOOKS AND PLAYS
BY DOROTHY O'MALIA

Books
- The Golden Key to Astrology
  - A complete guide on Astrology
- Lives I Have Lived
  - An experience in Reincarnation

Historical Fiction Novels
- Billings
  - and it's sequel
- Peggy
- Boss Lady
  - and it's sequel
- Petticoat Sailors
- Flight of the Golden Eagle
- Robin
- Clifton House
- Dorsey, The Honorable Lady from Colorado

Plays
- The General was a Bartender
- David—A story of Pope Jone
- Central City
- Speakeasy
- Corrigenda

Dorothy is now writing another historical novel set in the time of William the Conqueror.

ABOUT THE AUTHOR

Dorothy O'Malia was born in Silesia, Montana. She attended the Clifton Hughes School for Girls in Denver, Colorado.

She started her career working in the advertising department of the *Denver Post* and the *Rocky Mountain News*. She later studied business administration and held management positions in various hotels and country clubs in New Mexico and Montana. Later Dorothy moved to Sacramento where she owned a small hotel.

Dorothy became fascinated with astrology. She studied and practiced the Ancient Chinese Taoism Astrology. She was a long time member of the news staff of the National Broadcasting Company and American Broadcasting Company, Sacramento, California and conducted a daily astrology program on radio station KCRA. She has appeared on talk shows on the Columbia Broadcasting System radio station KFBK and made television appearances in which she discussed reincarnation and astrology.

Dorothy now divides her time between astrology and writing her novels.

BOSS LADY

Anne didn't want to think of the future. She didn't want to think of the nothingness that faced her. She attached her attention to a small thrush, looking up at her on the park bench. Standing there in front of her, unafraid, he looked first to the right and then to the left of this inanimate human that was no threat and hastily snatched at his unsuspecting prey, a nice fat worm making his way through the grass that did not quite hide him.

Children ran noisily through the park, disturbing Anne's from her benumbed state. She sighed and picked up her shoes, she couldn't get them on.

"These shoes were not made from walking," she said aloud.

"Did you say something. Ma'm?" A small boy who had lagged behind the others asked.

She looked at her watch, four o'clock, and said to the lad, "I'll give you a dollar to find me a taxi, would you do that?"

"Yes Ma'm I'll be right back." He ran off and in no time he was back, "there's your cab, lady," he said pointing to a taxi waiting at the curb.

She thanked him, gave him his dollar and walked to the taxi in her stocking feet.

The taxi stopped in front of an old mansion that had been converted into apartments to accommodate wartime housing. She entered the hallway and opened the apartment to the left on the ground floor. She looked around. Only this morning she had happily left here to go to work, her life in order . . . then on this day, May 16, 1944, it had all coming crashing down!

What a way to end what was to have been 'till death do us part'! There was nothing she could do about it. He wasn't here to shout at or to throw something at him! She still felt his presence in this cozy place they had thought of as home, how, in a few short hours could life have gone from these rooms, she asked herself as she dropped her shoes and purse on the floor and sank into the huge armchair they had so often shared and wrapped herself in her memories.

Just that morning she had carefully dressed herself in her newly tailored natural linen suit and went to work at the Hilton Hotel where she was bookkeeper and cashiered in the coffee shop during lunch.

After lunch Anne waited at the entrance of the Coffee Room for Mrs. Nation, an elderly resident of the hotel to come down for her noonday meal, before locking the door.

Jim, the head desk clerk at the El Paso Hilton, approached her with a letter in his hand, "this came for you in the hotel mail, Anne, "he said handing her the letter.

"Thanks Jim", she said glancing at the APO return address and wondered why Bill had sent the letter to the hotel instead of the apartment.

Her thoughts were cut off when she saw Mr. Hilton, tall, suave gray haired gentleman who owned the hotel, escorting Mrs. Nations toward the Coffee Room and slipped the letter in her pocket.

Mrs. Nations was a frail lady way past ninety years. She wore a long black faille gown, princess cut, styled of the 1890's. Nestled in the center of her snow white, upswept hair was a pert little black hat. She carried her cane in a courtly manner, rather then as a tool of necessity.

Anne held the door for them and Mr. Hilton seated Mrs. Nations in her favorite place, a small linen covered table just behind the grille that separated the cashier from the dining area.

Since Mrs. Nations tipped only a dime, waitresses resented having to stay over and wait on her. Anne, having to be there, to check out the Coffee/Grille Room receipts solved the problem by offering to wait on the lady, as she had to be there, and thus avoid the daily hassles

Anne had suggested Mrs. Nations call her order down before she left her suite and Anne had everything ready for her, including her pot of green tea, which the lady thought warmed her stomach before she ate.

Anne brought Mrs. Nations tea and asked if Mr. Hilton cared for something.

"No thank you," he told her, "I'll just chat with this lady for awhile."

Anne went back to her work. She still had guest charges to get to the front desk before checkout. She finished posting the signed checks and as Mr. Hilton rose, from his chair and bid Mrs. Nations a good day, he collided with Anne as she came from behind her desk. The checks she held in her hand went flying over the floor!

"Oh . . . I'm sorry," she said," "I guess I wasn't looking."

"Neither was I," he laughed as he bent down to help her pick up the checks.

"I know you're on loan from accounting, but what else do you do besides this and that and waiting on tables?"

"I just wait on Mrs. Nations. She's too old to fight the crowds down here at mealtime and I have to be here anyway."

"How long have you been with us?"

"Almost since the beginning of the war, when my husband went to France I decided to stay here. I love working around so many kinds of people "

"Is it the people or the business?"

"Well, I suppose it has to be both, where else would there be the coming and the going . . . of all sorts of people?" They had gathered the checks and Mr. Hilton reached for them, "I'll take them out to the cashier."

"Why thank you, Mr. Hilton," she said in surprise.

At the door he turned around, "by the way, what's your name? Your full name?"

"Anne . . . Anne Courtney."

Anne finished her work, called the bellman to assist Mrs. Nations to her suite and locked the door. She picked up the dishes from Mrs. Nations table, stripped the table and took the dishes and cloth to the kitchen.

She came back for the cash box, receipts envelope and her purse. In the back office behind the key rack, she opened a safe **deposit box** and placed the cash box inside. She slid the receipts envelope into the slot of another safe deposit box.

There was a letter opener lying on the work desk and she sat down, took her letter from her pocket and slit the envelope!

> Anne
>
> I won't be coming back. You asked me once why I married you. I honestly told you, I loved you. What I didn't say, was that I loved you because you were always so good to me. Now I have found that other love . . . that real love we all seek, so I'm staying in France when this war is over. Your allotment check **will** continue until I'm discharged then you can get a divorce.
>
> As ever,
> Bill

Anne sat stunned. Her mind a blank. This couldn't be true; it had to be a bad dream! She looked around her and automatically folded the letter and put it in her purse. Slowly she rose from her chair, the world was moving in slow motion. She sat down again.

Jim came back and poured himself a cup of coffee from the pot that was kept on a warmer in the back office.

"Through for the day, Anne?"

She didn't answer, just gripped the desk to stop this disembodied feeling.

"Are you alright, Anne? You're a little green around the gills," he laughed, "something you ate?"

"I don't feel so good, Jim. Will you call Lynn and tell her I've gone home?"

"Sure, you have to be careful what you eat in this heat."

Anne left the hotel. Outside she faced the distorted heat of the west Texas sun in a daze. She stood on the steps facing the Plaza Park and was completely disoriented.

She watched the Plaza floating in the sunshine. Nothing was real. In every direction objects, people, buildings shimmered in a macabre frenzy. Something inside her told her move . . . move . . . move don't stand here like a zombie, move. She stepped onto the sidewalk and turned to the right and walked away from the hotel.

Anne walked and walked and walked, not knowing where, nor caring. Exhausted and confused she saw a park ahead. There was a bench under a pine tree, the Indians called it the healing tree and she could well use it's healing properties to cure this ache, this insular hurt. Could this be part of loving? All she had ever known of love was the glory and sacredness, not this turbulence of rejection.

Her feet hurt, she took off her high-heeled shoes and walked across the cooling grass to the bench where she could rest her aching feet. She sat for a long time trying to deny the significance of that letter. She took it from her purse and read it again wanting to find one word that would that would belie it's content. One word that would give her a sign, a hope that he would be back. Yet knowing he was gone from her just as though he had been a casualty.

This heartache . . . this was hers and she realized this was a turn in her life, a place from which she had to start over and she would have to work it out herself . . . alone. It was getting dark outside, she looked around the room, she had left his things as he had left them. The book he was reading . . . his pipe . . . she rose from their chair and took her shower. As the hot water ran over her shoulders the tears came, first slowly and then the racking sobs, great shuddering sobs. She came from the shower, wrapped herself in Bill's big woolly robe still steeped in his smell, with letter in hand she cried herself to sleep.

The following morning Anne woke with the tear stained letter still clutched in her hand. Having cried herself out she applied icy cloths to her swollen face and wondered what she should do next. Go back to Denver where she and Bill had worked on the Denver Post before he was called to the service or go back to the hotel and let every day take care of itself.

Automatically she dressed, drank coffee and went to work. All that was left to her now.

When she arrived at the office, for she still had duties in accounting, her usual cheerfulness was missing. She found a note on her desk to report to Mr. Williford, the manager of the hotel immediately she came in.

She put her purse away, checked her appearance and satisfied with the pink shantung suit she wore, she went to Mr. Williford's office.

"Go right in, Anne, Mr. Williford is expecting you," Betty, Mr. Williford's secretary told her.

She opened his door. Mr. Williford sat behind an enormous mahogany desk, but then he was a big man, like a football player. He was good natured and handsome even with his receding hairline. He was well liked by all the employees and he gave Anne an easy smile when she came in.

"Good morning, Mr. Williford, you wanted to see me?"

"Good morning, Anne. Come in and sit down, we need to talk," he motioned her to a chair in front of his desk, "what did you do to impress Mr. Hilton yesterday?"

"I think I was the one who was impressed, Mr. Williford."

"Suppose you tell me what happened."

She told him about dropping the checks and Mr. Hilton helping her pick them up, then taking them to the front desk for her "I'm sure there's nothing impressive about dropping checks all over the floor."

"There must have been something else."

"I can't imagine what it could have been. Everything else was as usual. Why do you ask?"

Mr. Williford picked up a memo, "I received this memo from Mr. Hilton," he held up a scrap of paper." It says here, that you are to be taught the hotel business. Now that's a big order, Anne and women never get the top jobs, you have to own the hotel for that, if that's what you're looking for."

"I've never even given it a thought, Mr. Williford."

Mr. Hilton asked me if I liked this business and I'll tell you as I told him, Yes . . . yes what I've seen of this business, I like it very much."

Mr. Williford sighed and looked at the memo again, then he said thoughtfully, "you know, the best you could hope for would be a job like Lynn's, comptroller. From where you are now, that would take some time, you also have to be a CPA to be comptroller. Mr. Hilton refers to 'hotel business', that to me means management. What you would ever do with that, I don't know, I can't even imagine." He shook his head as if to clear it. Then glancing up at Anne, he asked, "you want to make a try for it?"

Anne sat stunned. At this moment, when she so desperately needed something, anything to keep her sanity after having lost all that meant anything to her. Surely God had not deserted her. Perhaps it would go nowhere, but for now, this would be her lifesaver.

"Mr. Williford, I don't know what happened yesterday that Mr. Hilton was kind enough to offer me this opportunity, but I will take advantage of it. I will do the very best I can. If this is to be my future, I can't think of a better umbrella to learn under, then the Hilton Hotel."

"Very well, but let me give you some facts about this business. It's a twenty four-hour a day job. You come down to the office at seven, hopefully have breakfast and read the paper without interruption. Then you go over last night's occupancy and what disturbance did we have the staff felt it was not worth calling me about and then find the visiting football team tore their rooms apart. At nine you go to accounting, go over the transcript and study the analysis the night auditor left, hoping there's been an increase in revenue."

Mr. Williford looked sharply at Anne' was she taking all this in, "do you understand what I'm talking about?"

"Perfectly,"

"You check all the departments. Listen to all the complaints. You may have some of your own, like where's the waste coming from? Why is the cost running so high? You check the front desk again to see how reservations are shaping up for the day and catch that football coach before the team checks out to be sure that last night's damages are paid."

"Just about the time you think you can get away to have lunch with a friend, there's a call from Dallas, Mr. Big Shot is flying in at noon and you have to be at the airport to shake his hand and convey him to the Hotel. Then that lovely couple, from Fort Worth, that take the third floor suite once a month, today her husband's waiting. God, those Colt .45's are messy" Mr. Williford shuddered.

"Your personal life is nonexistent," he continued, "hotel management is an all involving and transitory way of life, it's broken up more then one marriage, are you willing to live like that?"

"I don't think any of those things would concern me until I'm a manager. You don't seem to have much hope of that in the near future. Anyway, I don't have a private life," she murmured, looking at her folded hands on her lap.

"I thought you were married?"

"That was yesterday," Anne struggled to keep her voice from trembling, she opened her mouth and to took a deep breath to keep the tears from flowing.

"Did you get a telegram, Anne?"

"No . . . no, it was a letter, but I've heard there will be room for women in business once this war is over. Maybe the hotel business will give me that chance. So no matter how dark you paint the picture, it will give me something."

"Yes, I see," he looked at her thoughtfully, "so this comes at a most propitious time I take it?"

"I believe so . . ."

"Yes, well let me see," he rummaged around on his desk as though looking for something while Anne, with deep breaths pulled herself together.

"What say we start you out in Albuquerque? "

"That would be fine."

"It's Friday, can you be in Albuquerque on Monday? A change of scene is always good in cases like this."

"I'll be there."

"Report to Mr. Fletcher, you'll learn the front of the house there. There's a lot of moving around in this business, so learn to travel light."

She rose to leave, at the door, Mr. Williford called to her," this is your chance, Anne. See what you can do with it."

Anne went home, she had a weekend to separate what had been theirs, to His and Hers. She took the books and her clothes, sold the furniture and household items to the landlord, packed Bill's things, along with miscellaneous, in a big trunk and sent them to his sister in California.

Anne arrived in Albuquerque Monday afternoon. She walked into the high beamed lobby with an open mezzanine, carved wooden pillars supported arches all along the sides of a long lobby, with a bank of elevators at the far end.

She went to the desk, identified herself and registered. She was assigned a room and after refreshing herself she sought out Mr. Fletcher.

She started by learning the layout of the floors. She learned the front desk, checking in and checking out. She learned the transcript; a compilation of the day's business and the cashier's duties, posting on a Burrough's posting machine.

Anne kept herself busy around the clock dropping into bed exhausted at whatever hour she finished with whatever duties she was doing, all too often more then what was required of her. She began to believe she was more a troubleshooter, filling in wherever someone was missing.

After three months in ALBUQUERQUE Anne was to return to El Paso. Mr. Nelson, Food and beverage manager would teach her Food and Beverage service and control.

The night before she was to leave, the night clerk came down with a cold and she was asked to stay over and cover his shift.

It was early morning, nearing three o'clock when Mr. Lewis arrived. His reservation had been canceled as a non-arrival and there had not been any communication as to a late arrival. The man who came to the desk looked dead on his feet.

"I hope you've kept my reservation for me, I've been unable to let you know I'd be late" he told Anne.

Anne hesitated to tell him his room had been sold and she also remembered a Major on the fourth floor with a suite. While his numerous calls for service had come from room 420, nothing had come from 421 . . . maybe, he didn't know he had a suite. She rang room 420.

"This is the desk clerk, Sir. Are you using your living room?"

"I have a living room?" he asked sleepily.

"Oh. Oh . . . I'm sorry, I rang the wrong room," she hastily apologized; thinking if he didn't know he had a suite . . .

"You're forgiven, honey. One room is all I need, but don't ring anyone else at this ungodly hour," he said softly, then yelled, "it's three o'clock in the morning"

Anne jumped back from the phone as though she had been bitten. She looked at the instrument in horror!

"What's the matter", Mr. Lewis asked anxiously.

"I just found your room," she answered him, dazed.

"You expect me to sleep in whatever you found?"

"Oh, it's perfectly alright, I'll send the bellman up with you" she pushed the registration holder to him and took the key for 421 from the rack.

Ann rang for the bellman.

No bellman!

"Would you like to take a seat over there in that nice comfortable couch and relax while I find the bellman. You do look all in."

"Tell you what let's do, give me the key and I'll brave the wilds of the upper floors."

She handed him the key," are you sure you'll be able to find it?" He had given his address as Los Alomas and said, "Lady, what I've been through in the last twenty four hours, nothing could get worst."

Mr. Lewis took one of the elevators at the end of the lobby.

It was but a few minutes before the switchboard operator rang her. She picked up the phone," may I help you?"

"I found the room, I got in without any trouble. Where's the bed?" Mr. Lewis inquired.

"The bed . . . the bed, oh dear . . . the bed? Have you looked in the closet, Mr. Lewis? You know, like a Murphy."

He hung up without a word.

Anne turned to the switchboard operator, "the extra beds, in the parlor suites, they are Murphy's, aren't they?"

The night auditor was just coming through from the kitchen where he had gone for coffee and a piece of pie, and said," some times they're Murphy's, then again they could be in a chair, or a sofa or even in the wall."

The phone rang.

"No Murphy, no rollaway. The closet is empty."

"Have you tried the chair, Mr. Lewis?"

Anne was becoming quite agitated where the hell was that bellman?

"Listen, lady, I'm not paying to sleep in a chair!"

"Oh no . . . no, that's not what I meant. Some times a chair makes into a bed."

"You don't say. Hold on."

". . . find that damn bellman for me," she told the switchboard operator, then, "what did you say, Mr. Lewis?"

"What's your next best guess?"

"I'm looking for the bellman . . ."

"How can you be looking for the bellman when you're talking to me?"

"Via electronic communication, the Bell system."

"What's the matter with smoke signals?"

The bellman came from the elevator, "you ringing for me?"

"Where the hell have you been? Never mind just get up to 421"

"Ah ha, you found the Belmopan."

"I had to put General Sweeney to bed, he was falling all over the place."

"You didn't have to sing him a lullaby, now get up to 421 on the double. We can't find the bed . . . Yes, yes Mr. Lewis, he'll be right up . . . and Mr. Lewis, will you let me know where he finds it?"

Mr. Lewis laughed and hung up. The bed was in a panel, next to the closet.

Mr. Nelson welcomed Anne back to El Paso and asked, how did you like Albuquerque?"

"Mr. Nelson, I saw a lot in Albuquerque that has given me a whole new outlook on my future. I think women can be managers. There wasn't a thing I saw up there that would discourage me. I realize I need a little more training, but I can do it!"

"Why don't you look for something less, Anne?"

"What would that be, Mr. Nelson?"

"Well, a job like mine, that's management too, you know. There's plenty of time for the brass ring. Aren't you married, won't this interfere with your husband's ambitions?"

"Mr. Nelson, my husband's ambitions no longer concern me. Before I left for Albuquerque I had a Dear Jane letter. The edge of the hurt is gone now and I can go to bed without crying myself to sleep. I've accepted the fact that I have to go it alone and Mr. Nelson, that's what I'm going to do, go it alone! No more heartaches, no more personal rejections. The emotions go on ice. I'm setting my goal in one direction, to be a hotel manager."

Mr. Nelson looked at her with compassion and said, "I'm sorry, Anne. I didn't know . . ." Then, very impersonally he said," if that's the way it's to be let's get started. Food is probably the one most important factor in hotel management, beside cleanliness of course. You can lose your shirt on food alone if you don't know what you're doing, waste is your greatest enemy, but if you don't have a good dining room, you're finished before you start."

"So you'll be teaching me to avoid the pitfalls and set a good table, "she teased him, "so we get back to the woman's place in this business, housekeeping and cooking, just what women have been doing all through the centuries."

"Not quite the same thing and you're going to have to learn fast and on double time. Our hostess is leaving, her husband has returned from the South Pacific in pretty bad shape and she wants to spend time with him. You'll take her place during meal times, you'll also learn public relations fast that way, especially as it relates to food services.

"You'll work with me on banquets, conventions, social events, and private dinner parties. To know food, you have to also know the purchasing of food. The company is leasing a hotel in Denver, that's where you're going from here. You're supposed to be learning purchasing there, but their Mr. Dorhoff doesn't look too kindly on women . . . I doubt you'll learn much from him, so we'll take care of that here, although you'll still have to go through the motions there.

Anne worked with an eagerness that was pleasing to Mr. Nelson. He was relentless in his determination to teach her and ever so patient in his instructions. There was nothing too trivial in her questions for or against methods or policy that he failed to address, even when she disagreed.

"Now, let's get to employees. They have to be trained! Even in wartime they have to come up to the standard of the house. You have to be positive in your dealing with them and still earn their respect. You can't become too friendly, nor play favorites, that is a mistake too many people make and when you have a falling out they can really louse you up. But they do need to feel appreciated the same as you and I that's what you're going to learn the rest of your time here."

"You think I can absorb all this, in how much time did you say I had left?"

"November one you will be transferred to Denver. That gives you another month and the reason I told you, you have to learn fast.

The last few days came suddenly and Anne, while working in the dining room at dinnertime was called to the kitchen. One of the waitresses said Carlo; the Chef wanted to speak to her.

Carlo, the big handsome, Mexican Chef ran a tight ship. He had a fine hand with food, both taste and eye appeal, but he never asked for or tolerated interference in his domain. Puzzled, Anne went back to see what he wanted.

"Anything wrong, Carlo?"

"I gotta go out, Anne. I won't be gone more then fifteen or twenty minutes."

Since it was the middle of the dinner hour, Anne hesitated. Carlo always took the broiler station during dinner, as he didn't trust anyone else.

Anne asked him," can your sous chef handle your station while you're gone?"

"Yes, yes he'll do fine. I won't be gone long."

"Alright, but make it quick," she told him and went back out front.

Carlo was back in fifteen minutes. Anne breathed a sigh of relief for the dining room was beginning to fill up and she did not have the same confidence in the souse chef that Carlo obviously had.

Presently another waitress came from the kitchen to tell her she was wanted.

"What for this time?"

"The police are all over the place."

"Oh God, tell the desk to call Mr. Williford," and she went to the kitchen. The police wanted to arrest Carlo! He was still behind the range and came out when he saw Anne.

"What did he do?" she asked the officer.

"Stabbed his wife to death,"

"She was cheating!" Carlo explained to Anne as though she was the one he had to excuse himself," I caught her with another man!"

"How could you have caught her when you were here, working?" Anne demanded.

"My cousin came and told me," he said hanging his head.

"Damn your cousin!" Anne said angrily and stamped her foot, just as Mr. Williford came in the kitchen.

"What's going on here?"

The police told him they were arresting Carlo for the murder of his wife. That he had admitted it. Anne turned and left the kitchen, shaken, wishing she had not given him permission to leave, that he had not asked her.

Anne left El Paso the end of October and checked into the Cosmopolitan Hotel in Denver. This hotel would be the testing ground for a future Hilton Hotel in Denver. Mr. Beatty was Manager, another big, handsome, football type. Impeccably groomed and a friendly handshake with an engaging smile. Anne immediately felt comfortable with him. Not so the housekeeper. A heavyset woman who was extremely jealous of her bailiwick. She didn't want any young smart assed 'inspectors' or whatever they called themselves coming into her department. Seeking refuge from her vituperious tongue and generally nasty disposition Anne escaped into accounting and found Mr. Fels and Mr. LaChance. Fels was a Swiss educated genius in accounting, LaChance, the comptroller. They suggested she speak to Mr. Beatty to move her into purchasing.

"I'm having trouble with Mrs. Andrews," she told Mr. Beatty, "for reasons that I can only interpret as fear of being replaced, so I wonder if we couldn't get on with purchasing instead?"

Mr. Beatty laughed, "are you sure that's what you want?"

"It would be better then working with that she lion."

"You might consider her an angel compared to Mr. Dorhoff. That German is a terror." He leaned back in his chair and studied Anne. He saw a woman who had no fear of the powers that be, still she had backed off the housekeeper, a wise decision, "however, if you want to chance it . . . report to him Monday morning. I'll tell him to expect you."

Anne reported to Mr. Dorhoff the following Monday. She found a pleasant, short, stout man in his forties, with thinning light hair . . . If he had any dislike of her, or women in general he didn't show it and greeted her with a hearty handshake.

He gave her meaningless little duties, which Anne recognized as handouts to keep her occupied. If she was to learn anything from this man it would have to be by association and keeping her eyes and ears open. To further impede any tutelage, Mr. Dorhoff had built a network of German speaking sales people, with which he did business. They spoke only in German. Mr. Dorhoff never realizing Anne's Irish name hid a German heritage.

Mr. Dorhoff was very good at what he did. The stores were well stocked. Surely at the Cosmopolitan there was no shortage of any kind. Anne was learning a lot from Mr. Dorhoff without his being aware of it. She kept the comprehension of their common national language to herself. Especially so when she recognized the under the table transactions he was making.

Their desks faced each other; his had a small visiting area, where he 'entertained' his suppliers. Anne busily worked at the mediocre chores Mr. Dorhoff gave her and listened intently to the illicit negotiations being conducted. She kept these discoveries to herself, after all; a man with Mr. Dorhoff's talents might be a valuable employee whose behavior was condoned by silent assent. Surely the cupboards were well stocked.

She continued her friendship with Mr. Fels and Mr. LaChance and tried to have lunch with them every day, for they, more then any other encouraged her in her goal to be a manager. Always there were the insights they shared with her. More and more they opened the door to the challenging world she had chosen and saw no deterrent to why she could not be a manager.

Shortly before Thanksgiving Mr. LaChance asked her to have lunch with him outside the hotel. They went to the Navarre. When they were seated and had ordered, Mr. La Chance told her, "Anne, after the first of the year we'll be starting a training program for returning G I 's. We anticipate a greater traveling public after the war so there will be a need for new hotels and trained personnel. This is your opportunity to show what you can do."

How's that, Mr. LaChance?"

"My dear Anne, who but you for instructor? You start with these young men we're bring in for training. Go for it, Anne, I'll handle the details for you."

"Alright, you know I value your guidance and your advice."

"We'll shoot for the first of the year."

Anne went back to work elated and Mr. Dorhoff had a huge box sitting on her desk. She looked inside, Christmas cards! She looked at Mr. Dorhoff who sat across from her grinning.

"What do I do with these?"

"Send them out to our regular guests and suppliers.

"There's a list with addresses inside."

Anne got busy with them and in the days before Thanksgiving she had finished about half of them. When she came back after the holiday, she diligently worked on getting the remaining cards out. As she worked, she noted that many suppliers called to wish Mr. Dorhoff the season's greetings and slip him envelopes, heavily stuffed. When Anne had finished with the cards, he suggested she take her vacation and he would look forward to her return the first of the year.

"Thank you, Mr. Dorhoff," she set the box of cards on his desk, "wenn gehen diese raus?" (When do these go out?)

His mouth dropped open. He stared at her. She started up the stairs and slinging her coat over her shoulder, she looked back and smiled at him, "Froehliche WhienaChten." (Merry Christmas.)

Nonchalantly she went up the stairs; he was still staring after her.

During Anne's time off she moved from the hotel to an apartment. With the assurance of a prolonged stay in Denver she needed to get out of that one room.

The first Monday of the New Year, 1945 Anne came back to work. Her duties differed from anything she had ever done. She had three young men, discharged with leg injuries. Anne found herself not only instructing them in hotel procedures and conduct, but restoring their psychological confidence to overcome the, 'yours not to question why' syndrome they had been living with.

"Question! Question! Question! Everything I say! Not only to regain your own self assurance, but you must know before you can manage or direct others."

Anne enjoyed her work with these young men after she got the hang of how to deal with their injuries and their memories.

She learned from them too, for having coerced them to question; she had to come up with answers.

In May, the Germans surrendered at Rheims, Anne's work load increased. Immediately her young men were ready. They were sent out to hotels in the Rocky Mountain area as clerks and assistant managers.

Often while she considered one of her deserving young men for a specific post, she would dream of doing that job herself. She had all the qualifications.

She had lunch with Mr. LaChance and told him of her thoughts.

"I wonder what would happen if one day I were to say to Mr. Beatty, "I wish to recommend myself for this position"

"Why not?" Mr. LaChance prompted her, "you never know. But let me give you a bit of advice. Think of how you're going to take it if you're turned down. How will you feel about going on with your present job, will you still have the same interest? Secondly, Anne, be sure you have another place to go."

"I don't know how I'd take it. We never do until it happens to

us. I'll wait until something really good com~
you know."

In August, after the Bomb, Japan surre~
Cornell University was expanding their curricu~
ment. In Denver, there were fewer trainees, then in ~
really good did come along. The first post war hotel was be~
in Cheyenne, Wyoming. They needed an assistant manger.

Anne went to Mr. LaChance's office and showed him the order, "this is what I want, Mr. LaChance! What do you think?" She eagerly asked him.

"If this is what you want, go for it. Just remember what I told you about being turned down, but if you don't try or take that first step, you'll never know, will you?"

Anne dressed with great care the next morning; she wore a blue Chanel suit with a crisp linen blouse. Her hair was done in a neat French roll and she wore a tiny red hat, dipped over her right brow. "Very business like", she told herself as she checked herself in the hall mirror.

Confidently she walked into Mr. Beatty's reception room. Jane, Mr. Beatty's secretary, was busily typing. She looked up as Anne came through the door and whistled.

"My, aren't we looking elegant this morning"

"Elegant? I was trying for professional."

"Very well, professional. What's the occasion?"

"Is the Boss in?"

"In and busy, can I help you?"

"No, but the Boss can, that's if he will." Anne sat down on the couch in front of Jane's desk.

"Is everything alright with your apprentices?"

"I haven't heard any complaints, it's just that I have my eye on another job."

"You mean we don't keep you busy enough?"

"Jane, Cornell University is offering hotel management courses. People who are seriously interested in the field will be going there, so my job is almost done and I need a new challenge."

THE PARK HOTEL

It was three thirty in the morning when Anne drove into Great Falls, Montana, a town of fifty thousand. Central Avenue was the main street.

This was not where Anne had intended to come. She didn't know where she wanted to go. She was just too tired to go any further. She saw a sign for the Johnson Hotel and drove to it. After stopping the car and looking down the early morning main street, Anne stretched her weary shoulders and got out of the car. She entered a comfortable looking lobby and asked the young man on the desk if they had rooms. They did, but they had no bellman so he offered to help Anne with her bags.

"You want to bring all these in?" He asked as he looked at the pile of bags loaded in the trunk "

"Might as well," she shrugged.

"How long you figure on staying?"

"A day. A year. Who knows? I'm looking for a place to . . . to light, I guess."

"Well, you sure can't find a better place than Great Falls."

"Bucking for president of the Chamber of Commerce, are you?" She laughed.

"It's just that this is my home town and I think it's great."

"What's your name?"

"Brad Johnson."

"Any relation to the hotel here?"

"Yeah, it's my Dad's."

Brad helped her up to her room with her bags and asked if she'd like a wake up call.

"Don't even think about it. I'm going to sleep around the clock."

"O.K. Good night."

Two days later, the phone rang. Anne, still asleep, reached for it. "This is the desk," a gruff voice informed her. "Are you dead or alive up there?"

"You just brought me back to life. What day is it and what time is it?" She asked sleepily.

"It's Thursday morning, the 16th of May. You're in Great Falls, Montana and it's nine a.m."

"Thanks." She hung up.

Anne dressed carefully in a pink cotton dress with a flared skirt and tight bodice. Neat patent leather pumps and a matching clutch purse completed her outfit. She decided to forego her hat as she shook out her new poodle dog hairdo.

She came downstairs, laid her key on the desk and asked where she could get breakfast. The girl at the desk said the cafeteria next door was good. Anne thanked her and went next door. There she found the hub of the community. She watched the people and was impressed by the friendliness of everyone around her.

She finished her breakfast and went back to the hotel. Mr. Johnson, owner, manager, rancher, part-time desk clerk and part-time bartender was a long, lanky, gruff but friendly Rotarian. He greeted Anne with a friendly hand.

"So you're Anne, our sleeping beauty. What are you doing in these parts?"

"I thought I would stop here and rest, but now that I'm here and see the friendliness of everyone, I think I'll stick around," she laughed.

"What do you do, girl?"

"I manage hotels."

"My God, girl. I don't know that you're going to find anything up here. Most of our hotels are owned by the families who run them."

"At least you didn't cringe and say, A woman!"

"No, Anne, we have a lot of respect for our women up here. But I don't know where you will find a hotel to manage. What else do you do?"

"Mr. Johnson, I will manage a hotel. That's what I want, that's what I've been trained to do. So what is the biggest hotel in town that's not family owned? That's usually a good place to start."

"Now that would be the Rainbow," he slyly laughed. "They've got a manager. Not that they don't need one."

"Nothing ventured nothing gained. Thank you Mr. Johnson. I'll let you know how I come out."

"His name is Eagon," Mr. Johnson called after her.

When Anne reached the end of the street she asked herself, "What am I doing? I was going to take a vacation and here I am an old war-horse ready for action. I need to slow down," she thought as she entered the lobby. There was a young man at the desk being instructed by an older, handsome, well-groomed man whom Anne took to be Mr. Eagon. She approached the desk and introduced herself. "I'm looking for a position as assistant manager. I understand you do not have one at the present time."

"And I don't need one either. I could use a girl on the cigar stand though."

"Mr. Eagon, I've been trained to manage. I am not a cigar stand attendant."

"Looks to me like you're out of luck up here then . . . on the other hand, if you're as smart as you think you are, there's the Park Hotel." He laughed uproariously and rose from his desk, dismissing Anne. "Yes indeed, there's the Park!" He laughed.

Mr. Eagon walked Anne out the door. "Just down the street there." He pointed to the direction from which she had just come. "Turn right you'll see it at the end of the street."

Anne approached the Park Hotel on that sunny May morning knowing this would be her day. She would not be discouraged by Mr. Eagon's laughter or Mr. Johnson's kinder restrained mirth.

She came upon the lovely old light brick building next to a small park from which the hotel had taken it's name. A wide verandah encircled the building on two sides. One side faced the park. The other side faced Central Avenue.

Anne walked up the wide stairs onto the verandah and entered a delightful turn-of-the-century high ceiling lobby. In the center was a huge ornate registration desk. In all it's worn out splendor, it had graciousness about it.

Anne went to the desk and asked the young man behind this massive edifice where she could find the manager. She was directed to an office at the rear left of the desk. She passed a bar and a coffee shop before coming to an airless cubbyhole. Behind an old scuffed desk was a man in his sixties, heavy set, slightly red faced and going to baldness? He sighed and looked up at her when she came to the open door, apparently relieved to be disturbed from the papers he was puzzling over.

"Good morning," Anne said cheerfully.

"What's good about it? You looking for me?"

"If you're the manager, you're the one I'm looking for."

"You're in the right place, what can I do for you?"

"I'm looking for a job."

"Do you know anything about the hotel business?" He asked as he looked back at the papers.

"I know ALL about the hotel business."

"Can you make sense out of this damn thing?" He pointed to the sheaf of papers on the desk in front of him.

"Certainly. It's a transcript, isn't it?"

His chin dropped, his mouth opened and his eyes glazed with hope. He jumped up from his chair and motioned her to take his place. "You really know what to do with this damn thing?"

"Yes, Sir."

"Sit down. Sit down here." He practically pushed her into his chair. "You wait right here. Don't go away, I'll be right back."

He backed from the room as though Anne was some sort of strange creature. "Don't go away, I'll be right back."

Anne looked after him wondering what she had run into. She looked at the transcript of the daily room occupancy and wondered what his problem was. It was a very well done transcript. Occupancy was not even fair. She turned to the last page, "not even fair."

In moments, the gentleman was back with another heavy set man. He was a cigar-chomping, impeccably suited individual that put Anne in mind of a movie gangster.

She rose from her chair. Number I pointed to her as though she might have come from outer space.

"She knows all about hotels," he said in a monotone to Number II.

"Do you?" Asked Number II

"Yes, that's the reason I'm looking for a job here."

"We don't," they both said at the same time.

"You don't?" Anne asked, stunned.

"No," they shook their heads in a negative motion.

"Did one of you inherit this place?"

"You might say that," said Number II, grinning and taking a chair in front of the desk. Number I followed suit. "You see it wasn't supposed to be a hotel. Know what I mean?"

"I'm afraid I don't understand at all, but I'm willing to listen. Shall we start at the beginning? By the way, what are your names?"

"I'm Mike, I own the joint. This here's Lloyd; he's my manager. "Mike pointed to Number I.

"My name is Anne Courtney. Now Mike, did I understand you correctly? You did say this was not to be a hotel."

"That's right. You see, Annie, I didn't buy a hotel."

"What did you think you were buying?"

"A club," he frowned.

"The mystery deepens. Didn't you check out what you were buying? You really don't look like a man who wouldn't."

"Sure, sure, I came out and looked at the club. I liked it, I bought it and when I got back the Feds had closed the joint!"

"There must be a puzzle about to unfold here. How did you get the hotel?"

"I took it. The bastard had my money. "Mike grinned like a little boy.

"Legally?" Anne asked

"Legally? What the hell, he had my money!"

"I see." She looked from one to the other. "Neither of you knows anything about the hotel business?"

"Clubs are my racket. What do I know about hotels, except a certain kind I can't operate here and have my club? Understand?"

"Yes, I think I do. But why did you take the hotel?"

"Look, Annie, there's a hell of a big ballroom in this place. I'm going to make the best damn club this side of the Missouri back there. So I'm stuck with a hotel. O.K., I got a big family. I got three families. They all have to have a place to live."

"Three families under one roof? Is even a hotel big enough for that?"

"Yeah, and I want them all treated the same. No favorites."

"All right, Mike, you have a hotel. What do you want to do about it?" Anne sighed.

"What the hell, I gotta hotel. It's gotta be run like a hotel, not a flea bag."

"What about you, Mr. Lloyd?" Anne asked the other man. "Mike hired me for manager, but I'm really an accountant. I don't know anything about running hotels."

"I had to have a local man," Mike cut in. "Everyone here knows and likes Lloyd. The only reason he lost the election was because he was tired."

"What election?" Anne queried.

"County treasurer," Lloyd answered.

Anne resisted the impulse to ask why he didn't know what a transcript was, but felt the man deserved kindness. "You know of course that hotel accounting is a specialized field?" Anne asked as she handled the transcripts lying on the desk, and then added,

"Hiring an accountant to manage a hotel is par for the course. At least you're running true to form. Not necessarily the best choice."

"What's the matter with accountants?" Mike demanded.

"Nothing. They're necessary. But not as managers. They hate to spend money. So they let things run down. No aspersion on you, Lloyd, but most accountants make lousy managers. They don't

keep a place up. They allow it to get dirty to save money on supplies, manpower and promotion. There isn't time to keep a sharp
eye on accounts and generate new business too."

"Lloyd will generate new business just as soon as you start
running this place and he has the time. He's got class. Now that
you're here, he'll have time to generate new business. I kinda like
that word, 'generate'. What do you think, Lloyd?"

"I think we can work together, don't you, Anne?"

"Yes, Lloyd, I think we can."

"But I gotta know where my money's going," Mike reminded
her.

"True, you also have to get it coming in. This," Anne pointed
to the transcript, "tells me you just have about thirty percent occupancy. That's not going to cut it."

"Anne, if you know how to run a hotel, you're hired."

"What kind of a deal are we making?"

"You can be manager, but that's in here, between us. Out
there, as far as they're concerned, you're the accountant. Lloyd is
the 'generator' and manager," he laughed.

"Public relations man," Anne corrected.

"Public relations. I like that too, don't you, Lloyd? You both
keep outta my hair." He rubbed his bald head and laughed. "I'll
run the back of this here business and that's none of your managing business."

"What salary are we talking about?" Anne asked.

"$650 a month," Lloyd offered.

"Let's make it $750, Lloyd," Mike suggested. Mike rose to
leave. At the door he turned back and asked, "You know bookkeeping don't you?"

"Yes, but that will cost you another hundred."

"Good, good. Lloyd and you work things out so he can start
generating new business. You take care of the hotel, the coffee
shop, the Little Bar and the cigar stand. That's your managing
business. You keep outta my nightclub. Another thing, that
apartment in the basement the penthouse and my apartment on

the fifth floor, you leave them alone. If they want anything, give it
to them. If the fifth floor wants new curtains, the basement
apartment and the penthouse get them too. Now, for the Little
Bar. Try and get along with my bartender, he's a bastard." Then he
was gone.

"Oh my God," Anne said and Lloyd grinned at her.

"It isn't bad once you get used to it. Lucinda, that's the girl in
the basement she's his girl friend. Really nice lady. Denise, in the
Penthouse, is her sister. She and her husband are musicians. You
don't see much of her, either. Mrs. Mike has the fifth floor suite,
she'll not give you any trouble either. Just be sure you treat them
all nice."

"Will you introduce me to the staff?

"Yes, as soon as you're ready," Lloyd told her. Mike came back
and stood for a moment in the doorway.

"You don't play favorites with my ladies, understand?"

"Perfectly," she answered him with a smile.

"I think we got it made, Lloyd." He laughed and went on his
way.

"Where do you want to start? Lloyd asked.

"Why don't you introduce me to the staff today? I'll come
back tomorrow morning and we can make an inspection tour of
the house. That will give them a chance to accustom themselves to
the new girl on the block."

"Sounds good to me. We'll have to tell them something about
why you're inspecting the whole place."

"We can always use the cost of replacements for an excuse.
Then, of course, I have to assist you while you generate new business. It's a generally accepted procedure. What do you think?"

"Sounds alright . . ."

"Lloyd, I will be helpful and loyal to you. I give you my word.
If you need cover, I'll cover for you. "

"Why would you do that Anne Courtney?"

"In appreciation for giving me this opportunity. This will be
my first hotel, even though we do have to camouflage my role."

Without another word they shook hands. They understood each other.

Lloyd and Anne went first to the front office. Bob, the morning clerk, was a university student working in the summer. He was taking a business course but was not yet directed. He was a fine looking young man, always clean, neat and conservatively dressed. His hair was trimmed just right.

Juanita was a pert little Mexican girl, with a bright smile, flirting eyes and long shining black hair. She liked bright tight dresses and had a most seductive voice. She was paying for her trousseau. They were both friendly and interested in what Anne was doing.

"Anne is an accountant and will help where ever necessary," Lloyd told them. Then turning to Anne he said, "We'll have to find an office for you."

"Why don't we just place a desk behind this key rack. That will do very nicely for me."

"What, no private office?"

"I like to see and hear the action."

Their next stop was to introduce Anne to Jim and Velma Tucker, in the Coffee Shop. Velma was the businesswoman.

"Our lease is up in three months and we're be looking for another place," Velma told Anne very belligerently.

"I'm sorry to hear that Velma," Lloyd told her. "I thought you were happy here."

"Happy? Look at the place. It's a grease trap, a fire hazard . . . !

"It seems to me it wouldn't cost much to have it steam cleaned," Anne told her.

"Tell that to Mike. Lord, look at this cracked floor covering, these scarred booths and torn-up seats!"

"Maybe we can work something out Velma. Don't be too hasty," Lloyd told her.

They left the coffee shop and Lloyd asked Anne,

"What do you think? "

"Well, she's right you know."

"I know Mike wants to keep them, but you heard her."

"Is their food good?"

"Damn good, but they've lost heart lately."

"Let me think of something. You won't mind, will you, if I have a talk with them?"

"Certainly not, but I don't know how you're going to change anything."

"Lloyd, I really don't believe in leased-out departments. The hotel should be making the money the Coffee Shop can bring in and every department should pay it s own way.

"You're talking over my head, Anne."

"Let's go ahead with this. I've an idea gelling in my head and we'll talk about it later."

They came back out into the stately lobby she had so admired upon entrance. On closer inspection she found the corners and the marble boarders stained with the dirt and grease of mop splashing from at least year one. The carpet was threadbare.

They went into the Little Bar, which ran parallel to the lobby. There was a small hall between the Coffee Shop and the Bar.

The bar was dark and gloomy and there was a predominance of dusty Elk heads mounted on the dingy wall. A man with a shirt that appeared to have been slept in was behind the bar. He wore two-day-old stubble on his face. Lloyd introduced Phil, the "bastard" bartender.

"Anne will be taking some of the load off me, Phil, so I can start promoting new business," Lloyd told him.

"Quite a responsibility for a little lady like you, isn't it?" Phil said.

"Anne's an accountant," Lloyd told him.

"Well now, I'm glad to meet you, Miss accountant. We'll have to get better acquainted," he said sarcastically.

"I'm sure we will," Anne said and turned away. She felt an overwhelming sense of repugnance toward him.

Next they went to housekeeping. Maids were coming in and out of rooms. Anne counted five and wondered why five maids were needed for thirty-five rooms.

The housekeeper, a plump, round-faced little woman, wore a cotton print house dress and looked at Anne as though she resented her presence.

The engineer, a tall, sad-faced gentleman in the blue overalls of his trade was having coffee. All hotels with steam heat had to have engineers.

"I'm glad I caught you both at the same time," Lloyd said to them.

"Mrs. Hughes, Mr. Stanley, this is Anne Courtney. Anne will be helping me out and keeping the books. She will also see about replacing those sheets and blankets you're complaining about Mrs. Hughes."

"You didn't have to hire a bookkeeper for that. I could do it just as well myself."

"I'm sure you could, Mrs. Hughes, but I know you have your hands full with all you have to do."

Lloyd turned away from Mrs. Hughes and said to the engineer, "Joe, I hope you will give Anne all the help you can. There's a lot to be done here to bring this hotel back to par and she'll need your help."

"You know I would do that Lloyd," Mr. Stanley told him," and I'm glad to make your acquaintance, young lady. You Just tell me when you're ready to get started and I'll be right with you."

"Thank you Mr. Stanley, I'll try to meet with both of you tomorrow morning."

"Joe, can you find Anne a desk? She wants it behind the key rack. Do we have an extra desk?"

"Yes, I'll find one. You want a big one or a little one, Miss Courtney?"

"I answer better to Anne, Mr. Stanley. As for the desk, the bigger the better." She smiled, shook his hand and turned to speak to Mrs. Hughes. She had turned away.

"Well, now you know who everyone is. We'll see you tomorrow morning," Lloyd said to Anne when they came into the lobby.

"I'll be here bright and early."

"I don't usually come in until ten. We'll work everything out just fine, Anne."

When Anne returned to the Johnson Hotel, she asked if Mr. Johnson was in the house.

"He's in the bar," the girl on the desk told her. She went into the bar. Mr. Johnson was tending bar and Anne took a seat at the end.

"How'd things go for you, young lady?" he asked her.

First she told him about Mr. Eagon and then how she went to the Park and what she had found there.

"With all your training that should be another kind of education for you, from what I hear."

"I don't know what you've heard, Mr. Johnson, but there can't be too much going on there. Some unusual arrangements, but aren't there always-unusual conditions in hotel living? With so many people under one roof they all bring their individual problems with them."

"Yes, you're right. Can't help hearing things."

"I can promise you one thing, Mr. Johnson. If Mike leaves me alone the way he has promised to do, I'll run a clean hotel. It's none of my business what he does in his night club."

"I hope you can pull it off. Are you moving down there?"

"No, Mr. Johnson. I'd like to stay here, I might need a broad shoulder to cry on." She smiled at him.

"Good, good. We'll look after you here."

"Thanks, Mr. Johnson. Be seeing you." She got up and left the bar.

Anne arrived at the hotel the next morning just before the night clerk went off duty.

"Good morning. You're Jeff Adams, aren't you?" She said to the elderly man, a retiree.

"Yes, Ma'm."

us. I'll wait until something really good comes along, then I'll let you know."

In August, after the Bomb, Japan surrendered. The war was over. Cornell University was expanding their curriculum in hotel management. In Denver, there were fewer trainees, then in May something really good did come along. The first post war hotel was being built in Cheyenne, Wyoming. They needed an assistant manger.

Anne went to Mr. LaChance's office and showed him the order, "this is what I want, Mr. LaChance! What do you think?" She eagerly asked him.

"If this is what you want, go for it. Just remember what I told you about being turned down, but if you don't try or take that first step, you'll never know, will you?"

Anne dressed with great care the next morning; she wore a blue Chanel suit with a crisp linen blouse. Her hair was done in a neat French roll and she wore a tiny red hat, dipped over her right brow. "Very business like", she told herself as she checked herself in the hall mirror.

Confidently she walked into Mr. Beatty's reception room. Jane, Mr. Beatty's secretary, was busily typing. She looked up as Anne came through the door and whistled.

"My, aren't we looking elegant this morning"

"Elegant? I was trying for professional."

"Very well, professional. What's the occasion?"

"Is the Boss in?"

"In and busy, can I help you?"

"No, but the Boss can, that's if he will." Anne sat down on the couch in front of Jane's desk.

"Is everything alright with your apprentices?"

"I haven't heard any complaints, it's just that I have my eye on another job."

"You mean we don't keep you busy enough?"

"Jane, Cornell University is offering hotel management courses. People who are seriously interested in the field will be going there, so my job is almost done and I need a new challenge."

"I've never known anyone who was such a glutton for work as you are, Anne. Why don't you settle down like the rest of us, do your job, get your pay and be happy?"

"I guess that's the problem Jane, I wouldn't be happy."

"What is it this time?"

"That new hotel, up in Cheyenne."

"Don't we have a request for an assistant manager from them?" Jane asked, reaching for the correspondence on her desk.

"That's what I want," Anne said with decisiveness.

"What's driving you, Anne?"

". . . ghosts, I guess, of what might have been," she said thoughtfully, "anyway, I guess that's as good a reason as anything." Mr. Beatty came from his office, "hello, Anne, don't go away, I want to talk to you."

He showed the salesman out and took his seat along side Anne on the couch. "Who do we have ready for that assistant manager's position in Cheyenne?"

"What would you say to, myself?" She replied with a smile.

"I'd say you have to be kidding."

"I've never been more serious in my life," the smile faded.

"They won't accept a woman!"

"Have you considered asking them?" she challenged.

"No, neither do I intend to, so stop this nonsense."

Anne rose from the couch, fingered the desk set on Jane's desk thoughtfully. "Do I remain servile to this security I'm assured of, or is now the time to declare my independence? It isn't just a job I want, it's a position to prove . . . prove what? To whom? Myself, of course!" She turned and faced Mr. Beatty, "I've just remembered, it was just about twenty years ago that women won the right to vote and it all started in Cheyenne. They even went so far as to give themselves a woman Governor. Mr. Beatty, I don't think they would object to a woman assistant hotel manager."

"Don't be flippant, Anne. Besides what would we do without you?"

"You won't need me much longer, in the meantime you'll get along very well. But we're not finished with Cheyenne, they would accept a woman if you recommended me."

"It's against hotel policy," he answered becoming angry at her insistence.

"Is it, Mr. Beatty? If that were true, why was I trained for management . . . by this company?"

If you re unhappy with what you're doing, we'll find another place for you. Name it. The skies the limit, anything management!"

Anne breathed deeply, now she had to take the big step and she said, "then you really have nothing to offer me."

She picked up her purse from the couch, where she had left it and went to the door. She opened it and seeing the brass plaque with Mr. Beatty's name on it, with Manager underneath she touched the word, tapping it with her fingertip, "that, Mr. Beatty, is how I want to see my name. On bronze."

"There's the YWCA and there are hotels for women only . . . ."Mr. Beatty tried to placate her.

"No, Mr. Beatty. I want a commercial hotel"

Mr. Beatty rose from the couch and turned to his office, "there'll probably be a place for women in hotel management some day, Anne, but for now . . . get me that list for Cheyenne."

Before Mr. Beatty had a chance to close his door Anne said, "you'll have your list before I leave today. You'll also have my letter of resignation, so please have my check ready."

He turned around sharply, "don't be foolish, Anne you have a future with this company!"

"Not if it doesn't give me what I want. The only way I can see a future here is to go over your head, Mr. Beatty. I won't do that. I've been taught too well, what is ethical and what is not. Also, when Mr. Williford said, "here's your chance, see what you can do with it", I'm sure he didn't mean I could come back crying on his shoulder if I can't take the disappointments. So you see, I have to look for opportunity elsewhere. I truly believe there are people in this business who will accept a woman for what she can do, to me, that means managing a hotel."

"Where would you go? Where would you start?"

"I haven't the faintest idea. The Hilton Hotels have been my life for the past five years starting in El Paso in accounts receivable. I've never thought of anywhere else. That doesn't mean I can't!" She concluded defiantly.

Mr. Beatty looked at her in anger, "it's a damn fool who will take off, not knowing where you're going, what you're going to do . . ."he came over and put his arm around her shoulder, "why don't you take a couple of weeks off, come back refreshed, rested. We love you, Anne."

Gently she removed his arm from her shoulder,

"I'm sure every employer loves a work horse, until they bolt and show a mind of their own. As much as I'd like a vacation, Mr. Beatty, I have to find me a hotel to manage. "

She turned and walked out the door, closing it softly behind her.

Anne gave up her apartment and called Bekins to come for her furniture. Then she went to the beauty shop and told the hairdresser to change her image. She came out with a short shag hair cut. She ran her fingers through her hair and already felt a freedom she had not known for a long time.

She got into her red convertible, that she had picked up for a song, gripped the wheel with both hands and asked herself, "where?"

She took a silver dollar from her purse, spun it

On the dashboard, whatever direction the face turned, that was the direction she would take.

The face looked north.

"I'm Anne Courtney. I notice you do a very neat transcript Jeff." The transcript was lying on the desk that would be Anne's and she leafed through the pages, one for each floor. "I'm the new bookkeeper and I'll be assisting Mr. Lloyd," she said as she turned to the last sheet of the transcript where the computation of the previous day's business was listed.

"Occupancy isn't very good, is it?"

" 'fraid not, Miss Courtney."

"Can you think of any reason why it should be this low when there's an air base here and two good industries to draw from? It seems there should be more business."

Bob stood by and was listening. "Perhaps if we had clean rooms and radiators that didn't go bang in the night . . . people just seem to stay here once."

"All right, we'll just have to change that won't we? I hope both of you will take note of complaints and see that I get them. We'll work together to straighten these things out. O.K.?"

"Do you mean that or is it just so much talk the way everything else has been?" Bob asked.

"I mean it. As long as I'm here, I'll do all I can to upgrade this hotel."

"Then let's hope you'll be here awhile;" Bob said and went to the front desk.

After Jeff left Anne went over to the front desk.

"Bob," she said, "I'd like to work with you a couple of hours a day until I see how the desk is doing. I hope you don't mind. I'd just like to get the feel of it and see how reservations are handled."

"You might say they're not. We haven't any reservations."

"You surely can't mean all we have are drop-ins?"

"That's about the size of it."

"Well, we'll just have to change that."

"How are you planning to do that?" Bob asked, laughing.

"I'll think of something. In the meantime, you say the radiators bang and the rooms are dirty?"

"The windows are broken, the sheets are torn and the blankets are dirty," Bob said.

"Looks like we have quite a project ahead of us, doesn't it? I'd better have a look at the housekeeping, That's Mrs. Hughes department, isn't it?"

"Be careful, she can get pretty mean."

"I can too, when the occasion calls for it."

Anne started in the lobby, taking a yellow legal pad with her. The carpet in the lobby was threadbare. She picked up one edge and saw color on the tiles under the carpet and made a note of it. She then went to the furnace room and asked Mr. Stanley to accompany her, along with Mrs. Hughes, for an inspection of the rooms.

"I need to inventory everything, Mr. Stanley, and make note of what has to be replaced or repaired. I think we should get Mrs. Hughes to go around with us," she told him.

When they reached the linen room Anne asked Mrs. Hughes to accompany her and Mr. Stanley on an inspection tour of the rooms.

"I haven't time for any inspection and since when has the book-keeper any business making inspections? What are you looking for?"

"Mrs. Hughes, neither do I have time to waste. I know all your girls should have been assigned their duties, which can't be much with only thirty five rooms occupied last night."

"There's more than thirty five rooms, and there's all those permanent guests too," she said as she slammed a notebook on the table. "What do you want to see?"

"Everything. We can start with this room by taking an inventory of your linens and I want to see the condition of them as well."

"You want what?"

"That's what I want and you might as well get that chip off your shoulder if we're going to work together. I'm not going to fight with you every time I need information or wish to check your department."

Mrs. Hughes opened her cupboards and started to count the neat rows of sheets.

"Please spread out every fifth sheet. I want to see the condition of the linen."

"Why not just spread them all out?"

"Every fifth sheet will do."

As the torn sheets began to pile up, Anne asked," Don't you have a seamstress, Mrs. Hughes? I can see some of these sheets are beyond repair, however, those with rips could and should be mended before putting them back on the shelf to be used."

"I'm all the seamstress we need with a hundred rooms empty."

"Filling those empty rooms is something we'll start working on, and since I can't stand here all day looking at damaged sheets, I'd like you to remove them all from the shelves and give me a count of what is usable, including those on the beds. Now let us take one floor at a time and look at the rooms."

"Where do you intend to start?"

"Might as well start on top, the fifth floor. I believe we'll start with all the vacant rooms. I noticed nothing had been occupied last night on either the fourth or fifth floors, except Mrs. Mike's suite."

They went to Room 503. Mrs. Hughes opened the door; "here it is," she said.

"Very well. First I want to check off the condition of the furniture. Is it marred, broken or stained?"

Anne had a legal pad where each item in every room was listed.

"The bedside table is stained."

"Can we refinish it, Mr. Stanley?"

"Sure thing. We can sand it down and refinish."

"I see the lamp is also broken, Mrs. Hughes. It will have to be replaced."

"And where will you get the money for it?"

"Let me worry about that Mrs. Hughes. Now, what about the drapes?"

"There's nothing wrong with the drapes!"

Anne went to the window and shook one drapery that filled the room with dust. Coughing she turned away. When the dust had settled somewhat, she went back to the window and turned the drapery around. The lining was shredded. She made a mark under the drapery.

"Now, the windows, please. If you'll just raise the shades I can see them."

The shades were dusty but in fairly good shape, but the top window was cracked.

"I think a good wiping down with warm soapy water would take care of the shades, Mr. Stanley. Would you take note of the cracked window and have the panes in all rooms with cracked windows replaced?"

"I have to have a order from Mike for that Miss Courtney."

"You'll have it. I also think a coat or two of paint would do well around these windows."

"Yes, Ma'm."

"Now for the baths. There seems to be a lot of stains in the tub and the sink." She rubbed her thumbnail across a stain and it came off on her nail. She showed it to Mrs. Hughes, "All this needs is a cleanser and a little elbow grease, wouldn't you say?"

"Now for the carpeting. It's dirty, Mrs. Hughes, as is the woodwork and the room generally. I could smell the dirt and dust as I came in here. So how do you think a guest will feel coming into a room that smells?"

"These things don't last forever, you know!" Mrs. Hughes said defensively.

"Yes, I do know. That's why we're going over this place to see what can be restored or refurbished. If you will call one of the maids to come up here with a bucket of hot soapy water and a brush, we'll see what we can do about these carpets."

"I hope you don't intend for my girls to scrub these carpets on their hands and knees!"

"We'll see, Mrs. Hughes."

Mrs. Hughes left in a huff, and stomped into the linen room. She slammed the door, called the desk, and asked for Mr. Lloyd. Anne and Mr. Stanley, strolling in that direction, heard her yelling into the phone, "Mr. Lloyd, that woman's up here and I want to know who is manager here?"

Anne motioned Mr. Stanley to stay outside the linen room until she had hung up.

Anne spotted a maid having coffee.

"Is this the lady you're going to loan me?" She asked Mrs. Hughes.

"I suppose so," Mrs. Hughes said grudgingly.

"Please finish your coffee and then get a bucket of hot soapy water and brush and cleaning rags and meet me in 503. Anne said to the maid. Turning to Mrs. Hughes, Anne said, "I think those drapes should be taken down."

"What will I replace them with?"

"You have sheers for the time being, that will be enough, since it is spring."

Anne and Mr. Stanley went back to room 503 and Mrs. Hughes slowly followed.

"By the time the panes are replaced and the window trim has been painted, we'll have new draperies," Anne said cheerfully.

"In the meantime, Mrs. Hughes, see that the curtains are laundered and starched. We'll shut off one floor at a time." Just then the maid came in.

"What is your name, young lady?" Anne asked.

"Emma, Ma'm."

"All right, Emma, I want you to take a spot about 12x12 and scrub it real good. I want to see what that carpet looks like under all that dirt that's ground into it."

Emma scrubbed the square. Three times she changed the water. Finally a pattern began to emerge.

"Let's give it one more change of water."

Anne bent down and felt the nap. It was soft and thick and a pattern of old roses came through. Anne rose, smiling.

"Emma, do you realize how much money you have just saved this hotel? Anne asked. "If the other rooms are like this, it will be the entire cost of carpeting this hotel. Thank you Emma."

"Now, Mrs. Hughes, Mr. Stanley, this is how I want this whole hotel gone over, one floor at a time. Also Mrs. Hughes, I want the linen inventory by the end of the week That will be Friday."

She handed the legal pad to Mr. Stanley. "I'll appoint you to go over everything with Mrs. Hughes, Sir. Every five rooms you finish, I want to inspect."

Anne left them. In the elevator she ran into Michael Duffy. Michael was six years old.

"Hello, young fellow, who are you?"

"I'm Michael Duffy. Who are you?"

"I'm Anne Courtney. I work here"

"Oh, I live here and I've never seen you around here before."

"You'll be seeing a lot of me now."

"What do you do here?" The elevator door opened. They got out and he followed her.

"I keep the books and sorta stick my nose in everyone's business."

"Oh." She sat down at her desk and he came over and opened the drawers, she had put some peppermint candies in the upper right hand corner that morning and he saw them.

"May I have one?" He asked.

"Help yourself."

"How many can I have?"

"You take some and leave some for another day."

He took two and ran out of the office. He was a handsome, charming child. Every morning he came in for his piece of candy before going on to his adventures. Anne changed flavors every few days to please him and occasionally took him into the Coffee Shop for ice cream, where he described his encounters with the world.

After Anne's instructions to Mr. Stanley and Mrs. Hughes, she cornered Mike to have lunch with her and explained the condition of the hotel. Room by room she pointed out to him what had to be done to increase occupancy.

"I thought you said that should be Lloyd's job?"

"He can bring a million people in here, Mike, but if the sheets are torn, the windows are dirty, the draperies are shredded and the carpets are ingrained with twenty years of dirt, they're not going to come back."

"The sheets are always good. I don't see any torn sheets."

"That's because the good sheets are saved for you and your families. Another thing, I notice you don't eat here unless someone drags you in. Look around you at this dingy hole. It doesn't encourage people to come in and eat. This lease is about to expire. Why not take Jim and his wife on as employees and give them a decent salary and a commission for incentive? It will pay off when you open the Flame Room, as it will do away with any conflict of what and when to serve. We must control the food. Then when you order new dishes for the Flame Room you can order enough for the Coffee Shop too. When you have the upholsterers in, they could do this room too."

"You sure know how to spend my money, Annie."

"Oh, am I asking too much? It will be to your benefit, Mike."

"No, I like your ideas. I suppose you've something in mind for the Little Bar?"

"I don't know, Mike. I'm afraid I would have to lock horns with Phil, and to be truthful with you, I don't know how to handle Phil."

"But you have some ideas?"

"Oh yes. I'd clean it up, brighten it some and serve food at noon."

"Tell you what, Annie, you look around for a bartender and I'll take care of Phil. O.K.?"

Anne had what she wanted. She still needed to save Lloyd's face so she would talk it over with him.

Anne stood by the cigar stand and looked at the lobby. She needed a good porter, maybe two. She would put them under the supervision of Mr. Stanley, as he was one of the few staff willing to go along with her plans. While she was at it she would also put the bellmen under him.

Anne did not want to be known as a manager who would come in and fire all the old employees. She wanted them to do better and be proud of their work and their work place. She was also ready and willing to train them.

She had a talk with Lloyd, telling him what she had suggested to Mike and that he was willing to go ahead.

"My God, Anne, that's going to run into a lot of money."

"True, but look at the rewards. People will want to stay here. The place will be clean and the food will be good . . ."

"Maybe I've been too optimistic about the quality of the food."

"They will not have to worry about the payroll or paying their bills and the commission will give them the incentive for better food. We'll take that hundred item menu off and make it smaller and manageable. We'll also need to serve food in the Little Bar and the Shrine Club. They'll love that."

"You're going too fast for me, Anne"

"Don't worry, Lloyd. I'll take care of it."

"I don "t know, Anne . . ."

"We'll work together like a charm. Just keep your presence visible."

Anne sat at her desk thinking of the work ahead. She wondered why she hadn't fallen into a nice clean operation, but of course, a man would have gotten that.

She needed time to think after what she had put in motion, so she called in the commercial carpet cleaners. They would buy her thinking time.

She called on Denise, telling her the carpets were to be cleaned and asking her to decide when it would be convenient for them to come into her apartment.

Denise was so thankful about having clean carpets, she offered to send the children to her sister in the basement while they were being cleaned and dried.

Next she called on Mrs. Mike. She too was agreeable to any schedule. Anne told her they would be the first rooms to be done, if she would advise her when she was ready. Anne offered her another suite for her use during the drying process.

Mrs. Hughes called in reserve maids to wash the woodwork and scour the baths and showers. Mr. Stanley drained the radiators of condensed steam.

A lackadaisical staff found themselves in a flurry of cleaning. The housekeeper resented it most of all and Anne was to find this would be a pattern with housekeepers wherever she went. They were notorious in their protection of their run-down domains.

The front office system was in excellent shape. The lobby shaped up into gleaming marble on the floors and the sideboards. Mike suggested another carpet to replace the threadbare one that had been taken up before the winter came. "We don't need law suits from broken legs no matter how pretty you think it looks," he told Anne. A runner from the front door to the desk was installed.

By fall the hotel was shining clean and smelling fresh. New linen, draperies and curtains graced all the rooms. The furniture was polished, the lamps and light bulbs were working and the carpets were clean with a lovely pattern and a plush softness.

The Coffee Shop, after it had been steam cleaned, was given a fresh coat of soft yellow paint, new dishes, and renovated booths with brown Naugahyde upholstery. The menu was shortened. Special orders were available and the food was improved. The Coffee Shop more than paid for the expense, and the Tucker's were happy to stay under the new arrangement.

The antlers and the elk's heads in the Little Bar were cleaned and, re-hung on a bright new wall. To have discarded animal heads in a Montana bar would have been a sacrilege. However, the dust of ages was gone and hot prime rib was now being served for lunch.

The Shrine Club, except for carpet cleaning, was left untouched, as was the radio station. Lucinda's apartment was thoroughly cleaned and the basement was designated as the subterranean floor.

Mike took Phil into the Flame Room and Anne hired Jack, the relief bartender. He was a smiling, good natured Irishman with fine wit and fresh jokes. Anne was happy with the sparkling hotel that came out of the ruins to become a notable place to eat and stay.

While the employees never came to terms with 'that woman' running things, Anne thought she had at last, well, not won them over, but at least not alienated them altogether. She was wrong.

The torn sheets, the aged mops, and the thin blankets were gone. Reservations were met and she no longer had to be ashamed of the guest rooms. Then trouble came from housekeeping again.

The Hotel Worker's Union came down on her. She was over-loading her maids, they said. When Anne asked Mrs. Hughes how she had let this happen, she snickered and said, "Why weren't you inspecting?"

"Because I thought you could be trusted in spite of your dis-like of me," Anne said as she turned away in disgust.

On the floor of the linen cabinet Anne spotted some bunched-up sheets.

"What are these, Mrs. Hughes?" Anne asked as she picked them up.

"They need to be mended."

Anne spread them out on the table.

"What's the matter, don't you trust me?" She demanded of Anne. Do you think I'm stealing?"

"First, Mrs. Hughes, you know the conditions of your union contract better than I!. You knew how many rooms each maid could do. You have the authority to call in extra help when you need them. So why did you allow this reprimand from the union to happen? Secondly, you also know these linens should be used in rotation. As an experienced hotel housekeeper you should know that."

"Furthermore Mrs. Hughes, I will inspect this department whenever I deem it necessary. Do I trust you?" Anne continued. "No, not after today. As for stealing, until very recently there just hasn't been anything worth stealing in this place. Your past record tells me nothing, while these," Anne pointed to the sheets she had just spread out on the work table, "are comparatively new sheets. No rents, no tears, and these are lying here to be mended, you say."

"I don't have to take this from you and I won't have you coming up here and acting like the manager!" Mrs. Hughes fumed.

"It may be better to pretend that I am, Mrs. Hughes, because you will have me to deal with."

"We'll see about that, Miss! "

"Mrs. Hughes, I am willing to overlook what I might think and I advise you to do the same. For this is a warning, the only one you'll get. I can make a better case than you. Now, let's send these sheets out to be laundered and put back on the shelf. If you fail to appreciate what I have just done for you, I'd suggest you give Mr. Lloyd your resignation. Think about it."

Anne left the linen room and went into Lloyd's office. She sat at the desk and thought about Mrs. Hughes. She hated this sort of thing and then she thought, this is really the last holdout. She got up and went to the Little Bar.

"A good day to you, Boss Lady," Jack greeted her.

"Thank you, Jack. As one Irishman to another, what's wrong that I can't seem to reach Mrs. Hughes? I thought I had been fair to everyone working here. We've made it a better place to work and business has improved a hundred fold. They get more work and they make more money. There's hardly any complaints, not even about your sharp attire" she laughed. "Still that woman will challenge me when she knows she's remiss in her duties, as well as her ethics."

"You put the whole place in high gear, Boss Lady. Like you say, the house is full and business is good in both the bar and the restaurant. So, why doesn't Mike give you the title of Manager when that's what everyone knows you're doing?"

"I think you know the answer to that Jack. You're a sharp one, and I have no problem with it. As far as getting into high gear as you call it we all had to. We have a full house nearly every night even weekends our sample rooms are filled."

"They liked it the way it was. This was considered a nice quiet place. We put in an easy shift and got paid good money. You changed all that."

"That's what I was hired for. I couldn't have done anything else."

"I guess you couldn't. One thing you are forgetting is not everyone's against you."

"Thanks for that. When is your family coming out?"

"They'll be here next week, maybe," he shrugged.

Anne left the bar and went to her desk. Michael came in for a piece of candy. He looked cold from the outdoors where he had been playing in the snow, in the park.

"I think you'd better have a cup of hot chocolate instead of the candy, young man," Anne told him.

"Do you suppose I can have both?"

"Come along my greedy little monster, we'll both have some chocolate," Anne said.

They went into the Coffee Shop and slipped into a booth, with Michael facing the door. Anne ordered hot chocolate and then noticed Michael was sticking his tongue out at some one in the doorway.

"Michael!" She called.

"I suppose you know you're spoiling that child!" Anne turned around to see who was speaking to her. Miss Haskins and Mrs. Fischer, two elderly ladies who were permanent guests in the hotel were just coming into the Coffee Shop.

"A cup of hot chocolate on a cold winter day never spoiled a child," Anne replied to Miss Haskins. "However I will have to ask Michael to apologize for his rude gesture . . ." Michael, I believe you owe these ladies an apology."

"If you want me to," he answered, sliding down in his seat and pulling his chin into his coat.

"I want you to because it was very bad manners."

"All right . . . I'm sorry," he said as his stubborn little chin rose to thirty degrees northeast without looking at them. They nodded abruptly to him and found a booth.

"Michael, I've never known you to be rude. Why did you do such a thing? And your apology was less than gracious."

"I don't like them."

"That's no excuse to be rude, just leave them alone. Now, tell me what you've been up to today to make your cheeks so rosy?"

"I had a snowball fight" he confided as he sat up straight and leaned across the table.

"Was the opposing team . . . your size?"

"Nope, but there were two of them," he grinned, "and I beat 'em. You see they got me yesterday but I was ready for 'em this time. I'm faster than the both of them. I hit one right in the snazola. He went home crying and I ran the other one off."

"This all took place in the City Park this morning?"

"It's my park!"

"No, Michael, it is not your park. Suppose they didn't have any other place to play. Wouldn't it be nicer to have someone to play with? What did you do when you ran the other one off?"

"I came back here."

"Wouldn't it have been nicer to have two boys to play with? You could still have your snowball contests without hurting anyone."

"All right, I'll play with them tomorrow."

"It isn't going to be that easy. You're going to have to apologize again tomorrow to those boys and I'm afraid you'll have be a lot more gracious about it than you were to those two ladies."

"Why should I be as long as I apologize?"

"They won't be as forgiving as the ladies, I'm afraid."

"No, I suppose not . . . maybe if I gave them some candy . . . ?"

"You can't bribe your way out of this, Michael. You'll go out there and say, 'listen, fellas, I'm sorry about yesterday. I just wanted to get acquainted."

"O.K., then I'll kick 'em!"

"Do all boy games have to be so . . . so violent?"

"Oh it's just good exercise."

"Well you just get that well-exercised little body upstairs into a hot shower and keep warm for the rest of the afternoon."

"O.K." He gulped the rest of his chocolate and swaggered out.

Anne turned her attention to Lloyd. He had developed a pallor and she worried about him.

"Lloyd," she asked him one day," don't you think you should see a doctor? You know you're not looking at all well."

"I'm fine," he told her as he hung his hat on the hat rack by the door. Anne watched him as he checked the letters on his desk she had left for him to sign. Then he went to the Shrine Club.

At five o'clock on the dot each day, Lloyd would come in from the Shrine Club. Anne always had a taxi waiting for him at the side door to take him home.

Anne often wondered why Lloyd would let Mike use him until one day she came across the application for a liquor license. Lloyd's name was on it.

Once a month, for three days, Lloyd would stay sober enough to get out the profit and loss statement. This saved his pride somewhat, then he returned to his pattern. He would go from the side door to the office to sign letters, to the Shrine Club, and back to the side door at five o'clock where the taxi was waiting to take him home.

Mike and Anne were like birds of passage, occasionally meeting, crossing paths as they went about their business; He was usually calling it a day when Anne came to work. Mike, always the gentleman for all his rough ways, had a great respect for Anne. He admired the job she was doing, her willingness to stick by the bargain she had made and most of all her subtle protectiveness toward Lloyd.

Anne had arranged with the police department to pay Mike's parking tickets once a month as there were so many of them. She was sitting at her desk one morning, making out the list of dates and numbers of these tickets, when she heard a piercing scream! She jumped up to run to the lobby and nearly collided with Michael coming for his piece of candy before he started on his voyage of discovery for the day.

Anne rushed by him. There was another scream! Miss Haskins saw Anne coming and screamed even louder while her companion, Mrs. Fischer, commiserated with her as they examined Miss Haskins leg. As Anne came near Miss Haskins yelled at her, "he did it! He did it! That little delinquent you think so much of! He charged at me!"

"He did what!" Anne exclaimed.

"He charged me. With a hatpin! He stuck a hat pin in me!" She sobbed and slumped in her chair.

"A hat pin?" Anne repeated unbelieving.

"He stuck me with a hat pin." She groaned.

"Where would Michael get a hat pin?"

"Ask him, not me!" She suddenly sat up straight.

"I certainly shall. But what I'm asking you is why would a child attack you without reason? What did you do?"

"What did I do! My friend and I were sitting here talking, just like we always do. Every morning we sit here in the sun . . . and then . . . then he came at me. Just like the little demon he is and he charged me . . . with a hatpin!"

Anne sighed deeply. "How is your leg, or your knee now, Miss Haskins?" Anne inquired.

"What does it matter? What do you care?"

"I care a great deal. I'm very concerned, Miss Haskins. If you need to see a doctor, I'll see to it. So please let me know. In the meantime I'll talk to Michael."

Anne went into the back office. An angelic Michael was sitting at her desk beaming, a proud little smile on his face. Her Saint George looked up at her.

"Why?" Anne demanded.

"I didn't like what she was saying."

"That's no reason to attack people, Michael."

"She had no right!" He said stubbornly.

"Michael, where did you get a hat pin?"

"I found it in your desk," he smiled.

"A hat pin? In my desk?" Anne asked.

He held out a corsage pin. "Do you want to know what she said?" "No I really don't, Michael, because I'm afraid to ask." He was ready to burst then he was disappointed. "On second thought maybe you'd better tell me in case we're sued."

"Well, she's always snickering at you . . ."

"That's no reason to hurt the poor woman."

"Well this morning when Mom and I came down to breakfast, she said she wondered what all you were being paid for. Mom said it was bad of her to say such things, that she needed to be punished. So I stuck her!" He beamed.

Anne thought for awhile. She moved Michael from her chair and sat down.

"Have you had your candy?"

"Yes Ma'm," Michael answered as he watched her, wondering what might happen. He didn't want Anne mad at him. She was his friend. He could tell her things.

"Put the pin back in my desk, Michael. Get yourself some ice cream from the Coffee Shop and . . . and sin no more. Scoot."

Anne sighed as she watched him walk out the door and stuck his tongue out at someone.

Then Miss Haskins came in. "What are you going to do about that boy?" She demanded.

"Nothing, Miss Haskins. Probably pin a metal on him. You should be ashamed of yourself and that evil mind and tongue! Do you think a child doesn't understand when ugly things are being said? Even if they don't understand the underlying significance of what you're saying? So for your information, Madam, my life is more in keeping with that of a nun than a prostitute. Also, don't worry about the condition of my employment. Good day to you, Miss Haskins. It seems I have need of a cavalier, even a very small one."

It was May and Lloyd suddenly decided to leave. He recognized what he was doing to himself with his non-stop drinking.

Anne felt his loss, although he had spent his time downstairs. It was always a comfort to know he was there. He never ceased to applaud her for the work she was doing and admired her for working against great odds to challenge a man s world.

Things were never the same after Lloyd left. It seemed strange that a man who was seldom seen should leave such emptiness when he was gone.

Phil seemed to make his presence felt more than Anne was comfortable with since Lloyd left. He flattered her consistently, which was not his nature. He asked her to lunch, to which she always replied that she was busy. Finally, he came down to the hard facts. He simply came out and asked her for the combination to the safe.

She referred him to Mike but Anne knew she had made an enemy.

She didn't really mind because with the hotel in very good shape both physically and financially, she found she was losing interest.

Each morning she lingered longer in the cafeteria, where before she couldn't wait to get to the hotel.

Mr. Johnson must have noticed, although she had not mentioned it to him, for he asked her, "Are you losing interest in your job, Anne?"

"Why would you ask that, Mr. Johnson?"

"I don't see the excitement any more."

"You have a keen eye, Mr. Johnson."

Then one morning while she was taking her time getting dressed, the phone rang.

"Hello."

"Anne Courtney?"

"Speaking."

"Roy Smith here, at the country club. I'd like to talk to you about a job out here. Would you be interested?"

"I . . . I don't know." She answered cautiously.

"Lloyd said you might like a change."

"Lloyd said that? What is the job, Mr. Smith?"

"Accounting."

Anne was silent. What would happen to her dream of becoming a recognized hotel manager? She wondered. If she took this job would she be sidetracked away from her goal?

"Miss Courtney?" She heard Mr. Smith calling.

"Yes, Mr. Smith, I'm just thinking. I do need a change. Yes, I think I would be interested. Can I depend on like money?"

"I don't see why not. But why don't you come out and have lunch with Lloyd and me and we'll talk it over.

"I think that would be nice, Mr. Smith."

"I'll see you about one o'clock then."

MEADOWLARK COUNTRY CLUB

At the point where the Sun and the Missouri Rivers meet stood a gracious, rambling clubhouse on a high rock foundation. Anne walked up to the enchanting old weather-beaten building and searched for the entrance.

The front door did not seem to be in use, so she went to the back. She entered a small hallway with steps going up on the left. Straight-ahead was the slot machine room and a small bar.

She took the steps to the dining room. Except for six people at two tables, the dining room was empty. Anne looked around. The huge dining area was surrounded by a screened porch that seemed to wrap itself around half the building. A series of french doors opened onto the porch.

On the inside wall, opposite the porch stood a ceiling-high fireplace made of native stone and expanding over a third of the wall.

A heavy-set man very much the same build as Lloyd, excused himself from some ladies and greeted Anne. He held out his hand and said, "You must be Anne."

"Yes. Roy Smith?"

"Guilty. Let's go out on the porch and join Lloyd and one of our directors.

He led her to a secluded corner table. Anne greeted Lloyd and he introduced her to Mr. Burke, club treasurer. The table overlooked the nine-hole golf course.

A waitress came to take their luncheon order. The men ordered steak sandwiches and Anne ordered a salad.

Roy leaned back in his chair and said, "I'll tell you what we have out here, Anne. We have an excellent chef and no business. I'll introduce you to her later. We have six hundred and fifty members and should have more than the ten or twelve people we had for lunch today. We want to make some changes but we have to go slow. We can't be stepping on any toes. We have Mrs. Jerome, who is the widow of a former member as our social director. But as you see, we're still not doing so well."

"Now Lloyd, here, tells us you can get things done. We'd like you out here. Start out in the office, get to know the names of the members and get acquainted. I think we can gradually change things," Roy said.

"Sounds challenging, Mr. Smith. But you must understand I've never had anything to do with a country club."

"I don't think you'll find it too different from a hotel, Anne," Lloyd told her.

"Where does the money come from, Mr. Smith?"

"Food, dues, bar and slots," Mr. Burke, the treasurer, answered.

"You say you have six hundred and fifty members. What are the dues?"

"A hundred and twenty five dollars a month."

"The bar must be doing better than the food. What are the dues earmarked for? And the slots?"

"We're thinking about a redevelopment program."

"There must be green fees," Anne stated.

"That's for upkeep of the golf course," Mr. Burke said.

"Mortgage?" Anne looked at Mr. Burke.

"None. You did say you didn't know country clubs."

"You understand as the accountant I should know these things?"

Lunch came and they ate without referring again to the business at hand. The ladies in the dining room left and Anne excused herself from the table to look over the building. "What is the chef's name, Mr. Smith?"

"Gina."

"Would you mind if I go out and introduce myself?"

"No, go right ahead."

Anne looked around the large circular reception room, where the front door facing south was barred. The room opened into that immense dining room with the attached porch. A nine-hole golf course circled these rooms. Anne went to the north end of the dining room, with a bank of windows overlooking a swimming pool on a knoll.

Turning toward what she assumed to be the kitchen, she came to a small dining room. Another door opened into the kitchen, where the employees were sitting around a table having their lunch. A tall, stout Italian woman rose from the table and came toward Anne. "Are you Gina?" Anne asked. "I'm Anne, the prospective bookkeeper," she smiled.

Anne felt an immediate warmth toward this woman.

"Prospective, did you say? We heard you might be coming out here with us." Gina told her.

"I haven't decided yet. I'd like to talk to you first."

"Would you like a cup of coffee?" Gina asked.

"May we have it in there?" Anne pointed to the small dining room.

"Yes, of course."

"Cream?"

"No thank you, black." Anne went into the small dining room and sat down at the scarred table. Gina followed with two cups and a pot of coffee.

"You want to talk to me? I don't know anything about books," Gina said taking a chair across from Anne.

"Then we're even. I don't know anything about country clubs. I don't know if I even want to make a change. Perhaps I should say, I want to make a change, but I had never thought of anything like this. You see, Gina, I'm a hotel manager and I'd guess they'd want more than a bookkeeper out here."

"You'd guess right. You never know what you'd be doing out here."

"If I were to come out here, it would be important to have your support and friendship."

"They want you to do the same thing here that you did at the Park."

"It's an entirely different operation, Gina. At the Park I had one man to deal with and he gave me a free hand. With a Board of Directors, my God, Gina, I've never worked with a Board of Directors before. I don't know if I could."

"From what I've heard of you, I wouldn't take you to be a woman who would be afraid to tackle anything. As far as my support and friendship is concerned, if you treat our people right you'll have that without question. Now you go out there and tell those men you're ready to take this on. I'll give you all the help I can and so will they."

"Thank you, Gina."

Anne rose and went back onto the dining room porch where the men were having coffee while they waited for her.

"Gentlemen," she said resuming her seat "I don't exactly understand what my position would be. So, let's see if I can make it out. Officially I will be the bookkeeper, accountant if you like. I've never considered myself an accountant. Unofficially, I shall be hostess, bookkeeper, housekeeper . . . making the place attractive to members so they will come out and support the club. I don't think there's an official name for that yet."

"Speaking of stepping on toes as we were a while ago, what of Mrs. Jerome? I would think she should be doing the hosting?"

"Mrs. Jerome is in society. She has offered to give some time out here. We pay her a small salary, a pittance. I will deal with that," Mr. Burke said.

"Unless there's a source of income exceeding what you're making on food and the bar, I question how you can afford me. As I drove in, I noticed the buildings; golf course and tennis courts are in bad shape. Your other obligations, including upkeep on the swimming pool cost money, too. I would not like to take less than I'm making now."

"We'll meet what you're making. It's high for us, but if you'll give Gina a hand and help out in the dining room, we can cover that expense," Mr. Burke told her.

"Very well, Gentlemen, then if we've come to an agreement to more or less play it by ear for awhile as far as my duties are concerned, I'll pass as the bookkeeper, hostess and housekeeper at my present salary. When would you like me to start?"

"What about June first?" Roy asked.

"In two weeks, that sounds good to me."

Anne left and went home. She asked Jeanie, the desk clerk and Mr. Johnson's daughter-in-law, if he was in the house. He was in the bar.

"Hello, Mr. Johnson."

"Are you taking a day off?" He asked.

"You might say that. I'd like you to be the first to know I've taken another job."

"I thought you might be due for a change. You don't look very happy about it. Is something wrong?"

"No, nothing's wrong. It's just that I'm not familiar with the operation. It's at the MeadowLark Country Club."

"Isn't Roy Smith out there?"

"I'll just be the bookkeeper and jack of all trades. But you see, Mr. Johnson, I don't know a thing about private clubs."

"Did you tell them that?"

"Yes. They seemed to think it wasn't that much different from a hotel. While I can agree there is a similarity as far as the food operation is concerned, I've not had much experience with entertaining."

"I guess it depends on how high up you want to go with this dream of yours to become a hotel manager. Knowing catering will no doubt be to your advantage and that club out there would be a good place to learn. I'd say, not bad. Not bad at all. The only thing is they don't pay very good out there."

"I won t get a raise, but they've promised me the same money and I do need a change, Mr. Johnson."

"You know I wish you luck. You've done pretty well for your-self since you've been in Great Falls. I didn't think you'd do it that first day," he laughed. "You're still staying here?"

"You're not going to be able to get rid of me, Mr. Johnson."

Anne made the change the first of June. She and Mike parted amicably. He gave her a bonus and said he was sorry to lose her, but he understood.

In spite of the weathered appearance of the clubhouse, Anne felt the MeadowLark Country Club had a personality of it's own. The building was an architectural treasure of the single story Victorian elegance.

Her work started with billing and sending out dues notices for the membership and becoming familiar with their names. She brought accounts payable and receivable up to date. She had a porter scrub out her office and bought curtains for the large ex-panse of windows in her office. There were windows every where. She bought two pictures for two walls. One of a stormy sea with high angry waves going nowhere. On the opposite wall she placed a tranquil meadow scene, a few cows grazing on green grass and a peaceful pool under the shade of oak trees.

Her desk was centered, just in front of the windows, facing the door and looking out at a hallway onto a blank wall. She found a painting she could hang on that wall. Two large wooden tables stood against the sidewalls under her pictures, and the files leaned against the wall as one entered.

Ten days passed before she was nicely settled in her office and had the accounts in order. Gina came into her office on that sec-ond Monday morning and asked, "Are you all caught up?"

"It's a breeze," Anne said. "Ten days and all caught up and the nest made habitable."

"Good," Gina said. "Mrs. Albutross wants a luncheon for twenty ladies and they'll play bridge afterward."

"How does Mrs. Albutross concern me?" Anne asked.

"You're going to set it up."

"Gina! I don't know anything about bridge parties!"

"Then it's time you learned. They told me you knew everything."

"And I told you I didn't!"

"Here's where you begin to learn. Mrs. Balderdash wants to make arrangements for a dinner after Mrs. Albutross's bridge party. In the small dining room."

"Gina!"

"Do you know about this? Do you know about that?" Anne said mockingly to Gina. "You had better learn," Gina replied, "because Mrs. Caladonia wants a buffet luncheon with her bridge group on Tuesday."

So it went with Gina bullying Anne to accept greater responsibility for country club entertaining, but always with an eye to please the member.

Suddenly Anne was interested. Coming in one morning she said to Gina, "I've been thinking on how we may get people out here for dinners. That seems to be where we're falling short. Luncheons are so so and the downstairs food isn't doing badly. What do you think about sending a calendar out every Friday with next week's dinner menu as well as the activities for the week? I hope we don't need board approval for that."

"No," Gina said. "Just Roy's approval and it sounds real good to me. I'm glad that you're finally thinking about business," she added.

"I just had to adjust my mind to another way of thinking, Gina. When can you sit down with me and work out next week's dinner menus?"

"Let's see, tomorrow's Wednesday"

"I'll need time to get them copied and sent out," Anne said. "So we' II have to get to it if we want them out on Friday."

"I'll come in early tomorrow morning and go over it with you," Gina replied.

"Fine. Now, what did you say about Mrs. Doberman?" Anne asked, moving on to the next item.

"Now that you've adjusted, I need a dozen fresh chickens and a short loin. Will you order them for me?"

"That, Gina, I know how to do. Also, I found a list of preferred suppliers," Anne volunteered.

The next morning Anne and Gina worked out the next week's
menus for mailing.

When they were finished Anne told Gina," You know, I know
how to deal with the general public. A selected membership is
something my mind has to accept. Feeding the masses who come
into a hotel is one thing, but it takes a little adjustment for these
private dinners, private luncheons, tea parties and card parties."

"It isn't all that hard to learn if you'll just put your back to it"
Gina told her. "Don't forget we have the Fourth of July celebration
coming up. For that we have a traditional swimming party, barbecue and golf tournament."

"I don't suppose there's time to promote a beauty contest?"
Anne asked.

"That would take a month at least to arrange. Better forget
that." Gina advised.

Tables were set up around the swimming pool and the edge of
the golf course as near as one would want to be by the ninth hole.

The barbecue was set up in the parking lot, close by the
swimming pool. It was to be a gala Fourth!

The last day of June it began to rain and alternate plans had to
be made for indoor entertainment in case the rain didn't give up.

On the afternoon of the third the rain stopped but the tournament had to be called off as the grounds were too soggy. Indoor
plans were put in motion as it was also too cold for swimming.
The rivers were rising.

The kitchen crew worked all night with Anne to make a pseudo
barnyard appearance to the dining room and porch. The barbecue
would be in front of the fireplace.

It was almost midnight when Gina told her crew to go home.
Jim, the caretaker, she and Anne finished up. Anne suggested Jim
move into the basement apartment just in case the water rose
higher. If necessary he could then move his cot into the small
dining room.

They checked the Pro's cottage. It was locked and they couldn't get in. They knew he was in town on a drunk as his wife had just left him again.

Just as they went to their cars, the Sun and the Missouri Rivers jumped their banks and water rushed onto the grounds. They waited for the first onslaught to subside. "You'd better take the cars to high ground and leave 'em," Jim told them. "Take the pickup and get the hell outta here. I'll hold the fort down!"

"Just a minute, Gina, I can't leave the books here," Anne said. She ran back into the club house, grabbed the employees record book, the ledgers and the check book, then hurried out to the pick-up Gina was ready to leave.

From the highway they looked back. It seemed the rivers were emptying themselves onto the golf course.

"I hope Jim will be alright out there by himself." Anne worried.

"Don't worry about Jim. He's a survivor. There's plenty of food and the phone should stay in service for quite some time."

Anne went into the hotel and up to her room. She immediately called Mr. Burke.

"It had better be good this time of night," he said before he said hello.

"I'll make it as good as I can. We flooded out at the club around midnight. The rivers jumped their banks."

"What? "

"Everything's tied down and locked up. Jim stayed out there. We moved him into the basement. I have the books. There's nothing you can do before morning, so good night." She hung up.

Morning saw the grounds covered with nearly hip deep water. Only the clubhouse, sitting on it's rocky pinnacle was dry.

Mr. Brand, the President of the club, called Anne the next morning and told her to dismiss all the employees until further notice. He also instructed her to give them two weeks extra pay and tell them they would be notified of future plans.

"I'll call Roy myself, but you'll have to stay on. We'll get you out there by boat if we have to."

"I hardly think there's need for that. I brought the books and employee's records with me."

"Good, then you can work out of your hotel room until the water goes down."

Anne and Jim were the only employees left at the club, Jim on-site and Anne off-site. The Pro was still under contract. But as soon as he sobered up he decided to go on the golf circuit or what was left of it that season.

By the first of August the water was down and the road was open. Mr. Brand called Anne to attend a Board meeting at the club.

Anne was early. Jim had piled all the furniture in the south end of the dining/ballroom. As Anne walked through this empty space it had the sound and feeling of an old barn. Jim had left one long wooden table in the kitchen for whatever work area might be needed. Anne made coffee and placed chairs, pads, pencils, cups and saucers around the table for the twelve members of the board.

She heard Mr. Brand come in with Mr. Burke and went to meet them, guiding them to what had been the kitchen. "This is the only working space we have," she told them. "This will do nicely, it's a short business meeting." Mr. Burke assured her, "I see you made coffee, thank you."

The Board slowly began to drift in. When they were all there, Mr. Brand told Anne to pull up a chair to his right as she was to attend this meeting. Believing she was to take notes, Anne brought another note pad to the table and sat down.

"Anne will be staying on at the club to look after things. She will keep members informed of the club's progress, handle billings and write |letters to ask for continued support for the club while we are closed," Mr. Brand began.

He also announced that one of their members, Mr. Peters, had offered to loan the club money to renovate the clubhouse and add nine holes to the golf course.

Mr. Peters had chosen Anne to be in charge while this project was going on. In exchange for this loan, with negligible interest Mr.

Peters would be Chairman of the Board until all financial liability was satisfied.

"Why this woman? No one here knows her." One Board member objected.

"I believe that's the reason Anne was chosen." Mr. Brand told them.

No one could have been more surprised than Anne. She did not know this Mr. Peters and had never seen him or heard of him until this moment.

Al Brand stayed behind and gave Anne instructions on what her duties would be. First there were letters to write encouraging the members to stay with the club through a renovation period, and to pay their dues even though there would be no activity for approximately one year. The new club would reward their support.

"You'll be responsible for checking all construction invoices and paying the bills. Jim Burke or I will co-sign checks with you."

Mr. Brand left and Anne went to her office. It seemed this would not be an idle year after all. Her work was cut out for her, not what she had planned, but . . .

Now to get to that letter asking people for money for which they were getting nothing for at least a year.

Her thoughts were interrupted by a "Hello, you must be Anne I was told you would still be here."

"Yes . . ." she answered.

Coming in the door was a man six feet plus, dressed in a torn denim shirt and a battered hat with fishing flies so thick, Anne could hardly see the shock of white hair. He was a well-preserved seventy.

His jeans were as ragged as his shirt showing red and white shorts underneath.

Ragged clothes and beat up hat notwithstanding, there was a powerful energy about this man that Anne felt immediately. She rose from her desk, stepped around it and held out her hand. They shook hands while he scrutinized her with a studied look.

"I'm leaving for Hawaii tomorrow and I want to leave you my itinerary and a check," he said as he walked around her desk. Seating himself in her chair, he pulled a filing card from his pocket with dates and names of places.

"This is where you can reach me whenever you need to," he said. Taking a checkbook out of his torn pocket, he wrote out a check and handed it to her, along with his itinerary.

"That should get things started out here."

Anne looked at the check. She sat down. She looked at it again.

"What's the matter?" He asked.

"How many zero's are there in a million?"

"Well now," he laughed, "you're holding three million dollars in your hand. That's just to get things rolling out here. Hasn't Al been out to tell you the plan?"

"Do you mean that Board meeting that was held out here this morning?"

'The whole damn Board was out here, you say? Never saw such a bunch of people afraid to hire a woman."

"Hire a woman?"

"What did they tell you?"

"Just asked me to stay through construction."

"It amounts to a little more than that. But we'll let it rest there for the time being. That check is to get the construction started. You, Al and Jim will be the only ones to sign checks. Now Anne, you don't know me from Adam, but I know all about you. You and I have to have a little understanding. You have to be my watchdog. Have you any objection to that?"

"Generally speaking, no. Depends on what it entails."

"Fair enough. I've had you checked out pretty thoroughly, from Floyd Roberts who has known you for most of your life to Mike, who had some pretty nice things to say about you. How did you ever get mixed up with that mobster?"

"Mike treated me very well, Mr. Peters." She looked at the signature on the check to make sure she had his name right. "I wanted a hotel to manage and he gave me that chance. Even if we didn't call it that, I knew and he and Lloyd knew that I was the manager. That was good enough for me. I learned."

"That's where you learn. Where everything is wrong and you have to go in and straighten it out. You always handled yourself well. There's not that much difference in a hotel and a private club, just more emphasis on food and entertaining in a club. You do well in one; you'll do well with the other. Being a woman you picked a rough row to hoe, so you have to get off on the right foot. I want you to joined some clubs before we open next spring."

"It makes me wonder why a perfect stranger would give me this opportunity." Anne asked Mr. Peters.

"If you want to grow in management, in any business, you have to know the right people. And being one of those Russians from down there around Billings does not qualify you to manage a country club."

"I am not a Russian!"

"Same difference. That's where your people came from. That's neither here nor there, you have to know the right people. Edith, my secretary, will see that you're nominated to all the important organizations in town."

"Why are your doing this for me?"

"I'd like to see what one of you Russians can do. You've already broken the kitchen mold. You've got guts, now let's see what else you can do. Not only as a Russian, but as a woman in a man's world. You've got your chance, let's see what you do with it."

"You're serious?" She remembered she had heard this phrase before, in El Paso.

"Damn right, I'm serious. I never do anything half way. Go for the brass ring! I want you to start with the Business and Professional Women, the Soroptimist, the Toastmistress and, let's see; there's another one. Can't think of the name of it but Edith will know? I want you to sit in on every Board meeting. You'll be notified. Whether they're official meetings or not, you be there! You're my representative. My ears, my eyes. If they try to have secret meetings, there's someone who will let you know and you let me know."

"You check everything. Anything questionable you check with Jim. They don't know you and, being a woman, they'll try to put something over on you. I'm told you're a loner. That's good stay that way."

"Now this next item is important and confidential. Don't allow anyone to know what or how much is budgeted for anything."

Mr. Peters pulled a typewritten sheet of paper from his shirt pocket and handed it to Anne.

"This is the estimated cost allowable for each project. The golf course, the tennis courts, the swimming pool and our new clubhouse, which includes the Pro shop and locker rooms. The golf course is in three segments of development, so it's important to watch this first one, or they'll be in trouble right away when they start on the second segment."

"There's another eight million dollars in reserve." He laughed and Anne felt this was her testing ground. This is where he would find out if he could trust her.

"Believe me," he was saying, "if they get wind of that amount, they'll find a place to spend it. I've got to get away for a vacation and I can't be here to watch their every move. You're a stranger, Mike tells me you know how to mind your own business and keep your mouth shut. He says you're to be trusted. That's saying a lot from a man like Mike."

"You'd better know they don't think the same way about you in Denver. That woman, Miss Lacey, sure doesn't have any liking for you. Said you never managed anything. I didn't tell her you hadn't claimed to. Now, Mr. Beatty did say some mighty nice things about you. He didn't believe you had the guts to do what you did. That kinda surprised him. Guess they don't think much of women in that outfit. How did you get mixed up with them?"

"I worked for the Hilton Hotel during the war. When my husband didn't come back, I just sort of stayed on because Mr. Hilton gave me a chance to learn the business."

"I see," he rose from the desk. "Well, you've got everything straight. The budget and my itinerary. I'll see you when I get back." As he started out the door he stopped, looked back thoughtfully and said, "I'll send you someone from Seattle to help you."

Anne watched him go, then she looked at the check in her hand. She had never seen this man before. Still, he like Mr. Hilton, was giving her a chance, an opportunity.

She sat at her desk, laid the itinerary card and the check to one side and studied the allotment list.

She found that the $3 million was divided between the golf course and the clubhouse. In studying the golf course allotment, she saw it would take most of the money for survey, contour and drainage. There was also a note advising her Mr. Sturgis, the golf course architect, would be checking in September first and she was to give him the Pro's vacated house. Mr. Peters had paid off the Pro's contract, and the Pro moved on to Reno.

The clubhouse was to be completely renovated and Mr. Barton, from Seattle, would be the designer. A local firm of architects drew up the plans for the clubhouse. The Pro shop and the ladies and men's locker rooms were to be attached to the clubhouse. Mr. Peters would meet with Mr. Barton in Seattle, after which he would arrive in Great Falls and Anne was to make arrangements for he and his wife to stay at the Rainbow Hotel.

Anne gave a deep sigh and wondered if she was up to it. What sort of man would Mr. Barton be?

She would be able to discuss matters with Mr. Brand and Mr. Burke on all but the eight million. She looked at the check lying on her desk. It was Thursday and the bank was closed but she didn't want to keep this check overnight. She called Mr. Burke and asked that he arrange for her to get into the hank. He said he would and send someone out as well. He sent a Highway Patrol officer!

In the days that followed Anne saw golf committee people, construction people and the just plain curious.

Some thought there was not sufficient money for the entire program, and of course there wasn't. However, there was adequate money to get started.

Then good fortune met Anne again. Mr. Peters sent Mr. Barton, an interior designer from Seattle, to help her! In Mr. Barton, Anne found a friend. This was a person she could talk to. Mr. Barton

took Anne's mind off the petty things that arose such as speculation
as to why Mr. Peters had chosen her to be the watchdog over the
affairs of the country club. Rumors were rampart and Anne was
called everything from a Medusa to a Jezebel. Where she had been
graciously greeted wherever she went, now there was whispering
behind hands. It might have gotten to her had not Mr. Johnson
counseled her to hold up her head and pay no attention. This was
the price she had to pay for daring to rise above the crowd. As Mr.
Peters had warned her, she had picked a tough row to hoe.

Mr. Barton took her mind off these hurtful innuendoes and
got her on track, doing what she should be doing at the club. He
came in one morning and asked, "What are you doing about your
dishes, linens, and paper goods?"

"What am I doing? There's a committee for that, isn't there?"
She had learned that much about club protocol.

"Not anymore, there isn't. That's your job now. What are you
waiting for?"

"My God, what do I do?"

"There's an adequate allowance for those things in the budget
you have. How many tables do you need? I'm pretty busy so you
can work out a logo to place on everything but the kitchen sink. I
talked to Mr. Peters at great length in Seattle. He put up the money
and he calls the shots. He told; me he was grooming you for manager. He also asked me to help you all I could. I'm willing to do
that but I want your input. I'll listen to you and you listen to me,
O.K.?"

"You know what to do," he continued. "You learned all that at
the Hilton and you did a credible job at the Park your first time
out. This isn't any different. Get busy doing all the things you
would do if you had a hotel to open. I'll be here designing the
interior so we'll work closely. Decide on your table measurements
and order your linen. Get busy picking out a design for a logo we
can put in the dishes, matches, paper work, stationary, napkins,
silver and crystal . . ."

"I'd like a very personal design," Anne ventured.

"Have you thought of something?"

"Yes, but I didn't think I'd be able to use it. I'd like a MeadowLark sitting on crossed golf clubs, in earth tones. What do you think?"

"Not bad. I'll draw something for you then you can get busy ordering. Call a local crockery firm and order your dishes through them. *Always, always* order through local merchants, members if possible," he advised. It creates good public relations." He rose to leave and turned back at the door, "Remember, there's a six to nine months waiting period for custom dishes. I'll have your logo for you tomorrow."

The next day Mr. Barton came in with the logo and Anne was very pleased with the design. It was exactly as she had imagined it. She sent the sketch to Mr. Peters for approval. He wired back, "Order now!" A few days later she received another wire, instructing her to order a mosaic of the logo for the entrance floor.

Mr. Barton brought the plans for the clubhouse to the office. He spread them out on one of the long wooden tables in Anne's office and told her, "Here's your kitchen and dining rooms."

She checked the plans for the dining room and what would become two private dining rooms. She measured the tables and the rooms for total seating capacity. They would no longer have use of the porch, as it was to become a terrace.

She calculated the number of place settings that would be needed for three turnovers in the dining rooms.

Next time Mr. Barton came in he asked if she had finished her list of dishes.

"I've an order here that is enough for a regiment," she replied as she handed him her estimated order.

He glanced over it with a practiced eye and said, "you haven't included the 19th hole or the swimming pool. That's the downstairs bar. For the pool and the 19th Hole you need something that won't break. They can cut their feet from broken dishes and sue us. When they come in from the golf course exuberant from winning or mad from losing, they'll break the dishes."

"Where would I find dishes that don't break for goodness sake?" Anne asked exasperated.

"Try a hospital supply house," he recommended.

Anne found a hospital supply house that could furnish heavy plastic in attractive colors. She ordered them and Mr. Barton changed the building plan that would put an entrance from the 19th Hole to the pool. All was going well and the clubhouse renovation was on schedule. Anne had found it more comfortable to wear jeans on-site, instead of the fresh cottons she liked in the summertime and the tailored suites for winter. This became a cause for criticism. It was undignified, some thought. However, crawling in attics and basement tunnels in a dress was just not practical and she ignored the talk.

She saw little of the old staff, but she often called Gina to give her a status report on how the work was coming along. Roy came out to tell her he had purchased a liquor store and would not be coming back.

Joe Fraser, who had the contract for building the golf course, came out to the office one morning. "Anne," he boomed, "You know that million isn't going to be enough to build a brick shit house, let alone eighteen holes."

"I think we're all agreed on that, Mr. Fraser. But isn't the golf course to be in three stages of development?" She asked.

"I need to know what's in the kitty for the whole job."

"I can't tell you that since I don't know myself. I believe Mr. Peters specified what he wanted done by the time he came back from his vacation. He also felt that million was enough to get it done."

"I gotta have a better figure to work with than I have now!"

"Mr. Fraser, I can't believe you didn't talk to Mr. Peters about this before he left or at the time you contracted for the job. There must have been some sort of agreement as to what you could do with a million dollars. I certainly can't give you information I don't have. Besides, won't the money have a lot to do with how close you keep to your schedule?"

"Well now, can't you give me a ballpark figure?" He cajoled
"I don't know what park we're playing in." Anne countered.
He left in a huff. That afternoon, a handsome young man
appeared at Anne's door. A foreman, maybe. He was dressed as a
construction worker.

"Got any coffee here?" He asked.

"Coffee, I always have. No food, but plenty of coffee," Anne
pointed at the coffee urn she kept in the office. He drew a cup of
coffee and slumped down in a chair as though he was really ready
for this minute of relaxation from his hard work.

He watched Anne. She ignored him and went on with her typing.

"By the way, I'm Bob Fraser. What do you do with yourself
besides work?"

"Work." She smiled at him and went on with her work. She
wondered what he was up to since her abortive talk with his father.
She had heard of Bob Fraser. There were rumors of an impending
divorce.

"Haven't you a boyfriend?" He finally asked.

"Don't have time."

"Don't you ever go out?"

"Out?" She leaned on the typewriter. "I go to shows. To dinner. Now and then I even have a drink. I'm not in love. I'm not
interested in anyone. Anything else?"

"How would you like to go out to dinner with me?"

Anne looked at him thoughtfully and said, "Now why would
Bob Fraser want to take me to dinner? Why, we've hardly known
each other," she looked at her watch," I'd say ten minutes."

"I'd kinda like to know what makes you tick. Besides, you're
kinda pretty."

"It seems to me, I've gotten the impression somewhere that
you're still married."

"You mean you'd let that stop you?"

"You're damn right it would. Everyone in this town knows
you. Most people in this town have found me a favored past-time
for gossip. An unhealthy curiosity about how I got this job."

"How did you get it?" He asked.

"I must say one thing for you," Anne said laughing. "You shoot straight from the shoulder. Roy Smith hired me. It was convenient to keep me on because I'm a stranger. No ties to people who would try to use me for getting information. What do you think?"

"Ouch! Do you always hit below the belt?"

"You mean I hit a nerve?"

"No Anne, you didn't. But it is a matter of interest. Roy was here, then you're suddenly running things. I hear the same thing happened at the Park."

"Roy did hire me. A closed club does not need a manager. It does need a bookkeeper, an office girl. I assume the board decided to keep me."

Bob rose, drew himself another cup of coffee, took his seat again and said, "I can assure you it was not the Board who decided to keep you."

"Oh well, it really doesn't matter. The position I hold when the club opens will be the deciding factor whether I stay or not."

"The worst that could happen is that you stay in the position you 're in. Or are you thinking of yourself as a manager?"

"I've been reading up a lot on club management lately. I found managers of these clubs usually come from retired members, like bank managers, ousted city, county or state officials. None of them businessmen. They come in and they look around and think, 'this would be a cinch. Think of all the golf I could get in. Then it isn't long before they find they can't get on the golf course as often as they thought because all hell is breaking out in the kitchen. The kitchen was something his wife always handled but the kitchen help doesn't work for his wife. What does he know about kitchens? How did he ever get into this mess anyway?"

"What's the matter with the chef handling the disturbance in the kitchen?" Bob asked. "Isn't that what he was hired for?"

"At this point the chef is looking for a referee, and most chef's cannot fire anyone. This is also the time when they need someone like me, someone who doesn't have to get out on the golf course, or tennis court, but knows how to settle that fracas in the kitchen.

"Come on, now, you're making this sound like a three ring circus."

"That isn't the half of it if that manager has never worked with a Board. Bank directors are absolute gentlemen compared with country club directors. They aren't concerned that he was their bank manager, or was their elected representative. No, by God, he's their club manager now. He's there to serve them!"

"There are also nine committee chairmen who can come down on him. That is nothing to the fifty-six committee members. Count them." She shoved a piece of paper across the desk at him from which she had been studying the protocol of the club hierarchy.

"Am I bucking for manager?" She asked. 'When I look at this I wonder how long I would survive. "I take it you've never worked for a Board before?"

"No. When I worked for Hilton, you might say it was by directive. I was learning and I seldom questioned. I had a great deal of respect for the people I was learning from. At the Park I put into practice what I had learned. It worked. Neither Mike nor Lloyd interfered with me, we had an agreement. It would make it hard for me to have to ask permission for every little picayune thing that came along."

"I don't think you'd have to account to Peters in quite that subservient way."

"It's not Mr. Peters I'd be worried about. Maybe it should. Have you ever heard him bellow? When I heard it I was glad he was in Hawaii. Let's not forget there are also eight committee advisors and from what I've observed of them, they are experts in the field of everything and anything except running a club. They read a book, just as I'm doing, with one difference. I have hotel experience."

Bob stared at her with a look of disbelief as she went on. "So you see, Bob, I am something unique. I am a trained manager, but a woman. As a woman, I recognize I have to take second place. I have never worked for a Board. Your retired member, hopefully a good host, can blame a committee for his mistakes or shortcomings. While I, I'm afraid, have to take my duties much more seriously and personally. I will not be allowed the privilege of blaming anyone but myself for anything."

"Whatever plan Mr. Peters has in mind I don't know. I'm as much in the dark about my future at the Meadow Lark Country Club as we both are about your budget."

Bob laughed and thoughtfully looked at the floor. "O.K." He sighed and looked up. "Let's be friends. My marital status, although I'm sure you're not really interested, is that I am getting a divorce. Yes, it's been filed by her, in California. Now, how about dinner tonight?"

"If we can leave club business here. My loyalty is to Mr. Peters. That will not change no matter how many drinks or what my interest might be with one Bob Fraser."

"What time shall I pick you up?" He grinned.

"How about seven thirty?" She replied.

"I'll see you." He touched a finger to his hard hat with a mocking gesture. "Thanks for the coffee and the very enlightening insight into club management."

Anne was looking over the plans Mr. Barton had brought her. Having finished with the dining room plans, she was now giving the kitchen plans her undivided attention, when Mr. Barton came in.

"Do you know what you're reading?" Mr. Barton asked as Anne scrutinized the kitchen plans.

"Sure. I almost became an architect once."

"You're kidding. You do have a propensity for stepping into a man's world. Have you ever wanted to be a man?"

"Never! I love being a woman. I love my name. I love my birth sign. Doesn't that make me a well adjusted person?" She laughed.

"I didn't know they allowed women in that hallowed stratosphere of study."

"Women should never have allowed it to become a man's domain. Women are the ones who should be designing the homes for the future."

"Oh, why?"

"Well, just one minor detail. Women are taller these days than we were when the standard height for worktables and counters, as well as sinks were determined for the little woman. Kitchen and bathroom sinks are back breakers. They haven't changed height requirements in a hundred years. So we have to break our backs leaning over low sinks."

"Too bad you didn't have a chance."

"Oh but I did."

"How far did you get?"

"I learned to read a blueprint. This kitchen is all wrong. That doesn't come from architectural knowledge, but common sense from anyone who has worked in this industry. I hope you didn't design this kitchen, because then you won't like what I'm going to say."

"No, I understand a hotel man drew up the design for the architect. The architect's name is on the bottom left hand corner. He's a member."

"Have you checked it out?"

"No, kitchens are not my forte."

"This thing is set up all wrong. It's a long kitchen. That's not bad, however, the IN door has the hot food to be picked up. The OUT door has the cold food to be picked up. It should be the other way around so the hot food is picked up last and thus comes out hot. Of course the doors could be changed, but if you do that you have busboys colliding with waitresses with loaded trays. That's the beginning. The dishwasher is over here where the noise interferes with conversation in the private dining room. On the opposite side we have noise only in the office, which I understand it to be a storeroom. Who cares about noise in a storeroom?"

"You're the one who will have to tell Mr. Peters and you know the roof will come off."

"He won't be back until after Christmas. Let him enjoy his Holiday."

Bob Fraser picked Anne up at seven thirty that evening. They went to Black Hawk, a small industrial village, where there had been many roadhouses before repeal. They continued on with night-clubs and fine Italian dining.

Anne enjoyed his company until he gradually brought the conversation around to the club and the cost of the golf course. Then she suggested calling it a night.

The next two weeks Anne went to dinner several times with Mr. Prince Charming. For those two weeks Bob hinted, alluded and finally just came out and asked about the budget. Anne pleaded ignorance and the charming little dinners in Black Hawk ceased.

Another contractor skipped the subtle approach. He barged into Anne's office late one evening. A monster with a treat 'em rough and make 'em like it approach, he came at her and she feared she would be raped right there in the office had not Mr. Barton returned for something at the crucial moment.

"I don't think you should stay out here late anymore unless someone safe is out here with you," Mr. Barton said.

"My God, who would have thought it of him?"

Mr. Barton changed the subject to take her mind off of the incident.

"You never finished telling me about your architectural experience, and since Mr. Peters is almost due in San Francisco on the Lurline, I'd like to hear about it before he chops your head off," he laughed.

"I got the bug to want to be an architect when my aunt decided to build a new home in Billings. I was living with her and we would go over the plans every evening. I became absolutely fascinated. I went back to Colorado and signed up for architecture, literature and history, taking as little as I could of the latter two subjects so I could concentrate on the architecture. I was the only girl in the class. Let me tell you, I was not welcome! The professor let me know in no uncertain terms that I had stepped into a man's world! He told me it would be better if I reconsidered my choice . . . something more feminine. I tried to persuade him, very nicely, that I had considered my options very carefully and I wanted to take this course. When my tactfulness didn't work, I got stubborn. I told him I would not be coerced out of this class!"

"He said my presence was disturbing to the men. I offered to wear a Mother Hubbard gown in class. He didn't think that was funny or appropriate. So I suggested he come up with a solution that would not exempt me from class."

"Did he?" Mr. Barton laughed.

"Most assuredly. In the left-hand corner in the rear of the classroom, he built a cubicle. I could see the front of the classroom but no one could see me!"

"This is incredible. Did you stay?"

"Yes, I stayed but I'm sorry to say, for only two semesters."

"It must have been miserable," Mr. Barton sympathized.

"When one must tolerate, one begins to see the funny side of things. One can't let others know how much you hurt. I learned to read architectural plans, maybe more from my aunt than my class, which takes us back to these kitchen plans. Mr. Peters is staying at the Mark Hopkins. I'll send him these plans with my new and improved suggestions. Maybe he'll blow off steam before he gets here."

Two days after Mr. Peters arrived in San Francisco, he came storming into Anne's office.

"What is the meaning of this?" He roared at her and threw the plans on her desk. This was no time to retreat. She stood up and went to the table where the plans were laid out.

"As I advised you in my note, which accompanied those plans," she said pointing to her desk, "they are not made up right. The traffic pattern is all wrong!"

"What the hell do you know about it? The most reputable architect in the state of Montana made up those plans!"

"He doesn't know anything about food service!"

"And you know so damned much?"

"Mr. Peters, since I know you checked out my background with a fine tooth comb before you ever told the Board you wanted me for this job, you had to know I knew food operation! That means more than just serving! That means I also have to know where and how food is picked up to get hot food into the dining room hot and cold food into the dining room cold! I also have to know how to keep waitresses and busboys from colliding with loaded trays! This," she pointed to the print, "sure as hell doesn't do it!"

"If you're so damn smart, draw me a kitchen!" He yelled at her and stomped out.

"I will, " she yelled after him.

Immediately he came back and challenged her, "you haven't told anyone what the final budget is, have you?"

"The answer is NO! "

"I've been getting reports that you've been pretty chummy with Bob Fraser."

Anne paused. She should have known someone would make it their business to inform him of her activities. She took a deep breath before she answered, "I haven't told anyone anything! Not because I wasn't wined and dined, received improper proposals, both moral and monetary and fought off attempted rape and seduction. The answer is still NO. I did not tell anyone about your damned budget!" He grinned at her and left.

Anne was seething. Not only had someone carried tales about her, but he had dared to challenge her loyalty because he had no other ammunition.

"I'll show him," she thought. She looked again at the prints and went to the kitchen for some of the butcher paper they kept for covering the table where the workmen ate.

She spread it out and got her rulers and sharp pencils. "I'll show him!" She told herself again as she prepared to start work. She got a measuring tape. As she looked around the kitchen, she decided there was no need for that large expanse in front of the stoves. They could use a bakery very nicely, and there was room for a good-sized bakery if she moved the stoves into the middle of the room.

She moved the dish washing room into a pantry to break the noise. It was after midnight when she arrived home. She dreamt of the kitchen, rose and went back out to the club, where she worked through the afternoon until she had finished the plans. One last time she followed the traffic lines, the ease of coming into the dish washing room, the placement of the refrigeration and checked out the bakery. She drew arrows to show traffic lines. Satisfied, she went home. As she locked the door, she thought, 'That should show him!'

It was noon on Monday before Mr. Peters arrived at the club. Jolly and full of good spirits, he came into the office. Anne was waiting for him. She threw the new prints on butcher paper at him, just as he had thrown them at her.

"There's your new and improved kitchen," she told him smiling.

He opened the roll and looked at it with a grin before he spread it out on the table against the wall.

"Uhmmmm . . . . uhmmm I see . . . uhmmmm. You know, this is damned good. I can see how this would work better." He traced the service lines with his finger. 'Uhmmmm, why couldn't that architect see this?"

"Perhaps because he's never been in a kitchen or waited on table," she smugly told him.

"Neither have I but I think if I were designing I could see this, put myself in place of the people . . . but you know, that's no excuse. I paid Pat from the Rainbow as a consultant. Pat started in the Rainbow as a busboy he worked his way up. Call him. Call both of them and tell them to get the hell out here! You stay out of sight until I call you. Understand?"

Again he was looking at the plans as Anne went to her desk to call the hotel manager and the architect.

When Anne returned to the table, Mr. Peters was still muttering "Uhmmm, not bad . . . not bad . . . what's this, a bakery?"

"I thought we needed one as we use so many bakery goods and there was room."

Mr. Peters gathered up the plans to take them to the kitchen, reminding Anne to stay out of sight.

Mr. Peters was waiting in the kitchen when the architect and Pat found him. Anne had locked her door.

Soon she could hear shouting and table pounding. She knew she was right and there would be no repercussion from Mr. Peters, but what would these men do to her? She suddenly realized they could destroy all she had been working toward and Mr. Peters had planned for her, according to Mr. Barton

She heard Mr. Peters roar, "Anne, come in here!"

Anne went into the kitchen with some reservation, but ready to do battle if she had to. Mr. Peters was leaning back in his chair, at ease. The architect and Pat were studiously going over the plans. Mr. Peters was enjoying himself.

"Now gentlemen," he said as Anne entered, "Meet the lady who did this. Do we agree it is a masterpiece and that she knew what she was doing. She knows the path of picking up food, of keeping employees from colliding and she knows how to keep noise from the dining areas! So, who is going to manage this club? She is!"

His statement could be compared to a bomb falling in the room. Anne was as flabbergasted as the men sitting at that table. She probably had some reservation about what Mr. Barton had told her. A dream, yes, but this reality . . . she sat in the nearest chair, stunned.

This man, this self-made millionaire, a blacksmith son for whom she had the highest respect had just put her on a professional par with others in a way she had only dreamed of.

This man was giving her the chance for that bronze plaque on a door, a door that didn't exist yet.

"Alright, Anne," he turned to her, "get to work and hire your crew. This bakery you've added, I like that. There's a place in Portland. I want you to send whomever you hire there to be trained

. . . I'm not going to tell you who to hire, I want to see what you do."

Anne left the kitchen in a daze. She had carte blanche. First she called Gina to come to work. There was much they had to do, that had to be done in tandem. She told Gina, "Among your people there are good workers. That's what I want. You will hire the kitchen and dining room crew. I'll hire the bartenders and whoever we have for the 19th Hole. We have to play a lot by ear, take care of things as they come along. We can't be open before the fifteenth of June. You need to find a woman who would make a good baker and we'll send her to Portland to a place Mr. Peters recommended. But Gina, I need people who will stay on the job, people who are loyal to you and me. Can we do it?"

"I told you once, Anne. You do right by our people, we'll go all the way with you."

"That's all I can ask for, thanks."

Anne called Jack and asked if he wanted to come out as head bartender. "When do I start, Boss Lady?"

"Yesterday, and Jack, you can call your family in New Jersey to pack up and come out now."

After that the club seemed to buzz with activity. Mr. Barton had done a beautiful job with grays and burgundy for a color scheme. The private dining rooms were in burgundy and yellows. The dishes, with the meadow lark logo, were on cream colored dishes. The woodwork was in white. The lounge had thermal windows now, as did the terrace.

As the clubhouse took shape and there emerged the most beautiful club in the northwest.

The Board met and officially appointed Anne as manager. The President lingered behind to give Anne advice on how to handle the membership and how not to get herself involved in any of the cliques that would be anxious now that she was manager, to take her over.

Anne had a door now. It opened to one side of the main door, across from the lounge. She had her bronze plaque fastened to it.

Jim, the maintenance man, laughed as she gave it an extra polish with her handkerchief.

She went back into the employee's eating area, outside the pantry where dishes were stored. She picked up a cup of coffee and sat down at the table waiting for Gina to join her. She looked up at the notice she had posted the day before, that the table must be kept clear when not in use. She had signed it 'Anne'. Underneath someone had written, AKA, Mrs. Simon Legree.

Gina came in with her pads and charts on how the tables should be set up for the opening buffet.

Anne was initialing SL for Simon Legree.

"Oh Anne, I'm so sorry, they were just teasing, you know."

"I know, Gina, but it won't hurt them to believe I may be Mrs. Simon Legree." The second Saturday of June was suddenly upon them. The clubhouse was bursting with activity. Gina and her crew were there early that morning getting ready for the onslaught of members by noon.

The Pro shop and the 19th Hole were already in a flurry. Lyle, the new Pro, was being introduced to the golfers by Mr. Peters, who was also giving the golfers a Cook's tour of the sports facility of the new club. Anne was presently using the area planned for expansion for storage space.

Gina and her crew were in early and had prepared food for the 19th Hole. Jack had hired Jake, Gina's brother as another bartender. He would take the 19th Hole during the day, and Greg, Montana's junior golf champion, would convert the 19th Hole into a teen's club with jukebox, soft drinks and sandwiches in the evenings.

The swimming pool was a sapphire-like jewel on the knoll beside the clubhouse.

There had not been time to finish the tennis courts by the second Saturday of June.

It had been a marathon day of members showing off their club to friends and visitors, until about three in the afternoon when everyone left to repair for the evening events.

There was a dinner dance and the tables overflowed onto the terrace and the reception room, to leave space for dancing.

There was a group of four entertainers from Los Angeles, with a well-built variety show.

Mr. Peters had friends from Chicago, Detroit, Seattle and other points west. There was Phil Harris and Harry James, not for their entertaining ability, but as golfing friends of Mr. Peters.

Gina, Jack and Anne worked together like a charm. It was as though nature had put them together to complement each other.

Each morning they had a short meeting of the day ahead and once a week they had a meeting of the week and the month ahead.

There were weddings, wedding receptions, breakfasts, luncheons and dinners planned. The private dining rooms were reserved weeks ahead.

The summer progressed but the golf course was not ready and would not be for at least another year, even though a very hardy grass had been sown that would survive the zero winters of Montana.

Lyle began to plan tournaments for the Snowbirds. These were golfers who played throughout the winter on snow with black balls. They could play on the hard crusted snow without damaging the grass underneath.

Anne got the invitations out and set up menus and hot toddy stands all along the fairways where the cold might be most severe for golfers in their walk from one green to another.

As cooler weather approached, Anne noted that most of the club activities such as card parties and club luncheons were just once a week. Too often she noticed, other than the golfers who had an interest in watching their course develop, ladies and gentlemen spent their time in the 19th Hole, while the dining room was sparsely used.

To correct this she began to arrange style shows, musicals and dancing recitals on the days when there was no planned activity.

She wanted to bring seminar luncheons to the club on these off days. The Board denied her request for use of the club for any except members.

Anne was anxious that every day had some event going for she was cognizant of the heavy debt the club was carrying.

The accounting, except for the daily business in the club and the collection of dues, was not taken care of at the club. The club was operating at a profit, and she had an operating reserve in the bank. However, the major profit was drained off into another account somewhere else. She presumed it went to the debt account.

With her healthy reserve Anne felt the pride of having a good cash flow for the club coffers.

It was Spring again and the golfers were eager to get out on the course. Even though it was not ready, they would walk the course and their anxiety to play grew to a frustrating point.

Anne, always too busy to listen to gossip, went about her work unheeding anything except her responsibilities to the club. The MeadowLark Country Club had become a joy and a delight to her. There had not been any of the usual let down associated with the routine that sets in after the excitement of starting something.

So it came as a surprise to her one day when she overheard a conversation as she was taking inventory in the room off the ladies locker room.

A group of women, having just come in from walking the golf course decided to try out the showers. Anne had left a door slightly ajar, for the supply room was kept closed at all times and got stuffy.

The women spoke proudly of their club and how it was such a pleasure to bring their guests to such a lovely club and always know the food would be excellent.

Anne smiled as she listened to them, for this is what she had been working toward. Then came a discordant voice.

"Yes, we do have a lovely club. It's too bad we have to have a woman manager."

"Now Marilyn, why do you want to be like that? She's done a wonderful job out here."

"You can say that, she gives your company a good amount of trade. But what does she know about clubs?"

"I think she's proven that. Now why don't we just change the subject?"

"Well, Ray was playing golf down in Billings with one of those new oil men. He was in a foursome with Mr. Peters and the man said he had known her as a young girl and that she was one of those Russians from down there."

"It wasn't so long ago that certain members of this club were called Bohunks. I don't think that story should be repeated."

Another voice spoke up, "I agree with Marilyn, Doris. It really embarrasses me to introduce my guests to a woman manager."

"Then don't introduce her," Doris told her. "You certainly can't say she's pushy, quite the opposite."

"Mr. Peters would take offense . . . ."

"I doubt that. I don't think either of them care one way or another."

"I wonder what's between her and our Mr. Peters? Another one of those affairs like Walt and his hussy."

Anne heard the door to the locker room close and sat there in shock.

Walt was another oilman who had purchased a social membership for his mistress so that her child could have use of the club swimming pool. She never attended social events at the club.

Bent over her inventory sheets, Anne wanted to cry. But she'd be damned if she would give them the satisfaction! She had no cause to be ashamed of her family. As Mr. Peters had said, though, they were not country club material, nor did they aspire to be. They worked hard. In seventy-five years they had 'made it' in this country, being Germans from Russia. Family meant more to them than any outside social life. They were a homogeneous people. Education, their heritage and family togetherness had the highest priority among them.

Anne felt anger and disappointment. Why were women a woman's worst enemy? Was there a deficiency within them that could not allow another woman a measure of success? Were they frustrated in their own lack . . . of guts . . . or whatever was lacking in women who were afraid, even to be women, that they cast aspersions on those who could and did do things?

But there was no time for analyzing the prejudices of these women.

Anne had to get ready for the evening activities. There was a golf dinner for visiting clubs to play at the MeadowLark next year.

Mrs. Fraser called to ask if she might bring a guest without paying the guest fee. Anne explained to her the Board had set this fee and there wasn't anything she could do about it.

Mrs. Fraser reminded Anne that since she and her son had been such good friends . . . "wouldn't that stand for anything?"

Anne, understanding the inference and still smarting from the afternoon tete a tete said,

"I didn't know we were such good friends, Mrs. Fraser. However if he'll give me call, I'm sure we still have some contractors complimentary passes."

The call from Bob never came.

Since hearing the locker room conversation, Anne found it a little difficult to be as cordial as she had always been. There was a tendency to wonder who else was talking and expressing like opinions.

Jack wanted to hire another bartender so he could help Anne with the greeting of members and, he said, act as host.

Anne confided in Gina about the locker room conversation as well as Jack's 'offer' to act as host for her.

"Why don't you talk to Mr. Peters, Anne?" Gina asked.

"Oh Gina, I'd be ashamed to."

"It isn't your shame, Anne. The shame is on the people who are spreading these lies."

"Does that mean you have heard them too?"

"I've heard them and so has Jack. I think he thinks you will be let go because of it so I'd pull his teeth if I were you."

"Let me think on it." Anne told her and left the club for her hotel.

"Jeanie, is Mr. Johnson in?"

"He's in the bar, Anne."

Anne went into the bar where Mr. Johnson was reading a paper behind the bar.

"Hello, Uncle Johnson," she said.

"What are you doing home so early?"

"I need to talk to you."

"Don't tell me you got trouble out there in your million dollar nest?"

"You mean you've heard talk too?"

"Anne, my girl, whenever a pretty young girl holds a responsible position—and you are young for the job you're holding—there's always talk of some kind or another. I'm just surprised you haven't heard any."

"I did, a couple of weeks ago. I thought it was just a flash in a pan until today. Jack came to me and asked to hire another bartender. Now if we really needed one, Mr. Johnson, he'd have asked me in a different way. But he also wanted a new job as host, greeter at the club. For him to ask that means he wants to set himself up to take my place."

"You're not too far wrong. I've heard he's being encouraged by certain ladies."

The following morning when Anne came in, she called Jack and Jake into her office.

"I've decided to make some changes, move you two around a little so you won't be bored with the same old faces every day. Jake, you take the upstairs bar and Jack, you will take the 19th Hole. I think it will do you good to get away from the admiring ladies for a while and shoot the bull with the men"

Anne felt she needed Jack in case of illness, or for any other reason she could not be there. She believed in having some one ready to step in when necessary, but not one who would be intrigued enough to maneuver her out by playing into the hands of idle women. She was willing to make accommodations in accordance with her needs, which meant training Jack, as she felt he had the ability and the personality. He was lacking only in the education which Anne felt was essential.

She missed the Jack, who had been her champion, who helped her fight off critics, for now she found a Jack who competed with her. Still she felt he was an asset to the club and in the 19th Hole he seemed to be comfortable.

Then one morning Mr. Peters came into the office. He quietly closed the door and sat down beside Anne's desk. This quiet thoughtfulness was not his nature, at least not after he had come to a decision. It seemed what he had to say was not fully formed in his mind, which was also unusual for him.

"Anne, there's a lot of talk going around—of my so-called relationship with you."

"Yes, I know. At first I thought . . . or hoped it was an isolated bit of spite . . ."

"You, my wife and I know there's nothing to it. It's spite all right. I've thought it over and I'll tell you what I think we'll do . . . . I'll find a man, a bookkeeper. We'll play the little game you and Mike played. Call you the accountant. Since that's what you were originally hired for. We'll call him manager. You will continue on as you have. All these damn women want is a handsome face. You'd think there were enough in the membership!"

"What about assistant manager, Mr. Peters, in charge of catering? That way it won't be so hard for me to take. After all, from manager to bookkeeper isn't going to do my career any good."

"So it's that important to you?"

"Of course it's important to me. I intend to make a career of this work. Marriage is not in my plans, so what of the next job? I'll not be here forever. From manager to bookkeeper would kill me. From Manager to assistant in charge of catering means my time and efforts are more important in that area and would not reflect on my future prospects."

"That's a good idea since your work consists principally of the food operation."

Anne was disappointed. She was also resentful that this could happen. Not because her work was inadequate or inferior, but because she was a woman!

She called a meeting of the staff and told them because of the increased volume of the food department, it had been decided she would give her full time to catering.

"There will be a new manager," she told them, "I shall be assistant in charge of catering. That will mean there will be little difference in the operation of this club. Jack, I would like to talk to you in my office and Gina I would like also to talk with you today as soon as you have some time to give me."

Jack followed Anne into her office.

"Close the door, Jack."

"I'm sorry about what seems to be happening, Boss Lady," he said as he closed the door.

"Much of it was brought on by your acquiescence with the ladies, Jack. Now I would like to make myself clear as to where you and I stand with each other."

"First I believe you're a very good bartender and would probably make a very good host. I did have you in mind to train as an assistant for you have been that to me. In a pinch, Jack, there's no one I'd rather have at my back. When you start playing politics, watch out, you're not the type."

"There's one thing I want to make clear to you. The new man coming in will be a manager in name only, nothing else will change. Now if you think you can work with me, for I do value you, stay on board. Otherwise, I want your resignation."

"The rumors were…."

"I know what the rumors were. Since when couldn't you come to me and talk about anything. If you felt a threat to your job, my door has always been open. Whatever these ladies could have promised you they could not have delivered without Mr. Peters, O.K. So you see, all the deception in the world wouldn't have done you any good. Before this happened I could have asked that you be my assistant. But you see, I already knew of your . . . shall we call it rebellion?"

"I'm sorry, Boss Lady."

"We do understand each other now, don't we?"

"Perfectly."

"Are you willing to stay and assure me that I don't need to watch my back anymore?"

"Yes."

"O.K. Go to work. You've learned a lesson so try to remember, members can play you false."

Jack left and Gina came in. " Sit down, Gina. There will be minor changes here. A new manager will be coming in. Between you, Jack and 1, that means he will be manager in name only. However, we can't make waves. We'll continue with our business just as we've always done and make the best of this . . . Jack has promised to stay out of any more club politics. I hope he does, for I do feel I need him and I hate to make changes, especially now."

Anne's bronze plaque came off the door and Mr. Dennis put his brass plaque up.

Mr. Dennis was a short, slim man, impeccably dressed in greytones. He was a very handsome pipe smoker. He kept his handsome profile on view at all times, as well as his pipe.

A desk was brought in for him. It was placed along the opposite wall from Anne's and a little to the rear. He asked that it be moved forward. Mr. Peters came in and said, "it stays where it is!"

Mr. Peters closed the office door. "What I have to say will be said in front of both of you so there will be no misunderstanding." Mr. Peters did not sit down. "Mr. Dennis, you have been hired as bookkeeper, with the title and pay of a manager. You're well paid, in my opinion, for this little charade. You have agreed, and correct me if I'm mistaken, that Anne in fact shall remain the manager. It will be well to remember that, Mr. Dennis. You will sign nothing. The payroll will come out of my office. Anytime you are no longer satisfied with this deal you have made you come to me. Is everything understood?"

Both Anne and Mr. Dennis agreed that Mr. Peters' statement was understood.

"I want you two to try to get along," he said as he opened the door and left.

Mr. Dennis looked at Anne, measuring her.

Anne looked Mr. Dennis over and thought he might be an asset with his good looks. A host, to greet the people, would make them feel the warmth of the club.

However, Mr. Dennis did not exude warmth. He seldom smiled.

It took less then a week to discover he knew nothing of simple bookkeeping. When Anne asked for the previous day's reports, he hadn't I had time to do them. She hesitated to ask what he had been doing that an hours worth of work could not be finished and asked when they would be ready.

"Tomorrow morning, " he told her.

"Tomorrow! Tomorrow, Mr. Dennis, I shall want today's reports!"

"Sorry, I can't have them for you until tomorrow."

"Where are they?"

He pointed to an incoming tray on his desk.

Anne took them and made up the daily report.

She went home for the day and decided to go to a movie to relax. *Duel in the Sun* was not exactly a movie to relax by and so she drove to the club and walked into the office. Mr. Dennis was reading a paper and Mrs. Dennis was doing the daily report.

They both looked up surprised as Anne came to the door. Neither said a word.

"Well, I assume this is the reason I can't get a daily report when I should," she said as she closed the door. "So many charades here we don't know where one begins and another leaves off. All right Mr. Dennis, I hate constant bickering. So I'll let this past, just see that the reports from each department are on my desk each morning so I'll have some idea of what we've done the day before. If you don't know how or just don't want to belittle yourself to do such a simple thing as daily reports, we'll let it go at that. But I'll warn you, I'd better not see any additional remuneration on the payroll or elsewhere, and please, Mrs. Dennis, work behind a locked door . . . I thought you would make a good host, but I see I'm disappointed in that too. You can't seem to greet people. You don't mix." Anne sighed, "oh well I want to say you're not my problem, but I wonder how soon you will be. Goodnight."

After that midnight visit, Mr. Dennis began to take a more active role in his job. Occasionally he seated people in the dining room. Any conversation he started went no where, for he hadn't anything to say.

He attempted to take reservations for luncheon and dinner parties, saying to Anne sarcastically, "I hope you don't mind."

"Not at all, it would help me tremendously. Just be sure you get all the pertinent information correct. All you need to do with this form is read and write. Leave the menu area c ear for Gina and me."

Since Mr. Dennis did not mix, he grew bored. His wife was doing his work and he lacked the qualities that make a man a host. So he began looking for things to do. Good, except he began working on a new logo.

Anne watched him at work with whirligigs and calligraphic designs and said nothing. When a design began to emerge, Anne said, "Pretty. Where are you expecting to use it?"

"Here," he said.

"You have to be joking. Are you really expecting to replace our existing logo?"

"It's too plain."

"Do you realize the cost? What with the dishes, the linens, the paper good and the matches?"

"It doesn't have class."

"I suppose that Victorian scribble you're doing does? Well too bad buster, plain or not, what we have, stays!" Anne stormed out of the office.

"We'll see about that," he called after her.

Anne felt someone was encouraging this revolt and wondered who it could be. Not Marilyn again!

Several days passed. As Anne came into the office, she noticed a salesman from a competing match company sitting at Mr. Dennis desk, writing up an order for matches with the new design.

Anne sat at her desk, listening until the salesman asked for a signature. She swung her chair around, "I'll take that" she told the salesman. She looked at the drawing and said, "Mr. Dennis, Are you aware that we have an exiting contract with Diamond International?"

"We can work through them," the salesman said.

"We have a five year contract. I see no reason for changing our contract or our design," Anne said as she tore the contract in half and gave it to the salesman. "Out here we go through channels. I am the only one out here with the authority to sign contracts. Perhaps you didn't notice our logo when you came in. You can't miss it. You have to step on it as you come in the door. That logo, nor anything else out here can be changed without the approval of the Board."

"I'm sorry. I wasn't aware of that" the salesman apologized and retreated.

When he had gone, Anne turned on Mr. Dennis.

"How dare you put me in such a position! You know very well you can't sign contracts! I don't know who is putting you up to these little shenanigans, but by God, you're going to have to get up pretty early in the morning to put them over on me!"

"I'll be damned if I'll sit here and let you order me around. I'm the manager!"

"I'm sorry if you're uncomfortable with the deal you made. I could have worked with you; just sitting there with your damned pipe and letting your wife do your work for you. You could have had it nice and cushy, but no, you had to be Mr. Big Shot! Now, my advice to you is, you'd better make the best of things as they are, just as I have to. If you'd just get off your dead ass and get out there and shake hands now and then, I could forget this whole damn thing"'

Mr. Dennis got red in the face. His handsome features twisted in anger and he hit the desk with his fist. "You may have to put up with it but I don't! They don't want you here! We'll see what happens when the members find out about your little deal with your boy friend!"

"I wouldn't press my luck if I were you, Mr. Dennis. You really haven't that much to offer. You may be able to con your way into a good position without knowing what the hell you're doing, but you can't last long! I'm giving you some good advice. Listen, because if you don't and you keep playing politics with Marilyn and her mother, you'll be looking for another job all too soon!"

Anne had taken a shot in the dark regarding Marilyn for she had been looking for the weak spot that had gotten to Mr. Dennis. She had seen the signs of treachery between them, hidden but obvious to one who was looking. Mr. Dennis did not have the fortitude for face-to-face confrontations. He was a sneak. Nor did he have the brains for conspiracy without someone to guide him. Marilyn was a far-fetched guess as she was on dangerous ground herself after her last little campaign, but one could never tell. Now with Mr. Dennis' reaction Anne knew she had guessed right.

Mr. Dennis rushed from the office and went home. There was a Board meeting that night and Mr. Dennis attended.

The following morning Mr. Peters stormed into the office. He did not wait to get to Mr. Denise's desk. At the door he began to shout, "what the hell do you mean by going into that Board meeting and complaining!"

Mr. Dennis didn't know what hit him. Mr. Peters just paused for breath. "So suddenly the deal you made isn't your deal. It's Anne's deal, is it? Well that's too damn bad! We made an agreement one you agreed to before you were hired. Nothing was hidden from you. You knew what was expected of you and you couldn't even do your share of the simple bookkeeping, though you assured Mr. Burke and I you were an accountant! Don't think I haven't known for a long time that your wife comes in here at night to do your work for you. You may fool some people with your looks and pipe, but I doubt you had Anne fooled and you sure as hell didn't fool me! I look for people like you when I need a job done by a man who doesn't have self-respect. Anne has more brains in her small finger then you'll ever develop in a lifetime! What's more, if she wants to keep forty pair of shoes out here, considering the hours she puts in on her feet, that's her business!"

"Now get your gear and get the hell out of here!" Mr. Peters shouted as he went toward the door and opened it. He looked at the plaque and said to Anne, "Get this piece of junk off the door and have Jim put your bronze up again."

ANNE COURTNEY
MANAGER
went back on the door.

MEADOWLARK COUNTRY CLUB - PART II

It was the beginning of September and the fall and winter social season was ready to kick off—the last swimming party of the season-along with a barbecue.

There would be club-sponsored activities for the winter months as well as the parties the members would be giving and it was important they did not collide. Anne sent out a calendar of winter events to all the members so that they could plan their socials around those given by the club.

September would be the month of payback dinners to visiting clubs of the summer. A welcome dinner-dance to young people getting into sports at the local high school level was scheduled.

October was a more formal month. The dinner dances were formal for the ladies, but there seemed to be a dearth of tuxedos among the men. The month was brought to a brilliant end with the Harvest Ball.

November would pretty much follow the pattern of October, except for Thanksgiving. Dinner started at noon with a great showing of children and old folks, and lasted until close to midnight.

The December calendar was filled with luncheons, company parties and other business acknowledgments. On the afternoon of the 24th, the club closed until the morning of the 26th. It was time to start preparations for the gala New Year's Eve party. It was 1950!

In January a new Board was chosen, the first since the flood. While Mr. Peters would still be Chairman of the Board, the crew could not help but wonder what effect this new Board would have this year, or what this new decade would bring them. Anne in particular looked at her position. Mr. Peters had mentioned in passing that he would like to go to Coronado to retire among the palms and good golf courses of southern California.

However, the new directors had to be met with and their ideas of a social and golf calendar discussed for the coming year, particularly the golf as the course would be opened in the spring.

The calendar was roughly made up. Every other Saturday would be a club activity. Other Saturdays would be reserved for golf dinners. The ladies could have the dining room for luncheons. Dinners would be served each evening from five to ten, except when there was a banquet. This Board intended to have a more hands on policy with management.

When policy had been laid down by this new Board, Anne did not find it too difficult. She could work with it.

At the February Board meeting all started out well. The club was making money, members were using all the facilities, and there were glowing write-ups in most of the trade papers.

Then, Mr. Fraser took the floor. "I've had some . . . well; we can't call it complaints, that's not what it is. However, many of the members are thinking they'd like to have a working manager. A man."

"A working manager! What the hell do you think you have?" Mr. Peters exploded. She's out here eighteen hours a day! I don't see that she has that much idle time!"

"The ladies . . ."

"Do what you damn well please," he rose from the table, "but she stays!"

Mr. Fraser came into the office with Mr. Black, for back up. "Anne," he said sheepishly, "last year, you remember, you took charge of the food exclusively."

"There was a noticeable difference in the service and quality during that time. We feel you need to do that again. It's a full time job just to keep tabs on a very crucial aspect of club operation."

"I see. Who are you going to bring in this time?"

"A working manager. He'll take a shift on the bar."

"I see. Then I think I'll move my office to where it was when I was hired. Closer to the kitchen, you know! Will that be all, Mr. Fraser?"

"Yes, yes . . . You do understand?"

"Whether I do or not doesn't really make any difference, does it, Mr. Fraser?"

Anne moved her office into her old location.

Mr. Black brought Bill in to meet Anne. He was a bartender who had been in too many brawls from the looks of his battered face, and his stance, coming in like a tornado. Immediately he demanded the keys to the bars and all the liquor rooms, except the beer and wine cellar.

Since sales, inventory and purchase of liquor had never been in question, this struck Anne as very strange. She wondered why this man was making such an issue of this particular stock. It was disturbing to Anne and she questioned his motives. She also questioned why this Board, and particularly Mr. Fraser, would have found it mandatory to take her keys. She hoped she had misunderstood him and got another set of keys from the safe and gave them to Bill.

"All of them. Yours too!" He demanded.

"Mr., it will be a cold day in hell when I turn my keys over to you! Now, if you want to throw down the gauntlet if you know what that means . . ."

"Now Anne, he just wants your liquor room keys," Mr. Black interrupted.

"The liquor room keys are on that key ring; I don't carry them around with me. The only other set is in the possession of Mr. Burke. I believe he still is the Treasurer of the Board."

"You know, Anne, your attitude is not good," Mr. Black told her.

"Sorry about that. What would you like me to do, bow and kiss your feet for relieving me of my job, which I've earned?"

"You just stay in your kitchen and leave the liquor to me. I'm running things around here now, and you'll not run me off like you've done the others," the bruiser put in.

"Don't get too big for your britches, I've had to deal with loud mouth incompetents before."

"Don't think I don't know what you've done. You're pretty sly; I'll give you that. One of these women who can't get a man so you're . . ."

"And you're one of those bastards that can't think beyond what's in your pants! Now get the hell out of here! Until I've moved my office keep out of here, I wouldn't want to breathe the same air as you!"

"Anne, Anne . . . that's no way to talk."

"Isn't it, Mr. Black? I can't help but wonder who is responsible for bringing this . . . this into the club . . . ." She said derisively looking Bill up and down.

"It's not yours to question what the Board does," Mr. Black reminded her.

"Just get out, the both of you!"

Anne moved her office. When Mr. Peters came in that afternoon, he asked,

"What happened out here this morning, Anne?" Anne told him. Then said, "You thought I had broken the kitchen mold. Well, you should have heard that wretch putting me back in the kitchen," she laughed. "I don't see that he has that much going for him and he doesn't even have a pipe!"

"I want you to know that your job is secure, Anne. I still hold the mortgage, as they say. Just take it easy and see what happens."

"I'll get through it, Mr. Peters. I doubt he'll have much to do with me. I'll just stay in my kitchen."

Whatever Bill was doing with himself was hard to tell. Anne never saw him in the bars or associating.

It was coming to the end of February. The big event of the month was the Sweetheart Ball.

Bill was doing his own things. No one knew what as he didn't make friends with his bartenders and was seldom at the club, unless it was after Anne had left.

There were dues notices and statements to get out and accounts receivable and payable to make up. While Anne was going over the invoices she noticed a decided increase in liquor purchases. She wondered what Bill was stocking up for. There was more then adequate inventory. She stopped to wonder why he didn't realize that the person who did the books and did the food was the one who had control of the club. She shrugged and decided to keep a sharp eye on this liquor situation. At the end of the month, she asked Jack to offer to help Bill with the inventory. He told Jack he could take care of it himself.

He did not turn in the inventory to Anne, but gave it to the accountant in Mr. Peter's office, who gave it to Anne.

Anne took out her last inventory, added the purchases and looked for requisitions for anything taken from any storeroom she had set up. She asked Jack and Jake how the bars were stocked.

"Bill just comes in the replaces what has been used."

"Without a requisition?"

"That's right, Boss Lady," Jack told her.

The apparent sales did not offset the apparent use of stock. On inquiry of accounting, they said they had questioned Bill and had been told he was lying in reserve stock. She told Edith, "I'm concerned about that heavy liquor purchase."

"We'll watch and keep you apprised."

In March the large purchase orders continued, with no offsetting figures in sales. Anne went to the Pro Shop. "Lyle, do you have any large tournaments coming in that I should know about?"

"No," he told her. "You've been advised on everything coming into this department. Anything wrong?"

"Yes, anything wrong, Miss Nosy?" Bill had entered from the locker room.

"Not a thing. I just like to be ready if an unusual crowd comes in. You know, stocked for emergencies," she smiled and went out.

The end of April came. Anne did not bother to have the bartenders offer help for inventory. From her accounts she knew what should be in the storerooms. If he needed help he could ask. At ten o'clock she went home. At midnight Jack asked if Bill needed help. He told Jack and Jake to close up, as he wanted to get through with the inventory.

"Need help?" Jack asked.

"No, I don't need help. Just get out of here so I can get with it" he snarled at them.

It had been a quiet Friday night. Early the following morning there would be a small group of golfers, the first to try out the new course.

Anne arrived at the club at ten o'clock. She noted there were first golfers on the new course.

She came into the clubhouse. Jack and Jake were having coffee in the kitchen. The bars were locked.

"What's the matter fellas? Aren't we opening the bars this morning?" Anne asked.

"Bill isn't here and the bars are locked," Jack said.

She looked at her watch. Ten o'clock. She went to the phone and called Bill's number, a motel on the West Side of town. No answer.

She went into the kitchen. "There's no answer. He's probably on the way in."

They waited half an hour then she decided he could be at the club from any place in Great Falls in that half hour and she called Mr. Burke. The treasurer had keys to everything in the place.

Anne told him Bill was not there and they needed to open the bars.

"Didn't you keep a set of keys?" Mr. Burke asked.

"He said he wanted them all and with Mr. Black to back him up, that's what he got. The golfers are already out here and we can't wait any longer. They'll be wanting something stronger than coffee."

"Alright I'll be right out. Bill must have gone to Butte and didn't get back."

"Is that where you all picked him up?" Anne asked sarcastically.

Mr. Burke grunted something unintelligible and hung up.

When Mr. Burke got to the club and unlocked the bars, they were empty!

They hurried to the storerooms. Empty!

"Well," Anne said sitting down on a crate, that was all that was left. Looks like we got plum cleaned out."

"And it's Sunday!" Said Mr. Burke. Montana had State liquor stores, the only supply source.

"I guess it's time to find out if we have a friend," Anne told them and went into the 19th Hole. She called Roy and told him what had happened. "We need to BORROW some merchandise, Roy."

"Serves that bunch out there right. I'll bring you what you need Anne, give me an hour."

Roy saved the day. Mr. Fraser, Mr. Burke and Mr. Peters had a meeting in the office that would soon be Anne's again, while she helped the bartender stock their bars.

As Anne came out of the upstairs bar, the men came from the office and Mr. Peters called to her, "Anne, you'd better have Jim put your plaque back on that door."

The next day he came out with another plaque, which read, NON-ILLEGEGTMATI CARBOPENDUM

"I have to tell you, I was kicked out of Latin," Anne told Mr. Peters.

"Then don't let the bastards get you down," Mr. Peters interpreted.

At the next Board meeting Anne was again officially declared manager of the MeadowLark Country Club.

She accepted the appointment very graciously. Then she said, "Gentlemen, I have a few words to say on my reinstatement. Twice, I've been put in this ignoble position. Not because I failed in my efforts to make this club a place you could all be proud of nor because of my ability to manage. I've been humiliated because I'm a woman! I want you to think about that. For women are coming into the workplace as managers. We're tired of being the peons, doing work for some unworthy man, while we must go begging for recognition and pay.

"So the next time some members feel they would be more comfortable with a man at my desk, I'd advise you to look for a good man. I cannot spend my life pulling chestnuts from the fire for an incompetent manager. That means the next time I won't be here for you to fall back on." She turned to leave.

"What does this mean, Anne?" Mr. Burke objected. "You have a good job here."

"No, I'm afraid I do not, it's too unstable. I never know from one day to the next what my title will be. I do the work of a manager and still any time some one doesn't like a rule the Board has made and I have to enforce it, you bring in these pseudo, counterfeit managers who take the pay and the glory, and I'm left with a mess to clean up. So if you don't mind, we'll both start looking for another manager/managerial position."

"If it's more money, Anne . . ." Mr. Burke offered.

"No it's too late for that."

Mr. Peters was silent. He knew how Anne felt.

Five years had passed since Anne came to Great Falls. She had never had a vacation and she was tired. She also knew she needed a new challenge. Now there was nothing to hold her here, not even obligation.

She needed new horizons. Hotel and private club management was surely her niche, but it was for itinerants. It was easy to go stale, getting to know members and guests too well.

Anne wasn't sure when she began to turn things over to others. She had been given an accountant, a good man who was familiar with the business. Mr. Peters had found him.

She looked far afield and next time she thought, her role would be understood right from the beginning and there would be a contract.

She lost interest and Gina knew that this time it would do no good to cajole Anne toward renewed interest. Gina had seen the silent hurt Anne had gone through and she knew it was only Anne's regard for Mr. Peters and all he had done for her that made her stay on.

The summer passed. That fall Floyd Roberts came to Great Falls from Billings to play golf with Mr. Peters.

"Anne is thinking of leaving us. I wonder if you might have heard of any place her particular skills at turning sows ears into a silk purse would be appreciated?"

"Not off-hand. I'll look around."

In October Anne received a letter from Billings. The secretary of the Board of the Yellowstone Country Club invited her down to talk to them about a management position. They were a new club, just organizing.

It was with apprehension mixed with a little excitement that Anne went to Billings.

Her tenure at the MeadowLark came to an end.

YELLOWSTONE COUNTRY CLUB

It was late one evening, in the middle of October that Anne arrived in Billings. She checked into the Northern Hotel, ate a light supper and went to bed.

It was difficult to sleep as she thought of the interview ahead. She had never been interviewed for a job. She had always sort of fallen into them. She told herself she must put her apprehension aside and get some sleep. She had to be sharp for the next day.

When she awoke the following morning, Anne had breakfast and then called Mr. Kelly, secretary/treasurer of the Board of Directors to let him know she was in town.

He gave her directions to the Yellowstone Country Club and told her Mr. Jenson, their president would meet her there at one thirty for a meeting with the executive committee. Mr. Jenson, he told her, was a construction man who weighed about three hundred pounds.

Anne left the hotel at one o'clock to give herself plenty of time, in case she got lost for the drive to Rimrock Road. In the distance, she saw a gosh awful green building. She came to a weed-grown lane and stopped. Above the building, on the side of the Rimrock Road, was a sign at least fifteen feet high, which read, "BILLINGS CLUB."?

Anne checked her directions. Had she made an error? She looked around at the field of yellow prairie grass, with late blooming wild flowers peeping through the yellow foliage. Boulders covered the ground as though the earth had shook and formed a huge rock garden.

Stepping out of her car, she found a weathered wooden board that had fallen into the grass. She picked it up. It was a hand-chalked sign, which read, YELLOWSTONE COUNTRY CLUB, with an arrow pointing nowhere, but it had to be that building on the side of the Rimrock.

She had been told before coming to Billings the place had been an old gambling club whose owner had been killed in a robbery. A small group of business and professional people, needing a club in post war Billings, saw this as an opportunity to get suitable property for very little money as a sale for the estate was not forthcoming due to the tragic end of it's owner.

Anne got back in her car and drove up the lane. Her first impression was that the building needed a coat or two, or maybe even three coats of paint. She drove into the parking area and Mr. Jenson came out to meet her.

"Miss Courtney?"

"Yes. You must be Mr. Jensen"

"The ladies are just leaving from their luncheon. Come in and meet a few of them," He said.

He guided her into a downstairs hallway, which led into an office and up a staircase. She met Mrs. Jenson and three or four other ladies who wished to meet their prospective manager. Then he led her into a dining room with windows on two walls overlooking the Rimrocks and that gaudy sign.

Someone handed Anne a melting tomato aspic, which she set on the table. Instead, she took a cup from the arrangement of cups and saucers and poured herself some coffee from a candled pot on the table.

Mr. Jenson offered Anne a chair as the committee began to wander in. Then he introduced her to each one of the members.

Mr. Fraser, first vice-president was a valued member as he was from an old family in Billings. His status had the pioneer luster. He had crossed the line in joining this new club, giving them respectability. He was tall, suave, and dark as his Scots ancestry was mingled with the French.

Mr. Gunter, a brilliant young executive, an asset to post-war Billings, was welcomed to the community as an up-and-coming young man. An oilman, extremely handsome, with a beautiful wife and two handsome young sons, he would have been welcomed by the other club.

Mr. Miller was a fat and pompous man. When he finally sat down in the last chair at the table, he puffed on his fat cigar and blew smoke in Anne's face. He would have been a comic-opera character were it not for a touch of shrewd knavery about him. She felt she should have walked out of that room and returned to Great Falls.

Mr. Anderson was an attorney. He was a man with political aspirations as was his grandfather before him. He had been left poor by a freewheeling father, whose debts Mr. Anderson was paying off before he could make a bid for state office. He was young and handsome with reddish hair and somewhat careless in his dress.

Ken Kelly was an accountant. A congenial, hard-working Irishman, he had his fingers on the pulse of business in Billings and the state. He seldom attended club functions and never allowed himself to become involved in club politics.

Mr. Kelly told Anne this club had been made necessary by the new oil and business people who had arrived in post-war Billings without acceptable social credentials expected by the other club. Billings did not have a place for these young new professionals.

So they got together and formed a club of their own. They purchased this old, almost abandoned site with good space for a golf course.

Knowing they had a lot of hard work ahead of them, and being young, they could look forward to making something worthwhile out of this place.

Anne sat looking out the window, fascinated by the sign against the wall of rock.

"We're going to take that down." Mr. Kelly said, nothing Anne's attention to it.

"We can't afford to take it down now but it can be disconnected," Miller offered as he leaned back importantly.

Kelly ignored Miller and went on. "We're starting a new club here. Our members are young. Most of them are just starting their own businesses and professions and cannot give a lot of time to the club . . ."

"That's no reason we have to have a manager," Miller insisted. "One of our retired members can do the job!"

"Who would you suggest, Mr. Miller?" Anderson asked.

"Well, as I'm the only retired member . . . so to speak, and I'm helping out anyway . . . I'm retiring the first of the year, turning the business over to my boy," Miller rambled. " I'll just take over the management."

"I believe we discussed the possibility of a member manager. We decided it was not in the best interest of the club. It leads to too many problems. Cliques get started and there's always bad feelings," Mr. Gunter reminded Miller.

"I agree," Mr. Kelly spoke up. "It was decided by the majority to consider hiring a professional manager."

"Unheard of!" Miller jumped to his feet and pounded the table. "Where do you think you are? New York? San Francisco? This is Billings! Cow Country! Billings, Montana!"

"Tom, we have a cross section of the people in this area who are without a club, so let us not forget what brought this club into being. Now, Miss Courtney, one of our members, Mr. Roberts, has been playing golf with Mr. Peters in Great Falls. I believe you know both gentlemen?"

"Yes I do."

"Mr. Peters informed Mr. Roberts you were looking for a change. That's the reason we wrote you."

"That's true. I feel I need a change. Sometimes people in my position grow stale when they're too long in one place."

"You'd hire a woman?" Miller yelled from across the room.

'We've heard good things about this woman. So please sit down, Tom, while we talk to her."

"We have heard you've done a very commendable job up there," Mr. Anderson said.

"Who wouldn't, with millions, how many millions behind her? I'll be damned if I want a woman running my club!"

"That's just it Tom. It isn't only your club. It's our club. Now we've asked this lady down here to talk to us, to ask her if she is interested in making a change," Mr. Gunter patiently explained.

Anne sat there listening to them, to the ranting of this buffoon. She felt as though she was watching a play, a comedy. Then her mind wandered.

Mr. Haver, the new accountant in Great Falls, could take the management very well. He was personable, with good experience behind him. Anne had considered this before receiving the letter from Billings. She had spoken to Mr. Peters about it when she discussed the fact that she had not had a vacation in over five years. Then the letter came from Billings, asking her to come down to talk to the board in mid-October.

Now here she was, looking out at the Rimrock wall and listening to matters that should have been settled before her arrival.

Mr. Miller came back and sat down at the table. He rolled his oversized cigar, fondled his oversized belly and flashed his oversized diamond. His shifty little eyes appraised Anne and then, out of the blue, he condescendingly agreed to support her appointment as long as she adhered to the policies of the club.

"What else would I do, Mr. Miller? A manager carries out the policies of a club," she told him.

She sensed trouble with this man and thought 'what you really mean, if I carry out the policies of one Tom Miller'. Come what may, Anne was not about to play that game. If she wanted this job, it was clear she had better not show her feelings.

Did she really want to leave Great Falls badly enough to take this on? She wondered. Well, she'd just have to wait and see what they had to offer. She still had her job at MeadowLark.

She watched Miller fighting with himself about how much he'd have to give up on his dream to manage the club. She could sense his thoughts on how he would manage Anne. He had already gotten off on the wrong foot with her.

She had a challenge here. There was no routine. Everything was in shambles. She would play it by ear and just keep her mouth shut until the contract was signed. She brought her attention back to the table.

". . . this is not a million dollar club," she heard Miller saying for the hundredth time.

"Mr. Miller, the Meadow Lark was not a million dollar club when I went there. It took four years to make it a 'million dollar' club, as you like to phrase it. It was a major challenge. Aside form being established longer than this club and the fact that they had a golf course, there was little difference. The clubhouse was in similar condition. It was one man's dream, money, and foresight that made the Meadow Lark a 'million dollar' club. I was fortunate to be a part of it."

She faced Miller straight on. "Those were good years. We worked toward a goal." She turned toward the rest of the committee and said, "Even then, members had to support the club the first year without any of the benefits."

"Well, you've got hard work here. Look at that golf course!" Mr. Miller said pointing out the window.

"What golf course? You certainly don't expect me to move those boulders," Anne laughed.

"It's no laughing matter!" Miller thundered as he pounded the table.

"That's enough, Tom," Mr. Gunter reprimanded.

"Do you think you can do here what you did in Great Falls?" He asked Anne.

"No, Mr. Gunter. We can come a close second, if the members will support the club and if we plow everything back in or the first year or two. Now, allow me to ask some questions. How many members do you have?"

Kelly handed her the membership list and the profit and loss statement.

One hundred members with twenty-five to go, Anne read.

Initiation fees had made the down payment on the property. Dues were twenty-five dollars a year.

"I see your numbers go to one hundred and twenty five. Do you plan a membership drive?"

"No!" Miller shouted. "The membership is closed at a hundred and twenty five! The dues are frozen for five years! You'll just have to get along . . ."

"Is this true, Mr. Kelly?" She asked the secretary/treasurer and looked around the table at the others. She hoped that just one man would tell her differently. The faces were a blank.

"Gentlemen, surely as businessmen, you know this won't pay your taxes or your mortgage. What about your insurance? You can't even afford a manager. If you think you can operate on this scale, you'd better let Mr. Miller do it. I can't believe this, it has to be a joke."

"You're not a million dollar club anymore, Miss Courtney," Mr. Miller said. "You'll have to live within your budget!"

Anne rose to leave. "It isn't my budget that is the issue here, Mr. Miller."

"Please sit down, Miss Courtney. What can you do with this club?" Mr. Gunter asked.

Anne sighed, but stayed on her feet.

"Gentlemen, I would have to have a staff. I could start with a small one. I would depend totally on the food and bar income. The food and the bar will have to attract members. I have to have a good chef, probably our greatest expenditure. I do not believe in volunteer help from the membership. Service would deteriorate to the point where a few would always be waiting on the others and besides, I would lose control. I would expect to pay wages."

From their expressions, she hurried on to avoid interruption and ticked off on her fingers what she would need. "So I would expect to pay immediately a chef, dishwasher/swamper, two waitresses, a bar man and a maintenance man. I would expect to be paid myself."

"How much would you expect, Miss Courtney?" Miller asked sarcastically.

"If we come to a mutual agreement, I would take half of my present salary, which is all you can afford, and five percent of the food and beverage revenue."

"The operation of a club is a full time consideration and the food and beverage is where our cash flow will come from. The pool, tennis courts and the proposed golf course need not concern us until January. But you need more members. There should at least be as many members as you have seating capacity."

Miller stood up and shouted at Anne, "You've got a dining room, bar and slot machines to work with."

"You have neither food nor bar business according to this profit and loss statement" Anne said.

"This is a private club!" Miller shouted back.

"A private club, Mr. Miller costs more to operate than a greasy spoon," Anne retorted.

"I suppose you want a percentage of the slot machine revenue, too!" Mr. Miller sneered.

"No, Mr. Miller, I only said food and beverage. There's legislation in Helena now to prohibit slot machines. You won't have them very much longer."

"That will never happen in private clubs," Mr. Miller ridiculed her.

"I believe the legislation was particularly aimed at private clubs," she said as she walked to the window and looked onto the rock wall again and the awful sign. They sat there, thoughtfully. They had come this far; there was no turning back. They had come face to face with the reality of the responsibility they had taken on.

"What the hell does she know about what's going on in Helena?" Miller shouted.

"She's right you know," Mr. Anderson told them. Anne turned from the window. "I make it my business to know what's going on in my industry, as I'm sure you gentlemen have made it your business to know the ramifications of new laws in your industries."

"Well, there's enough activity here anyway, especially with the golfers next summer," Mr. Miller told them.

"Don't even think of golf next summer," Anne responded. "Let me paint a picture for you. Your membership is limited. At least you could have set the limit to what the building would accommodate, which I would guess to be around two hundred and fifty. You limit this club and you'll find another one starting up, just as you did."

"The building is run down. It needs repairs. It needs paint. Oh God, how it needs paint! You're opening a new club and it has to be attractive to new members. I understood you to say this club was for those who were excluded from the other club for one reason or another. The golf course isn't ready. Your members will still want a place to go where there are social activities and where the food is good and the bar is well stocked. They'll want to go where they'll meet the people they want to know. A place, gentlemen, where members are proud to belong. But first things must come first. You're planning on revenue from facilities you don't even have! Construction on a golf course, except for removing those boulders, can't start till spring, and there will be another two years before you can play. As for the swimming pool, there's little or no revenue from that until social programs can be built around it. You're a new club, meant to attract young people who have never belonged to a club and do not know the responsibility of belonging to a private club."

"I suppose you can do a better job . . ."

"That's a foregone conclusion, Mr. Miller," Anne interrupted. "The Yellowstone Country Club is an embryo and what I am saying is you do not have the membership that will support this club. Members on the rolls are not enough. Members have to use their club. They have to support it or you don't need them as members. There'll be about twenty five percent who will never use it."

"Gentlemen, I'm pointing out the reality of this. If I'm too outspoken . . . well, if we are to work together, we have to understand each other. I can make the best of things for awhile, as long as I see progress . . ."

"That's more like it. Let's adjourn!" Miller jumped up and started to leave.

"Miss Courtney, we have also spoken to a man from Portland," Mr. Kelly told her. "If you'll stay awhile, we'll discuss your salary. Then if you would, please stand by and wait for a call this evening, after our meeting with the full board."

Mr. Miller stopped by the door as he was leaving and bellowed, "What do we need her for? Let her go back to Great Falls!"

"We'll call you one way or another, Miss Courtney," Mr. Gunter assured her as they filed out of the room.

Anne and Ken Kelly sat at the table and worked out a salary agreement. He told her there would be a two-year contract if the Board voted in her favor. Mr. Kelly asked if she would take a raise in salary after a year instead of a percentage.

"No, Mr. Kelly, I've already offered to take half of what I'm earning now. I believe that is more than enough of a cut. I wouldn't want to go up against a new president and Mr. Miller when the time comes to get that raise. Frankly, Mr. Kelly, I have to be a glutton for punishment to even consider this position. But you see the MeadowLark is all routine now, no challenges. I need something I can get my teeth into."

"I'm sure this is where you will find it," he laughed.

Mr. Kelly walked Anne out to her car when they were ready to leave. She felt she had been through a wringer. That awful man. Why hadn't they sat down with someone who could have told them about clubs? She wondered.

Anne returned to the hotel, took a bath, dressed, and went shopping. In the morning she would go back to Great Falls and forget this farce.

It was nearing midnight when the phone rang. It was Ken Kelly.

"You're in! The Board voted in your favor . . ."

"Mr. Kelly . . ." She was going to tell him no way did she want to tie herself down to the Yellowstone Country Club, but he actually sounded pleased.

". . . But watch out for Tom, Tom Miller. A word from the wise, be careful . . ."

"Mr. Kelly . . ."

"I don't mind telling you, Miss Courtney, we're glad to have you aboard."

What was the use? She wanted to say thanks but no thanks, but she was made to feel so wanted. What could she do?

"Thank you, Mr. Kelly. I'll be careful." As she said those words, Anne wondered how she could be careful of a rattlesnake.

"Can you come into the office in the morning before you leave to sign your contract?"

"Certainly," Anne said.

"How much time do you have to give them up there?" Mr. Kelly asked.

"I can be back in two weeks."

"We were hoping you could start sooner."

"I came for an interview, Mr. Kelly. Even yesterday I had no reason to believe I was anything but a candidate for the position."

"No, of course not. I'll see you before you leave in the morning. Goodnight."

The next morning just before Anne planned to return to Great Falls, she went to see Mr. Kelly. He handed her an eight-page contract. It appeared to be a standard contract that allowed an attorney to earn his fee. Then, she came to page 8, paragraph 54!

"What's this, Mr. Kelly? Is this something new? I've never seen it before."

"What's that, Miss Courtney?"

"Page 8, paragraph 54."

"Oh my God, Miss Courtney, I'm so sorry. I was hoping you wouldn't notice that."

"Can I be hearing you right? You didn't think I'd read this contract?"

"You see, Tom included that at the last minute. The meeting was running late and we would have been there all night had we not agreed."

"So it was easier to insult me than to lose a little sleep?" Anne retorted as she laid the contract on Mr. Kelly's desk.

"I really think this should be deleted. I wouldn't have any trouble with it if I knew what it meant. I believe it's a moral clause. Spell it out for me. Do you have to find me in bed with a member or will a kiss do? One man's interpretation of questionable morals would be entirely different from another's. I'm sure Mr. Miller could make a handshake look like a licentious act."

"What do you mean?" Mr. Kelly asked.

"If I were to sign this contract in its current written form, who will stand behind me when Mr. Miller starts his attacks on me?" Not waiting for an answer, she continued "And I can assure you he will, or this paragraph would not have been placed in this contract."

"Miss Courtney, I promise you this Board will not act rashly on any charges brought by Tom Miller."

"But then, we would have to wait and see, wouldn't we, Mr. Kelly? I suppose anything I cross out will have to come before the Board. I can live with paragraph 54; however, I will cross it out in red, for the record. Mr. Kelly, I've decided to leave the MeadowLark regardless of what happens here. I need a long vacation and they have a good m an up there."

The phone rang. It was for Anne. Mr. Kelly handed her the phone. Mr. Miller was on the other end.

"Can you come out immediately?" Mr. Miller asked.

"Mr. Miller, it says here in this contract, which I have yet to sign because the last paragraph is an insult that I believe was put there at your insistence, that my management skills are not re-quired until November 1."

There was silence and Mr. Jenson came on the phone. "Miss Courtney, we need you out here. We need you at once! If you must go back to Great Falls, could you put it off until next week?"

"What's so serious in a non-operating club that you can't wait, Mr. Jenson?"

"Please come out, Miss Courtney."

"Very well," she sighed as Mr. Kelly handed her the contract.

"O.K., let's see what happens when I need you," Anne said as she signed herself to a two-year commitment.

Arriving at the club with Ken Kelly right behind her, Anne found Mr. Jenson, Mr. Miller and a Mr. Nickles in the dining room waiting for her.

"Good morning, gentlemen. What seems to be the trouble?" She asked cheerfully.

"Mr. Miller," Mr. Jenson said apologetically, "has just informed me that he has . . . that he has taken a banquet, a rather large banquet, for Mr. Nickles, here, for this Saturday evening."

"Where's the problem? Let Mr. Miller take care of it," Anne shrugged.

"You don't understand, Miss, Courtney. It's a rather large banquet," Mr. Jenson insisted.

"When did you make this commitment, Mr. Miller?" Anne asked, looking from Mr. Miller to Mr. Nickles and wondering who Mr. Nickles was. Mr. Nickles started to answer, but Mr. Miller motioned him to silence.

"A couple of weeks ago," he answered belligerently.

"I see. No Problem then? You surely had someone lined up to take care of it. Seems you really haven't that much of an emergency," Anne said as she pulled a chair from the table and sat down.

"Did you, Tom?" Mr. Nickles asked.

"Well, I thought I had the ladies. Damn it, I thought it was a chance for the club to make some money!"

"I'd change it to another place but with just two days left well, it's a little late for that," Mr. Nickles apologized.

"What happened to your ladies, Mr. Miller?" Anne inquired.

"There were too many people, they were afraid they couldn't cope."

"How many people do you have coming Saturday evening, Mr. Miller?" Anne asked.

"Two hundred." He answered so softly Anne could hardly hear him.

"Two hundred! I haven't seen dishes enough here for fifty let alone two hundred! You haven't any crystal, linen or silver. What did you expect to feed them on, Mr. Miller?"

"Silver! Crystal! I told you were not running a million-dollar club here! You can use paper plates!"

"It will be over my dead body! If I decide to stay here a few extra days to do this, I'll do it right or not at all. I do hope you understand this is a country club! Now, who are they and what did you promise them?"

This time Mr. Nickles answered. "We're the International Harvester Company. We requested prime rib."

Anne turned to Mr. Miller. "Prime rib on paper plates! Oh my God, you have to be out of your mind!"

Ken Kelly came running in. "What's the matter?"

"Can you do it, Miss Courtney?" Mr. Nickles asked.

"I'll do it Mr. Nickles," Anne said.

Turning back to Mr. Miller, she said "Have you any more little surprises up your sleeve for me?"

"That's all I can think of," he smirked.

"Then you'd better do some fast thinking while I look around," Anne retorted.

She took off her coat and went into the kitchen. The men remained seated at the table in the dining room.

The kitchen was surprisingly well laid out and complete. The white paint was stained but not greasy. A cook was behind a worktable in front of the range, peeling apples.

"Good morning," she greeted him. "I'm Anne Courtney, your new manager."

"Yeah, I heard you were here," he answered sourly.

Anne ignored his rudeness and asked, "What's your name?"

"Nick," he answered.

"Well, Nick, I hope we can work together. I understand we're going to need prime rib for two hundred guests Saturday evening."

"We've got plenty," Nick replied.

"Oh. Then Mr. Miller did order the prime ribs for the dinner on Saturday."

"There's plenty in the walk-in."

Anne looked around for the walk-in. She saw it on the porch, a screened-in area off the kitchen. She went out onto the porch and opened the walk-in. She saw six loins hanging, still in their wraps. Nick followed her and stood in the doorway of the walk-in, watching her.

She looked for a germicidal light. It was over the doorway where it should have been. It was on.

"How long have these loins been here?"

"A week."

She began to tear the wrappings from the meat.

"Why are they still wrapped, Nick?"

"They keep better that way."

"How long have you been around kitchens?"

"Longer than you have," he flung at her.

"Then you haven't learned anything, have you? I won't ask how long you've been a chef, for that, you're not. Otherwise, you'd know with these wrappings still on this meat you'll have spoiled meat."

She pointed to the light over the door. "That, Nick, is a germicidal light. It keeps meat from spoiling after it is unwrapped."

She ran her hand over the loin she had just unwrapped and found it sticky and slick. On closer inspection, she found it had a slight odor. She unwrapped the six loins and found they were all in the same condition. Anne bent to pick up the wrappings she had torn from the loins and thrown on the floor. In a twenty-gallon vat of navy bean soup, there was a mouse floating on top! At her look of horror, Nick took the mouse by the tail and flung it out the back door.

"Good as new," he grinned and went back into the kitchen.

Anne stood frozen, shocked at what she had just witnessed. She went into the kitchen, stood in the doorway and for a moment just stared at Nick. At first she couldn't speak. He picked up an apple, and with unwashed hands, resumed his peeling, smirking at Anne.

Anne marched over to the table. "Get your gear and get the hell out of here? Get out before I really get mad!"

"You can go to hell! The Board hired me and no damn woman is going to tell me what to do!" Nick yelled.

"Let me tell you something. This damn woman is going to kick your ass out of here and don't think she can't! There are at least three Board members out there in the dining room. If you have anything to say, go say it to them! But don't you ever set foot back in this kitchen as long as I'm here!"

"That won't be long!" Nick thundered.

"It'll be longer than you have left here. I'll be back in ten minutes and I'll expect you gone!"

Anne turned and started for the door to inform the Board of Nick's dismissal.

A hail of oranges, apples, pots, pans and various other kitchen utensils came flying through the air after her! Everything Nick could lay his hand on came at her.

Too surprised to run, she turned, too stunned to be frightened. Keeping her eyes on his, this madman, she slowly walked toward him.

She heard the door open behind her but she dared not take her eyes off Nick. Nick looked around for an exit. Anne heard Miller yell but she still kept walking toward Nick.

"What's going on here!" Miller yelled.

Anne didn't answer. She just kept walking slowly toward Nick. It was like herding him toward the back door. Suddenly he turned.

Seeing the open back door, he ran. Anne let out a deep breath and leaned her head against the lintel.

"What's happening?" Miller demanded while the others looked at the debris covering the floor.

Anne took a deep breath. Slowly turning around, she said, "I just fired a cook."

"You did what?" Miller yelled at her. 'That was a damn good chef. What are you going to do now, with that big banquet coming up? What are you going to do about that?"

"Mr. Miller, why don't you just let me take care of that. I believe that's what you just hired me for. As for the 'chef,' his food was filthy. Also, there are six loins out there that must have cost around eight hundred dollars that may be spoiled because he didn't know how to take care of them. You should have known they did not need to be delivered ten days ahead of use."

"Now look here, don't talk to me that way! And anyway," he continued, "Nick made the best navy bean soup I've ever tasted. Maher of fact, he made some for Mr. Nickles' dinner. It's always better after it sets for a couple of days," he assured Mr. Nickles.

"Gentlemen, I have a lot of work to do. Mr. Nickles, was there anything else on the agenda for your dinner?"

"It was to be a dinner dance," he said.

"Very well, that's what you shall have. I'm sorry the navy bean soup was spoiled. We'll fix something nice," Anne said.

"Miss Courtney, do the best you can. Regardless of how it turns out you have my appreciation for your efforts."

"Thank you, Mr. Nickles. I'll do my best."

"What are you going to do about a cook?" Mr. Miller demanded.

"I learned from the man who was responsible for teaching me this business to be damn sure that I can do everything I'm asking others to do. If that means I have to cook, I can cook! Now, get out!"

Anne looked at the litter on the floor and turned sharply after hearing someone behind her. There stood a meek, shy woman and her giant husband. They seemed to come out of nowhere. They looked half-starved.

"Can we help you, Ma'm?" The man asked.

"Who are you?"

"We're sort of caretakers. We live in the cottage out back. We'd be pleased to help you, Miss."

"Thank you. I'll be glad to have your help. You can see what a mess I have here. Would you mind taking care of that first? By the way, what are your names?"

"We're Jim and Lizzie Slater," Jim said.

"I'm Anne Courtney. Do you know where everything is?"

"We sure do, Miss Anne," Jim said.

"When you're through with this, fix yourself something to eat and we'll talk later about compensation for your services."

"You mean you would pay us?" Lizzie asked.

"Well, Lizzie, I don't believe people should work for nothing."

"Oh thank you, Miss Anne, thank you."

"You must be southerners," Anne said, and patted them on the back and said, "You know you're a God-send. Surely the man upstairs is looking out after me and perhaps you too.

Anne left them and went to the office and called Jack, in Great Falls.

"Jack, get down here as fast as you can. I need you."

"What are you paying, Boss Lady?"

"What you're worth. Just get down here. And Jack? Hands off my job until I'm ready to give it to you."

Anne had confided in Jack she was looking for another place. He had told her he would like to go with her when she found one.

"Pick me up on the afternoon flight. I'll be there, you can count on it."

Anne gave a sigh of relief and looked up the number of the packing house and asked them to send a butcher out.

She called the unions for waitresses and cooks and dishwashers and musicians. She would let Jack take care of the bartenders. She called Dohrman's and asked them to send someone with their in-stock patterns in dishes, crystal and silver. Then she called a linen supply house for linens and uniforms.

The butcher came out and looked over the loins.

"We can save them," he told her. "There's a lot that will have to be trimmed which will make smaller portions."

"Since the price is smaller too, we'll just give them larger salads and bigger baked potatoes."

"I'll leave you a stronger lamp for the walk-in, so you shouldn't have any more trouble."

It was Wednesday and they could keep the club closed. But on Thursday they would have to at least open the bar. They could serve hors d'oeuvres, sandwiches and coffee.

Late that afternoon she went to the airport to pick up Jack. Anne was very thoughtful.

"What's the matter, Boss Lady?" Jack asked with a grin as he got into the car.

"We got problems."

"We?"

"Mister, you wanted to work with me. That makes it we."

"Tell me just one time there haven't been troubles," he said,

"So I had to keep Phil off your back with the little bar at the Park. Then all the time at the MeadowLark, we had to clean up after those phony managers left. You say this is a new place. No past history, so what's up?"

"Oh you dreamer, just wait and see. In the meantime, have you ever thought you might like to be a chef? I could teach you. Of course we wouldn't have time to give you an inch on your hat for preparing vegetables. Or two inches for sauces and another two for fish and fowl. Let's see, that's five inches and still no mushroom," she teased. "I need a cook, a chef."

They were turning down the lane, approaching the clubhouse when Jack exclaimed, "My God, what is it? A honky tonk? Boss Lady, you've got more class than this." Anne stopped the car and Jack got out and looked around. "Pretty good size rock garden, he said, "What are they going to do with it?"

"I understand when that big sign was on after dark, it didn't look too bad," Anne said. "Too bad they changed the name of the club. It was a gaudy old clip joint. They bought it for a song. The former owner got himself shot. This is the sort of place women can expect to manage. I thought it a challenge before I saw it. Still, there are things we can do like paint and shrubbery. I was not prepared to deal with Miller. I should have headed for the hills. I was going to but this dinner-dance came out of the woodwork. I couldn't let Miller serve those prime ribs on paper plates. Jack, I just couldn't let that happen."

"No, I don't suppose you could, but you sure get yourself into some doosies."

"Getting back to a cook/chef what do you say?"

"Tell you what, Boss Lady, it never appealed to me as a profession. I like being a bartender. Of course, cooking might come in handy someday . . ."

"This is that someday. Anyone can tend bar. You know, it's lucky we have a good man in Great Falls."

"You think they're going to hire Havor for manager?" Jack asked.

"I think so. But here we are in Billings. On Saturday mind you, on Saturday and this is late afternoon on Wednesday—That's like day after tomorrow and we have to wine, dine and dance the International Harvester people."

Jack groaned, "oh great, I see why you didn't tell me before I got here. It couldn't have been the Shriners or the Elks, where we could pour the booze heavy and they wouldn't know the difference . . ."

"No such luck." She told him about Nick.

"I always come to late for the fun," Jack lamented.

"Just exert all that Irish charm with the folks in front of the house since you can't cook and I'll get things resolved in the back. I've talked to two cooks. So far, neither will do, so just don't be too surprised if you get a call to carve the prime rib."

"Don't worry, Boss Lady," he gave a deep sigh, "everything will go fine. It always does, doesn't it?"

"There's always a first time. Saturday night I'm just hoping they will all be well-fed, and we can send them home happy," Anne said.

They walked into the club.

"I've ordered an orchestra. There's a little stage for them," she said pointing to the stage against the front wall of the ballroom. "There's two bars. I'd like you to have two bartenders and I want you to hang loose in case I need you. This has to be a success, Jack. Against impossible odds, it has to be a success."

"Quit worrying, Anne, we'll make it" Jack said.

"It has to be good. A dinner party that will be talked about."

"From what you've told me, it will be talked about," Jack laughed.

"As you can see, there's very little stock in the bars and even that is the cheapest rat gut!" Anne said disgustedly. They went behind the bar where there were no more than twenty bottles of cheap liquor.

"That's another thing. We can't sell this sort of muck to our members, let alone our guests. You'd better make up a list of what we need and I'll go up and get a check from Ken Kelly.

Anne left Jack to get acquainted with the lay of the club while she went into town to see Ken Kelly. She was ushered into his office just before he was leaving.

"I have a want list here, Mr. Kelly. I'd like to get a check from you before you leave today," Anne said. "By the way, here is Jim and Lizzie Slater's social security numbers. Their services will be charged to maintenance. I'll need a blank check made out to Montana Liquor Control Board. I'll need, let's see, how much can you spare for petty cash? I'll need a check for Dohrman's. Here's Jack, the bartender's, social security number and his rate of pay."

"Isn't this a little high?" Mr. Kelly asked.

"What?"

"Jack's wages."

"Jack is a married man with two children, not accustomed to lower southside living. He will also be my assistant. You know, Mr., Kelly, you're already getting me at half price. In Jack, you're getting two in one."

"You're paying more to Jack than yourself."

"I have only myself Jack has three people besides himself to support. We do what we have to do," Anne said.

"This will have to go before the Board," Mr. Kelly said.

"Very well, but I shan't want to go before the Board each time I hire someone. Now, when we get a chef, I suppose I'll have to go before the Board again?"

"I suppose so. Now this petty cash, there's petty cash out there."

"There's exactly seventy three dollars in the till. Fifty-three has been rung for sales. That leaves twenty dollars for petty cash. Mr. Kelly, I need more than twenty dollars for petty cash and I need money for two cash registers."

"What's the mater with the liquor stock that is out there? I can't give out blank checks," Mr. Kelly said.

"I don't know where you got the stock that's out there, probably from some skid row joint going out of business who had a fire sale. I wouldn't pour it to my worst enemy."

"This presents a problem."

"Whatever that problem is, I hope it can be settled before Saturday. The liquor problem must be settled by Friday. If I have to fight for operating money, Mr. Kelly, remember I have first count," Anne laughed and walked to the door.

"How long will you be at the club tonight?" Mr. Kelly called after her.

"Most of the night at least till midnight," Anne said.

Anne returned to the club. Dohrman's had delivered their order and she and Jack set about washing the dishes.

"You know, Jack, this is no way to start a club. You know this could be a dismal failure. We can't serve that stuff on the bar. Mr. Kelly was hesitant about giving me a check for liquor. I don't know what his reasons are but we can't serve two hundred people, even as little as those people drink, with what we have. It isn't fit to drink."

"Come on, Boss Lady, it's not like you to be this way."

"I'm not worried about the food. At least we have something for them to eat it on. I do worry that Miller could come out here and have it all sent back. The help is all new. I'll have to be in the kitchen, so you'll have to watch over the dining room."

"Look at it this way, Boss. There's two and a half days, three if we work tonight. That's seventy two hours."

"You think we'll luck-out?" Anne laughed.

"Do you realize how many times we have lucked-out?"

'That's true, but we had Gina," she answered.

Anne heard someone coming. "Is that the patter of little feet I hear?" She asked.

Anne went into the dining room. There stood a tall, dark-complexioned man with laughing eyes. "Hello, you Anne?" He asked.

"Yes," she answered. Jack came in from the kitchen. "This is Jack Mahoney," she said.

"I'm Dave Fletcher, one of your members. I heard you had a dilemma and came out to offer my assistance. I used to be a bartender. If that will help take some of the pressure off."

"Mr. Fletcher, that certainly will take some of the pressure off. We haven't had time to hire anyone for the bar yet though Jack will be in charge of the bar, I'll probably need him to help me in the kitchen as we haven't found a suitable chef either."

"When will you need me?" He asked Anne.

"How about Saturday evening?" Anne said.

"Gotcha," he said and left.

Just then more footsteps sounded on the stairs. Mr. Kelly, Mr. Gunter and Mr. Anderson came into the ballroom.

"It looks like we're going to need some coffee, since I wouldn't serve what we have in the bar to anyone," Anne said. "Gentlemen come in and sit down. Jack, we'll use the new cups, saucers and silver."

Jack brought the cups and saucers out. Anne poured the coffee.

"New dishes, Anne?" Mr. Gunter asked.

"New dishes, Mr. Gunter. I got them from Dohrman's this afternoon.

"I have a list of wants, I think Ken said you called them," Mr. Gunter said. "Who are Jim and Lizzie Slater?" He asked.

"They're a couple who believe themselves to be caretakers without pay. I hired them as maintenance people. They live in one of the cottages out back."

"I see. Do you think they'll be able to do the work required of them?" He asked.

"I'm sure they will," Anne said.

"Very well, we'll o.k. that 'want'."

"Next is Jack Mahoney?" He asked.

"This gentlemen is Jack Mahoney, bartender and assistant to me as I need him."

"The pay is quite high."

"As I mentioned to Mr. Kelly, we have a man who is two and three in one. I believe he's worth the salary I've requested for him."

"Petty cash?"

"I cannot work with twenty dollars in two cash registers. I refuse to work with less than one hundred dollars in each register. Even that is not enough if members want to cash checks."

"Blank checks?"

"I have asked for one blank check for the Montana Liquor Control Board. We need to stock our bars. I will offer nothing but the best in alcoholic beverages. As you all know, the Montana Liquor Control Board is a cash business. I cannot say charge it. Neither do I know what this first consignment will come to in dollars in cents. So I need a blank check for them. If I do not have the confidence of the Board to write checks for which I am more than willing to have a co-signer, I cannot operate."

"Is that all, Miss Courtney?" Mr. Gunter asked.

"No, I expect to hire a chef as soon as I find a good one. I hope I do not have to go through a third degree as to the wages that person will be paid. If you'll excuse me, I'll get another pot of coffee."

Anne and Jack went into the kitchen to give the committee time to come to a decision. When they came out, Mr. Gunter said, "By the way, Anne, we're the house committee and we do not find your 'wants' outrageous. We will approve them. I have to commend your courtesy in bringing these to Ken and making yourself available for us this evening. I have to agree with you that the liquor out here is lousy and I hope you do put in better brands."

On Saturday evening Mr. Nickles came out early. Finding Anne in the kitchen he told her, "Miss Courtney, I know you're in a bad spot. Is there anything I can do?"

"Thank you, Mr. Nickles. I think we have everything pretty well under control, unless . . . you can help, Mr. Nickles. I can't be out front, so you can do something. Would you mind greeting your people when they arrive? Just consider it your ballroom, for it is, tonight. I'll be back here if you need me."

"Why, how very thoughtful of you. I'll be happy to greet our people. You know, there are always those who monopolize me at these functions and if I have a job to do, it will give me an opportunity to greet each one when they come in and go on to the next one, that would really please me, Miss Courtney."

"Thank you, Mr. Nickles."

Anne gave a big sigh of relief and Jack asked, "What did he want?"

"We won't have to worry about checking people in. Mr. Nickles has offered to do that."

The union had sent out excellent help. They became permanent employees and the International Harvester dinner went off without a hitch.

When the ballroom had been cleared, seating arrangements grouped in the dining room and the little bar, the music began.

Anne and Jack eyed those same dishes and decided to look at them a little longer while they had a cup of coffee.

"I want to see your Mr. Miller's face when he sees we did not fall on our faces," Jack said to Anne.

"Don't speak too soon. He could still come flying through the door and I can guarantee you it won't be pleasant."

"What's with that guy?"

"He wanted to be manager. The Board voted on an outsider to avoid the cliques that get started."

"That's the reason you were hired at the Meadow Lark too, wasn't it?" Jack asked.

"I've an idea that had a lot to do with it. At least I was advised not to make friends with the members."

"Well, to work . . ." They had started to place the dishes in the dishwasher when the door flew open and Mr. Miller stormed in.

"What are you doing back here? Who is this man? Your place is out there and . . . where did these dishes come from?"

"No word of thanks, Mr. Miller? No appreciation for a job well done? Is that all you can do-criticize?" Anne asked as she continued to load the dishwasher.

"You can expect to give an accounting for how you got those dishes! And how you're going to pay for them!" He slammed out of the kitchen.

"He must be crackers!" Jack said indignantly.

"That may well be. It certainly means we have to keep our guard up," Anne said as she leaned against the dishwasher.

"That is mine enemy. One to be watched and I can't do anything about it." She went back to loading the dishwasher. "I wonder if I'll last two years. It might be a good idea, Jack, if you keep a sharp eye on how this place is run. The time has come for you to learn something about the business end of this industry. You might have to take over, unexpectedly. I'll not take too much off that man and I doubt he'll take too much off me," she said as she closed the dish washing machine and turned on the switch. "Time for another cup of coffee."

Before Jack could answer, Mr. Nickles came into the kitchen.

"I just saw Tom Miller come through. He was very red in the face. Is everything alright?"

"Everything's fine, Mr. Nickles. I think he was just disappointed not to see a can full of paper plates," she laughed.

"Miss Courtney, you deserve a medal. A Purple Heart." He came over to her and gave her a big hug. "This dinner was outstanding and I'll write to your Board of Directors to that effect. Not one person knew there had been an emergency."

"You know, you helped too. By the way, this is Jack Mahoney, the man who should have been on the bar tonight. But as you see, we all do double duty here."

Mrs. Jenson's group made curtains for the dining room. Jack, the Slaters and Anne painted the upstairs room.

The dining room, ballroom and restrooms were finished by Thanksgiving. Anne had found a local treasure, Freda. Her wizardry in the kitchen made invitations to the club most sought after.

Thanksgiving was a family day. The club celebrated by placing a whole turkey with all the trimmings on each table.

Mr. Gunter had kept his promise to Anne that she would not have a fight on her hands for Freda's wages. Although Mr. Miller attempted to instigate dissension over it.

By New Year's Eve, the club entrance and the small bar gleamed in newly painted splendor thanks to the work of the Slaters, Jack and Anne. The office downstairs was cleaned and records were orderly. The shower and locker rooms had been shut off and left as they were. Anne would like to have seen them gutted and room made for the social events she was working on. She hoped to bring young teenagers into club activities.

Nothing was done with the green chipped paint on the club's exterior. Anne bought evergreen shrubs which Jim and Jack planted around the building, improving it somewhat.

The club began to have an atmosphere of lively activity. Long hours and careful planning all contributed to a smooth operation.

Jack brought his family to Billings. Freda was in command in the kitchen. Jack was in charge of the bars. Anne turned her attention to creating incentives to promote membership participation in the club.

Most of the members were young people just having their first experience belonging to a private club. Few could allow time from their new infant businesses to give to the club. Therefore, many committee dudes fell to Anne. More and more committee chairmen would come out of meetings say, 'Let Anne do it. She knows how.'

While it worked well from Anne's standpoint not to have the Board review all her plans and make changes here and there if they felt something else, it also had its negative side. It gave Mr. Miller the fuel he was looking for.

Anne recognized this. She documented everything she did as she waited for a confrontation she knew would come sooner or later.

She mailed a social calendar the end of December. On Mondays the club was closed.

Tuesday was ladies bridge and supper day. Wednesdays were reserved for a style show, a recital or some other forms of entertainment. There were always dinners with some item of variation. There were dinner specials, either Italian or German entrees. Thursday was the day for buffet and Friday the club brought fish in from the West Coast-succulent seafood seldom served in the restaurants of Billings. Friday was also popular with members because of the folk dancing, which was taught by a couple whom were members. They had been dancers before the war. Saturday was for the more formal dancing. Families were encouraged to participate in the family-style dinners that were the Sunday trademark.

Right after the New Year, Mr. Miller, who seldom came to the club, but was aware of all, that took place, came into the office shouting and waving a calendar at Anne.

"Who gave you permission to send this junk mail out to the members?"

"I wasn't aware I needed permission to send notices to the membership, Mr. Miller."

"Members don't want to be bothered with this junk mail. I want a stop put to it once!"

"I suggest you take it up with the House Committee, Mr. Miller. They approved the calendar. They thought it was an excellent idea to remind members of club events and the dinner menus." The Board also told Mr. Miller, "As long as the profit and loss statement is in the black, we're going ahead just as we are. Anne is doing a good job, Tom. Leave the woman alone!"

Still Anne began to hear occasional grumbles about club policy. People wanted to know who was making policy.

The first of the year brought an end of the slot machines in private clubs. Anne did not feel this in her operation, as she had not depended on that money.

Anne tried to encourage the involvement of committee chairmen to offset trouble with Mr. Miller. They always responded, "You know how. You do it."

In February, Anne sandwiched a Sweetheart Ball for teenagers between a music recital by courtesy of a local music academy. She scheduled a Hawaiian Night for adults, which was an overwhelming success with Jack's exotic drinks, Freda's pineapple roast pork wrapped in grape leaves instead of the traditional palm.

Jack and Jim had constructed a "pit" on a serving table, which would make it easy for Freda to carve the meat.

The Hawaiian music with Hawaiian guitars was well received. Molly and husband, our former dancing teachers, instructed the members in the Hawaiian dances.

In March, an exclusive local dress shop brought in the new spring and summer fashions for a style show. Then there was the St. Patrick's day gala with country and Irish dancing, corn beef and cabbage and, of course, the green beer traditional for that day.

On April first, there was a costume party with prizes for the most original costume. In the middle of the month, as Anne always tried to have two club parties a month, there was the spring clearance sale dinner dance. All liquor was at half price.

It was late that night when Molly, after a few too many drinks and after all the help except the bartenders had gone, came to Anne. "I need some black coffee and a quiet place to talk privately," She said. "I have something to tell you. No one must hear, hear?"

"Where do you suggest we hide, Molly?" Anne laughed.

"In the kitchen," she said. "I need some coffee."

"Be my guest. I don't often entertain the kitchen," Anne said. She asked Molly to sit down at the small table Freda used for her bookwork. She brought cups and saucers and a small pot of coffee. She poured coffee for both of them and sat down.

"Anne, I like you. I think you're doing a scrumptious job out here, but lady, you've got enemies I wouldn't want to have. They're . . . they're . . . I'd hate to tell you, because I can't think of a word bad enough."

"Oh?"

I suppose you already know anyway. That Tom Miller and his scruffy crowd are out to get you. So . . . watch your step, lady. He's holding meetings at his house, where they're trying to dig up dirt on you He calls his little group of cowardly sneaks an 'ad hoc' committee, whatever that is. But it's really a bunch of sore heads that want to get you ousted."

"I know he doesn't like me, Molly, but isn't that a little drastic?"

"Lady, he's a dirty bastard and he likes to see people squirm. I know I'm drunk, Anne, but I'm telling you the truth and it's best that you know."

"Yes, Molly, it's best that I know. Thank you. We'll keep this between ourselves, O.K.?"

In May there had been no effort on the part of the golf committee to begin the cleaning of the boulders on the grounds.

Anne was planning a spring festival for May when a letter was received by the House Committee of the 'ad hoc' decision, a committee of dissenters who had been thwarted when Miller didn't become manager.

The House Committee met at the club in Anne's office. The complaints were:
1) Anne had too much authority and not enough surveillance in matters pertaining to the club.
2) An audit should be done and Anne should be held accountable for all expenditures since the beginning of her stewardship.
3) They questioned the bartender's salary and the relationship between the bartender and Anne.

"This is ridiculous!" Ken Kelly exclaimed. "This woman has given an accounting of all business matters each and every month that she has been here. I have thoroughly checked over everything myself for this very reason. What in the hell is the matter with Tom?"

"I, for one, think he should be asked to resign. We've had nothing but trouble from him and now he questions the amount of Jack's salary."

"I'm more worried about the rest of that list. I hope you don't decide to sue us over this stupid innuendo," Mr. Anderson told Anne. "I'm not into suing, Mr. Anderson. I have to consider the source, and then, of course, it will depend on how much credence you put to this."

"All I can say is this woman runs the cleanest operation I've ever seen. Seems we'll have to have a talk with Tom and short, of asking him to resign, we'll have to tell him to lay off!" Mr. Gunter told them.

Anne came out of the meeting with mixed feelings. These picayune issues should never have had the dignity of a hearing.

"We're bringing this to your attention, Anne, so you'll know what's in the wind. I've no doubt that we can stop Tom this time. We have to believe he will strike again," Anderson said as she was leaving.

"All the more reason to ask for his resignation," Mr. Gunter told them.

Anne went upstairs where Jack was stocking the bar. She would pour our her frustration on him, she thought. However, there was a stranger at the bar, so that had to wait.

"I need a drink, Jack," she told him.

"You! Drinking! It must have been a rough meeting, Boss Lady," Jack exclaimed.

She sat at the end of the bar, tapping her fingers on the surface and wondering what to do next. Should she stay and let this man destroy her? She wondered, for that's what she felt he was about.

Jack placed a scotch and water in front of her. "What's the trouble, Boss Lady?"

"Miller," she shrugged, "what else?"

"Come up on this end of the bar and meet a member. This is his first appearance out here. Doctor Storm, this is Anne."

"So you're Anne? The Anne I've heard so much about," He grinned at her.

"At this point, what you might have heard scares me," Anne said.

"I had to come out and see for myself. What I've seen isn't bad to look at."

"Why the sudden interest, Doctor. I do believe I've seen your name on the membership roll. In fact, I've typed your name any number of times when sending out dues notices other junk mail."

"You've done a good job out here. I didn't think anyone could make this place look like anything except a blacked-out clip pint."

"Surprising what a little paint and a lot of elbow grease can do. Just think what we could do with a hundred gallons of white paint."

"The garishness is gone. Maybe it's those shrubs; you feel it as you approach the place. That neat little sign out at the entrance and the light help so we can see in the dark where to turn off. When you get inside, the whole atmosphere is different."

"Thank you, Dr. Storm. I needed you today and I do hope you'll be using the club."

"Don't let the doctor fool you, I'm nobody. Oh sure, I have all the right letters in back of my name, but it's my wife you want using the club. Now there's your somebody. But then, I doubt you'll be seeing her, she belongs to the other club."

"Then why did you join this club? To see how the new rich live?"

"Not exactly."

"Then why did you join? I understand they have a nice golf course over there."

"Business," he laughed.

"Of course, how stupid of me. You almost had me thinking you would use us for a hide-away."

Jack was looking at his watch. Anne asked, "Want me to take the bar, Jack? I imagine your wife is holding dinner for you."

"I don't know about that. The bars are stocked, but I need to get home for a shower and change of clothes."

Dr. Storm finished his drink and left with Jack. When he reached the top of the stairs, he turned around and said, "I'll be seeing you, Anne Courtney."

"Yes, do come out more often, so we'll know you when we see you."

"Oh, you will get to know me, never fear, Anne Courtney."

Anne cleared off the bar and heard some ladies coming up the stairs. Mrs. Jenson came in first with a friend.

"Oh God, Anne, give me a drink. What a day! I must talk to you, Anne. Do you think any part of that back forty will be decent enough for a June wedding?"

"If your husband would bring out one of his bulldozers," Anne answered. "Otherwise, we'll have to resurrect a comer with the help of the local florist. As you can see, the grounds are going to take some doing."

"Well, do the best you can. My husband's daughter is getting married the sixteenth of June, she tells me."

'This is terribly short notice for the middle of June, Mrs. Jenson. As long as it's for Marilyn, it seems to me Mr. Jenson would be glad to help out by clearing a space for an arbor and seating space for your guests."

"That'll be the day," Mrs. Jenson said. "Doesn't your budget allow for clearing a space?"

"I'm afraid not."

"My God, Sally, I don't know how we will get everyone to-gether," she said to her friend. "There's Marilyn's mother, God knows what man she'll be dragging around by that time. Then there's Greg's mother and her new husband. Greg's father . . . Sally, have you heard he's taken up with some floozy? He'd better not bring her out here. Do you think he'll marry her?"

"He wouldn't dare!" Sally what's Her Name said, aghast at the very idea.

"I'll reserve June sixteenth for you, Mrs. Jenson. Let me know the number of guests as soon as you can," Anne told her.

On April Fool's Day, there was a costume party. It took the flavor of a Lil Abner party without planning. The next fortnight, a Mexican Fiesta was planned.

The club had come to life. The only fly in the ointment was Miller. His spiteful swipes at Anne grew daily. While she told herself not to anticipate trouble, she knew there was always another shoe to fall. She was just beginning to see the results of the hard work they had put into the club, It was too rewarding to let that fat man bother her, she told herself. She had to concentrate on getting word out that the club had opened its membership to another one hundred members. She needed to plan guest luncheons and dinners for the new prospective members. This included social members, members who didn't have use of the non-existent "golf course."

Of course, as there was no golf course . . . Anne suggested to Mr. Jenson when he complained of not having a golf course that it would only take a weekend activity to bring his bulldozer out and start moving those boulders. She even promised them a good free dinner. Mr. Jenson laughed.

Under the new social membership, Mrs. Kent, Dr. Storm's mother-in-law joined the club. She also belonged to the other club, and was known to entertain a great deal. She liked the little dinners and luncheons.

Since every Wednesday was a club-sponsored luncheon, Mrs. Kent had her Wednesday luncheons at the other club. On Thursdays, Mrs. Kent held her luncheons at the Yellowstone.

Anne had seen little of Dr. Storm, though she had noted he began to take an interest in the golf Committee meetings. The golf course had yet to have a boulder turned. Though there was little progress, there were many meetings.

On the first Thursday of May, Anne was in her office putting the finishing touches to the Spring Festival Ball when Mrs. Jenson came into the office.

"Anne, can we sit down and make arrangements for Marilyn's wedding?"

"Certainly, Mrs. Jenson. I have the sixteenth of June blocked out for you. Do you have your guest list?"

Mrs. Jenson started rummaging through her purse.

"That date is correct, isn't it, Mrs. Jenson?"

"That date is all right. What did I do with that piece of paper? Marilyn's mother hasn't given me her list yet. Damn that woman! You know she's just trying to throw a hatchet in the whole shebang. Say's she's not ready. We'll have to work around her." Mrs. Jenson was still searching her purse for an elusive scrap of paper." Well, I don't know. Greg's mother hasn't made up her list yet, either. She's a hypochondriac, you know. Greg's father . . ." She stopped looking for an instant and looked at Anne. "Do you know he married that floozy! He took her to Europe for a honeymoon, no less. Said he'd be back in time for the wedding. We'll have to wait for his list, too. Well, since we don't have theirs, I guess mine isn't going to do much good."

" Perhaps we can decide on a menu today?"

"I'm going to leave the menu up to you, Anne. I wouldn't know what the hell to feed five hundred people." She went back to searching her purse.

"You did say five . . . five hundred people?"

"More or less. That's a ball-park figure," she said, going back to look in her purse.

"Your husband had better get those bulldozers out here, Mrs. Jenson, because the clubhouse doesn't accommodate five hundred, nor four hundred people. If we had those locker rooms available, there would be no problem, but I'm afraid we're as hard pressed to accomplish that as we are to get those boulders moved?"

"Then, what do we do?" Mrs. Jenson asked.

"Pray that we have good weather that day and we can have an outdoor buffet somewhere." Anne replied.

"But that's an excellent idea," Mrs. Jenson snapped her purse shut, rose from the desk and hurried out the door.

Upstairs Mrs. Kent was checking her tables.

"Good morning, Mrs. Kent," Anne smiled. "Is all in order?"

"I always like to check my tables in plenty of time before my guests arrive," she answered very pleasantly.

"I have been meaning to call you, Mrs. Kent," Anne said to her. "I wonder if you would sponsor a style show for the club?"

"Oh, I don't know, Anne. You know I don't have anything against you, no matter what is being said. People do talk about women in business, we all know that. But I can't sponsor you, Anne. You do understand, don't you?"

"No, I do not! I am not asking you to sponsor me, Mrs. Kent."

"Then, why . . . ?"

"I was not speaking for myself. I was asking for your club!'" Anne told her with concealed anger.

"I hardly call it my club, Anne. Why . . . why I've only been a member for a very short time, really less than a year."

"Everyone in this club has been a member less than a year. It has been in existence less than a year. Since you're one of the few members with an understanding of club responsibility, I thought you might set an example for the new younger ladies. They need to learn club responsibility from one of their own social circle, shall we say. I'm sorry you thought my intent was personal," Anne said and turned to leave.

"It would reflect favorably on you, though, wouldn't it?"

"Well, we certainly can't have anything reflecting favorably on me, now can we?"

"Anne, I simply can't take sides, " Mrs. Kent said with some embarrassment.

"Take sides? I don't believe I understand you, Mrs. Kent."

"This tug of war that is going on with you and the Millers," Mrs. Kent responded.

"You know, Mrs. Kent, I'm aware that Mr. Miller would like me out of this club for reasons known only to himself, I'm sure. There's no tug of war. I'm not interested in continued work under the conditions I've found here, so I will not ask that my contract be renewed. Mr. Miller has also caused the Board, who is duty bound to support me because of no wrong doing, some discomfort. This club, no matter who is manager, needs new members that will support it. While I am here, I have an obligation to make this club pay it's own way. So I feel it is my duty to ask members such as your self to not only lead the way for younger, inexperienced members to participate in the club functions, as well as learn to sponsor them."

Anne turned and walked away, seething. She was at the head of the stairs when Mrs. Kent called her back.

"Anne, if a member of the Board were to make the request . . ."

"Thank you, Mrs. Kent."

". . . another thing, Anne. My son-in-law . . ."

"Your son-in-law?"

"Dr. Storm. My daughter is very unhappy."

Anne looked at Mrs. Kent, unbelievingly. She took a deep sigh and said, "There is nothing, nothing, Mrs. Kent, that I know of that should cause your daughter unhappiness."

"He spends a lot of time out here. He never cared for the Hylands, or anything like that before."

"I'm speechless, Mrs. Kent. I've seen your son-in-law out here just exactly once." Anne walked out.

Mrs. Kent did sponsor the style show at Mr. Gunter's request. The next day Marilyn Jenson's mother came in.

"What arrangements has that woman made for my daughter's wedding?" She demanded and Anne felt relieved that she was not the only THAT WOMAN in Billings.

"The date is all that has been settled, Mrs. Jenson. I presume the young people made that themselves."

"I should be making arrangements!" She bristled. "That woman is always taking over. Then she never gets anything done and someone else has to do it for her! I'd like to see just one time that woman would mind her own damn business!"

"I believe Mr. Jenson asked her to make the arrangements, Mrs. Jenson."

"I know that bitch better than you do, Anne. She was my best friend, so don't try to cover by her, or him either for that matter!"

"I'm sorry, Mrs. Jenson."

She walked to the window and looked out. When she turned around, she had a look of satisfaction on her face.

"I'll show 'em! I'll just go to Hawaii next month. That's what I'll do. Those kids are just going to have to change their date! They're probably sleeping together anyway. They can have their wedding in July. They can wait until I get back."

Suddenly the door flew open and Mr. Jenson stormed in.

"What are you doing here, Katherine?"

"The date of Marilyn's wedding conflicts with my trip to Hawaii," she said with a smug smile on her face.

"What trip to Hawaii?" He bellowed.

"The one I just decided to take, Lover Boy." She smiled up at him all sugar and sweetness. She took a hold of his necktie in an attempt to draw him to kiss her.

He slapped her hand away. "You'll do anything, anything, won't you, to spoil things for everyone, even your own daughter!"

"Too bad, lover." She started for the door with him after her.

"You're damn right, it's too bad. You can change your date for Hawaii or you won't be at your daughter's wedding!"

She turned back to him. "I'm not changing anything," she told him as cool as cool could be. "You could have talked this over with me, to see what my plans were. But no, just like everything else, I'm the last to know."

"You and your god-damned melodramas," he started. "You change the plans for your trip or pay for the wedding. Make it easy on yourself!" He told her in such anger that Anne was afraid he would strike her in his rage.

"Well, I never! You see what a temper he has? I don't see how you can work with him. That's the reason I had to get a divorce," she said as she flounced out of the room.

Anne sat back in her chair and breathed deeply. My God, what a mess. Thank heaven she did not have to contend with that.

She went upstairs to check the dining room and the bar. She had gone over the menus with Freda and relieved Jack at the bar when two young people came in.

"Miss Courtney?" The girl asked timidly.

"Yes, I'm Anne Courtney."

"I'm Marilyn Jenson and this is my fiancée, Greg. Miss Courtney, we have to change the date of our wedding. Our parents can't get together until the sixteenth of July."

"I'm sorry. It will be no problem to change the date."

Anne watched them walk sadly, hand in hand, down the stairs.

Jack came back and Anne went to the office to do the work she was unable to do because of the disturbance that afternoon. She was sitting at her desk, feeling sorry for those two kids, when Dr. Storm walked in, hi-ball in hand.

"How did you get in here without my seeing you?"

"Hello, Anne Courtney. I came in through the kitchen. Sure does smell good up there."

"Thanks for the new member you apparently invited to join."

"If you're thanking me for my mother-in-law, don't. She joined to keep an eye on me."

"Oh come now, why would she think she has to keep an eye on you when this is only the second time I've seen you out here?"

"I've decided to head the golf committee."

"I hope you're a man to get things done, Doctor. What does the committee have planned for moving those boulders?"

"Takes time to clear boulders."

"Not if Mr. Jenson would loan you a couple of bulldozers for a two weekends. You could be playing on that dream course in a couple of years if everyone would get the lead out."

"You're an efficient little rascal, aren't you? No use asking Jenson for anything. The rest of us thought we could use a little road work this summer."

"I hope you all have strong backs," she told him.

"You're supposed to be overjoyed that I'm using my membership."

She leaned on her hand and said, "I wonder to what cause. Of course, after you've herded a few of those men helping you around that rock patch out there . . ."

"Not yet, there's a meeting about that tonight."

"You know you could have that whole Committee in traction by any Monday morning . . . just an idea for drumming up business."

"There's another method to my madness for that, you'll have to wait to find out."

"You're not that hard to read, Doctor. And I have work to do." She looked meaningfully at her littered desk.

"I like watching you work," he grinned at her.

"In that case it can wait until you're gone. As much as I like your presence, I'd prefer it in a less personal capacity."

"I'm glad your work can wait." He rose and closed the door.

"You see, being a good doctor like my Dad, who was on old country doctor, I learned early to read people. So I noticed when I walked in, your eyes lit up. Your smile came from inside. Considering the verbal discouragement I got, I'd like to see if the emotional reaction would be the same."

He went around the desk and pulled her to her feet. "You know, Anne Courtney, you're very beautiful," he whispered as he gently pulled her to him, holding one arm in back of her and taking her pulse while he kissed her.

"You see how it works? Your pulse is jumping just as mine is. The first time I saw you, Anne Courtney, I thought you were the loveliest woman I'd ever seen."

He kissed her again. This time there was no time to take her pulse for she could not help responding. He continued whispering to her, "then lately when I began to dream about you, well . . . you see, I had to do something."

"This should not be happening," she whispered.

"Why not? I can sense that you feel the same way I do, that you will love me."

"Dr. Storm, I put love out of my life sometime ago. The Miss is a misnomer and one lost is quite enough to last a lifetime. With you there could be nothing but a fling and I'm not into that, no matter how my pulse reacts to you. My work, while it is an antidote, is a very satisfactory antidote."

"Antidote, Anne?" He still held her in his arms, looking at her intently. She had wanted to return that last kiss with all the fervor in which it was given. But having gone through the loss of Bill, it was a hurt she never wanted to experience again. She pulled away.

He let her go.

"One day, Anne Courtney, you will love me."

He picked up his glass and left, leaving the door open.

Anne sat down at her desk, shaken. She had forgotten the rapture of a man's nearness. The feeling of strong-arms holding her. She shook herself free of the feelings Bob Storm had roused in her and promised herself she would avoid him like a plague.

She threw herself into her work more than ever, busying herself with the Spring Festival that would be held in the middle of May.

The work on the golf course started slowly. Mr. Jenson, in spite of Anne's constant reminders through hints, suggestions and out right requests remained oblivious of the need for his bulldozers. Anne felt that as President of the Board, he should have offered the use of his equipment. There were members who were ready and willing, why not Mr. Jenson?

From her own pocket, Anne bought plants and wildflower seeds which she and Jack and the Slaters scattered on the grounds. By June, there was a lovely rock garden where the golf course should have been.

She bought flowering shrubs that would withstand the winter cold for the north side of the lane. Miller's house was less than a half mile as the crow flies from the club, to the north. Anne had paid for these plants and flowers from her own pocket knowing that Miller would object.

June was filled with graduation and going away parties. Those leaving were headed for vacations or distant schools.

By the first of July, there were dropouts on the golf course and it never got off the ground.

Everyone seemed to be very pleased with the club, except Mr. Miller and his clique. He was still finding fault.

He counted every broken dish and glass and brought them to meetings as trophies. When that was not enough, he began to watch for any personal friends that Anne might permit to use the club facilities as her guests.

Anne had neither the time nor the inclination to make friends since she had been in Billings.

However, she did have club affiliations from Great Falls. She had been elected Treasurer of the Business and Professional Women, but had resigned when she came to Billings. Since she had been a past officer, she was often invited to events, which she did not attend due to her busy schedule in Billings.

Just after the Fourth of July parade downtown, there was a barbecue in the parking lot of the club and a square dance that night. During the dance and just before a midnight supper, Greg's father came to Anne and asked, "What kind of arrangements did Suzy Q Jenson make for the kids' wedding?"

"It has been changed to the sixteenth of July, but here it is the fourth and I haven't any other information."

"That's going to have to be canceled, too. Greg's mother had to go to Rochester. Something's wrong again."

"I'm sorry. Suppose when everyone is ready, we start at the beginning and work something out."

"Sounds good to me," he said and walked away.

Greg and Marilyn came to see Anne the next day.

"We have to cancel again, Miss Courtney," Greg said.

"Yes, I know. Your father informed me yesterday."

"Do you think this wedding will ever take place?" Marilyn cried.

"Not when you have as many people to please as you two seem to have. With everyone trying to spite someone, it seems to me that sooner or later you're going to have to take things into your own hands."

"That's a good idea, Marilyn, let's elope!" Greg caught on fast.

"Let's try one more time, honey," Marilyn said.

Anne could sense Marilyn's dream of a beautiful wedding with bridesmaids and rose arbor evaporating. But one more time. One short time to hold onto that dream. She turned to Anne.

"What about August twenty, Miss Courtney?"

"I'll put you down for that date. I really hope it works this time and weather holds."

"Do you realize this is the third time we've sent out invitations! I swear, Miss Courtney, we must be the laughingstock of Billings," Marilyn cried.

"I don't think so. I believe all your friends know what the conditions are, that a lot of unexpected plans are coming to light," Anne told them.

"That's not all the trouble we're having and the reason we thought an outdoor wedding would be best. Pop refused to walk down the aisle with me if Mom's at the altar. He says he won't stand beside her and she insists on being at the altar. Claire says she won't step in the same building with Greg's new stepmother. She even refuses to sit in the same pew with Greg's stepmother, or behind or in front of her . . . what will we do?"

Anne didn't answer. Then Greg asked, "What would you do, Miss Courtney?"

"I'd elope."

"But we have to try one more time, Greg," Marilyn said.

Business fell off some in August. Mrs. Kent curtailed her luncheons as so many of her friends were on vacation or otherwise occupied. The golf course committee and the members working on it gave up as there was so little interest in the project and there were other golf courses in the area they could play on. Besides, there were the rodeos and trail rides. Anne suggested as they now had the money in the coffers, they should pay for the clearing. However, there was resentment of Mr. Jenson's failure to do his part in helping as the rest of them had done.

The Board talked of hiring a pro. Anne argued this was putting the cart before the horse and that a Pro was not necessarily a course architect. Then they decided to wait for next year. There simply was no leadership on the Board. Those who could didn't have the time, which left those who couldn't, and nothing was done.

On the first of August, Marilyn and Greg canceled their wedding plans without making another reservation.

After Labor Day the golf Committee told Anne they had decided on a stag party to raise money. They asked if she would take care of it.

She called the manager of the Elks Club and asked him out to lunch. She told him the male members wanted a stag party and since she didn't know the first thing about stag parties, she wanted him to point her in the right direction.

"We usually use a group from Denver. Our members have always been satisfied. I'll give you their number. Just tell them I recommended them," he said.

Anne got in touch with the Denver group and made arrangements for their appearance.

After the stag dinner was served, Anne sent the waitress's home. The busboys cleared the dining room. Those who were old enough to serve drinks she kept on and the others she sent home. When she came into the bar to tell Jack she was leaving, Dr. Storm was sitting at the end of the bar. She nodded to him and told Jack, "You take it from here, Jack."

"I'll look after everything and see it's cleaned up before I leave," he said.

"This thing could go on till morning," she told him. "Just lock up when you're through and I'll be out early with a cleaning crew."

Bob Storm pushed his drink back and followed Anne out.

"Aren't you staying for the party?" She asked.

"Prancing naked women don't appeal to me. I'm thinking you're much too tired to drive yourself home."

"Thanks, but no thanks. Right now, I don't need you complicating my life."

"I'll just follow you to see that you get home safely."

She looked at him as he opened her car door for her. His eyes were laughing. "Oh hell, I'll leave my car at my apartment. We can go for a moonlight drive, that's all!"

It was a warm clear night. One could smell the breath of fall in the air. Anne parked her car and Bob parked behind her. She locked her car and started back to his. Suddenly she stopped in her tracks! Page eight paragraph fifty-four!

"What's the matter?" He got out of his car and came toward her. She looked at him hesitantly and then said, "I just remembered something. It doesn't matter."

"Where would you like to drive?" Bob asked.

"Anywhere. I'm in your hands. I don't remember when I've gone for a drive, just to be going."

"I know all the best places," he laughed at her.

"I'll bet you do."

"Relax, Anne. Don't be so serious. Enjoy life."

"Do you enjoy life?" She asked.

"I try to. Most of the time I do."

They drove to the top of the Rimrocks, found a place to park and watched the city below. They talked of many things, cabbages and kings, but not of themselves.

"Pretty, isn't it, down there? Like a jewel box," he said.

"Are you always poetic this time of night?" Anne asked.

He reached for her hand and didn't answer. They just sat there, holding hands, silently watching the city.

"I think it's time to go," Anne sighed.

He reached for her and said, "You know those sighs I hear so often are a sign of unhappiness." He drew her to him.

"Don't tempt me, Bob. Don't stir up emotions that are better left alone. We can't mean anything to each other, so let's not start anything."

"How do you know it can't mean anything?"

"We both know there's no future for us. Besides, conditions at the club are such that it would be . . . it would place us both in jeopardy. I almost wish you wouldn't come to the club . . . not alone, anyway."

"Who would I come with?" He asked as he kissed her cheek, her forehead . . . brushing his lips along her cheeks.

"I mean it, Bob," she told him, but unable to break away.

"Is that anyway to talk when I'm trying to make love to you?"

"Please don't Bob . . ." she succumbed to his kisses.

They drove to Laural, a hamlet to the south of Billings and found a small discreet inn.

It was just before dawn that Bob drove up to Anne's apartment.

"We've started something that has to stop-before it's too late," She told him.

"It's already too late, Anne."

Anne began to think a lot about Bob and about how vulnerable she was now. She knew any involvement could only lead to disaster.

"I have to look around for another place," she told herself. "The next time Miller strikes will be a good time to resign." She would leave the club with a good social program, and a good balance sheet. Jack could take over and Kelly would be happy to give him guidance. The club was well stocked with supplies and other inventory. She could take that long delayed vacation. She didn't need money at this t me for she had worked this last—good heaven—ten years! She had saved her money. Now she had to get to the club for she had a Montana Highway Patrol, a state gathering, coming in for a dinner dance.

The regular club activities would be starting. The Harvest Ball was coming up. There was much to keep her busy and no time for Bob Storm, no matter how delightful that evening with him had been.

Mrs. Kent came in to make arrangements for her Thursday luncheons and card parties again. It amused Anne that she was always there early on Thursdays, which was also his day away from the office. He was usually at the club.

The first Friday of October found Anne preparing for the club dinner-dance when two friends from Great Falls arrived at the club.

They asked her to come to Great Falls for the installation of June Jenkins to the Business and Professional Women's Association. Since Anne had been a past officer, they wanted her to be there and to speak for June, as incoming president.

She thought about it and decided it would be nice to see old friends, especially Gina. She knew Jack and Freda could handle the dinner dance and the Sunday brunch on their own.

The club would be closed on Monday and she would be back Monday night.

Anne neared Billings early Tuesday morning, just before daybreak. Across the plains, from a distance of about ten miles, she could see the garish old sign above the club, flashing through the night, BILLINGS CLUB!

It had never been taken down nor had Miller had the power turned off as he had assured the Board he would do. Could someone have hit the wrong switch? She wondered.

Who could have turned that sign on? Surely it could be seen all over Billings. Why hadn't someone turned it off? How long had it been on?

She drove directly to the club. All the doors stood open. She thought of the Sangre de Cristo Indians. She had, since her time in New Mexico, developed an interest in them and loved the mountain range named after them. What force, what condition . . . Why had everyone just walked out leaving glasses on the bar and food on the tables? It appeared someone had quite a party!

Anne began to realize she was finding it easier to escape into that old mystery than face the one she had here. Who had this surprise party and then just walked out?

First, Anne turned off the sign. Then she called Jack.

"Boss Lady, it's in the middle of the night!"

"It's damn near morning and this you have to see to believe. Just get out here, fast! But tell me first, how did that old sign happen to be on?"

"What! What sign?"

"The one that flashes BILLINGS CLUB through the night sky!"

"Boss Lady, when I left around midnight Saturday everything was in order. I could not have missed that sign, nor could anyone else in Billings."

"Just get out here before there's another murder!"

Miller lived less than half a mile to the north of the club. The sign was between the clubhouse and his home. He had a key to the clubhouse, as did all the Directors. Why hadn't he turned it off? The out-of-the-ordinary flashing light should have awakened him.

Just for the benefit of the doubt, she was willing to believe someone had hit the wrong switch. She went into the kitchen and made some coffee. Except for the sign, she left everything as she had found it. She thought she should probably call the sheriff and report vandalism, but decided to talk to Jack first. Then she would call Mr. Gunter.

Jack came in the back door, looked around and whistled.

"This isn't half bad. At least I was able to find the coffee," Anne said. "Look at the dining room and bar," she said, "and keep in mind that all the doors were open."

She offered him some coffee and they went into the dining room.

"My God, what a party someone had!"

"It's who? That's what I want to know."

"This place was dean when I locked up, Boss Lady. I'd never leave a place looking like this."

"Let's go back and find out if Jim or Lizzie heard anything or saw anyone," Anne suggested.

Anne and Jack went out back and knocked on the darkened cottage door. "Its Anne, Jim, are you awake?"

Jim came to the door with a .45 in his hand.

"My God, Jim. What are you carrying that thing for?" Anne asked.

"I heard a noise up at the house about two hours ago, people laughing and talking. I knew they didn't have any business there and I couldn't leave Lizzie. You know what happened here several years ago. So I've just been sitting with this, waiting for you to get here." Anne looked at Jack. "What do you think?"

"What time was it, Jim, when you began to hear the noise?" Jack asked.

"It must have been a little after one. They were there about an hour, then they left . . ."

"You say 'they', Jim. How many would you judge there were?"

"About three of four, Miss Anne. They were laughing, having a merry time, making a lot of noise. They took the path to the old sign that was blazing away. Maybe you'd better call the sheriff, Miss Anne."

"Try to get some sleep, Jim. We've a mess to dean up, but I want at least one Director to see it before we start cleaning up."

Anne and Jack walked back to the clubhouse.

"I smell a rat and it smells like our Mr. Miller. He probably thought I wouldn't be here till noon," Anne said. "You go home, Jack. I'll wait and see what happens. Someone has to come out of the woodwork and I'll lay you odds, it will be our friend"

"I'm not about to leave you alone. I'll stick around with you. You know there will be repercussions."

"You can bet on that. Let's see where they come from."

Anne fixed breakfast and at seven o'clock she called Mr. Gunter to let him know what had occurred.

"Did you call the sheriff?" He asked.

"No, I believe it's an inside job. I wouldn't want to bring any notoriety to the club."

"I'll be right out," Mr. Gunter said.

Mr. Gunter was stunned by the condition he saw and was about to leave when Mr. Miller came in, not all surprised by the desecration and waste of food.

"We'll see how much longer you'll be here," he greeted Anne. "What's all this mess?" He asked.

"What do you know about this mess, Tom?" Mr. Gunter asked. "Don't you have anything to say about this?"

"I'll say plenty on Sunday. I've a petition out for a vote of confidence!"

"You what! Don't you know you have to have the vote of the Board for that?" Mr. Gunter asked.

"When the Board doesn't do anything the members have to take things in their own hands?"

"What members, Tom? Your little cadre of malcontents?"

"You'll find out on Sunday and we'll see how much longer she'll be here."

"I hope you enjoyed your little impromptu party, Mr. Miller. I'd say you went to a lot of trouble," Anne told him.

"I'll see that you never work again in the State of Montana!" He yelled at Anne and made his exit.

"Coffee, Mr. Gunter?" Anne asked.

"No, I've got to get to the office. What is with him? Such vindictiveness I've never seen before. Why? Is there anything I should know, Anne?"

"I can't think of a thing, Mr. Gunter."

"I'm glad you called me. We'll have to be ready for whatever he brings against you. I'll have Anderson come out and talk to you. I have to be going."

Anne poured herself another cup of coffee.

"Maybe you'd better have a drink," Jack suggested.

"You know, Jack, I thought the next time he struck I'd just resign. But with a petition for a vote of confidence, I'll just have to fight. He didn't even deny he had left this mess. Did managing this club mean so much to him that it would account for this sort of thing?"

Jim and Lizzie came in and they started on the clean-up.

Later that afternoon, Bob Storm came in. Jack, Jim, Lizzie and Anne were busy cleaning.

"What are they trying to do to you, Anne? I had a phone call this morning of a meeting out here on Sunday."

"What would they have done without the invention of the telephone? To answer your question, I really don't know. I've done what I had to do. I don't see how I could have done anything differently."

"I don't think you need to blame yourself. There's a skunk in the woodpile and his name is Miller."

"It got around town awfully quick."

"The telephone brigade must be going through the membership list. They're telling everyone there's to be a meeting here on Sunday. A vote of confidence for our manager, by the membership."

"He's been like a sinister shadow following me since the first day I've been here."

"Well, what are you going to do?"

"Fight the bastard. What else can I do? I can't just lay down and play dead."

"I'm right behind you, Boss Lady. One hundred percent," Jack said.

"Thanks, Jack. I'll need every bit of that one hundred percent. But if I'm ousted, I think you should hold yourself in preparedness to take over."

"Boss Lady, I'll fight right alongside you to the bitter end."

"That sentiment is pleasing to me and I appreciate the confidence you have in me, but there's more at stake here. You wouldn't want Miller as manager here, would you? So hold yourself ready. Between you and Freda, you can do it."

"What will you do if you lose you vote of confidence?" Bob asked as he pitched in to help them with what was left of the cleaning.

"I've some money saved," she shrugged, I'll take a long vacation. I haven't had one in . . . my God, it's been ten years!"

"I've got to get home," Jack interrupted. "I'll take a nap and be here by the time dinner starts."

"Why so solemn?" Anne asked Bob after Jack had gone.

"I'm just thinking. Why don't you run away with me?" He asked softly.

"What!"

"You heard me. You don't have to stay here and take all this crap," Bob told her.

"But I've nothing to hide. Nothing to be ashamed of. Running away would be like admitting some sort of guilt. Guilt to whatever drummed-up charges Miller will have dreamed up."

"Anne, for months I've been coming out here, seeing you work your tail off and getting nothing but abuse. I walk into a room and I have to hide my feelings. I love you Anne. I can't go on hiding that. Neither can I stay away. This is a chance to get away from everything here . . ."

"What do you mean?" Anne asked.

"We don't have to stay here. We can go anywhere in the world. I'll take care of you. You don't have to fight reprobates like Miller."

"But I can't. Not now."

"When is there a better time?"

"Bob, I've been wronged. I can't run now. I can't turn my back . . ."

"Yes, you've been wronged by people who are not your equal. Let me take you away."

"You don't understand. My integrity is being questioned. I can't run away from that. I have to see this thing through." Anne wanted to cry but she couldn't.

"Anne, don't you know this is the best of times to tell them to go to hell?" Bob persisted.

"Not until any charges have been cleared, whatever they are. I may run away with you, but not until my reputation is clear. Besides, I'm still married. I've never gotten a divorce, for this very reason. To keep me from marrying again. Now there's more reason than ever. My self respect depends on fighting this . . . my future . . ."

"Your future would be with me! Put those bastards behind you! What the hell do you care about what they say? We're both residents of Montana, we can divorce tomorrow."

". . . and another cause for scandal," she said. "I can't let that man destroy me. You have to understand that if I were to marry you tomorrow, it would give credence to anything that man says. I'd still have to live with myself Maybe you know what he'll say tomorrow, I don't. There's nothing to charge me with. But neither did your mother-in-law have reason to come out here when she did to try to bargain for your wife's happiness, as though I could give it to her."

"What are you saying? What are you talking about?" Bob asked, perplexed.

"That I have to see this thing through."

"I mean about my mother-in-law?"

"Oh, that. I don't suppose you could have known about that."

"My God, what's going on here?"

"I don't know about you, but I feel as though I've walked into a jungle. There's a mad animal out there that doesn't care where he strikes. The only thing . . . but that's so flimsy . . ." She hesitated and thought about chapter 8, Paragraph 54.

"What are you talking about?" Bob demanded.

"Did anyone see us that night we went to Laural?" She asked.

"I don't think so. You can never tell about those things. Why?" He asked.

"The only thing I can even think of that Miller can use against me is the morals clause. It would be a shot in the dark unless someone saw us," Anne responded.

"Morals clause, what would anything like that have to do with you?" He demanded.

"That's the sort of thing women in business have to put up with when they're managing someone else's business. It means if anyone saw me or thinks they saw me, for instance, kissing you, I would be automatically fired, according to my contract, on a moral charge."

"I don't believe this!"

"You can believe it."

Saturday night was the Harvest Ball. A few members slowly drifted in. They made a point of not talking about the Sunday night meeting. The ball was poorly attended and by midnight everyone was gone.

"Want a sandwich, Jack?" Anne asked. "There's lots of food left. Thank God Freda didn't prepare too much."

"Coffee, tea, or milk," she mimicked.

"I'll just have a beer." Jack said.

Anne went into the kitchen to fix sandwiches. Jim and Lizzie came in.

"Would you two like a sandwich?" She asked them.

"That would be nice, Miss Anne. There's something we'd like to talk to you about," Jim said.

"Must be serious from the looks of you," Anne said.

"I guess it is. You see, Miss Anne, we're wondering what's going to happen to us, Lizzie and me, if things don't go well for you tomorrow," Jim said.

"It's hard to say, Jim. I would certainly recommend that you be kept on. I don't know though what my recommendation would count for."

"We don't want to stay if you go. They never treated us right before you came . . ."

"Where would you go, Jim? What would you do?" Anne knew it would be difficult for these two to find another job. Neither were in the peak of health. At least they been properly fed and didn't look like the two skeletons she had first seen a year ago.

"We'd like to go back home, to Kansas City. I thought as we were here so long without pay until you came, maybe you could ask the Board for some 'back pay'? Just enough to get back home. We saved a little, but we'll need that to find a place to live and.."

Lizzie picked up the sandwiches Anne had made and went into the bar with them. Anne went to the cupboard where she kept her purse and took it out.

"Jim, I don't know what will happen and I'm in no position to ask the Board anything right now." She took out her billfold.

"I wouldn't depend on the Board. Everything is in an uproar. Here's two hundred dollars, that should get you to Kansas City . . ."

"Oh Miss Anne, my God, Miss Anne, you're an angel . . ." Tears came to his eyes.

"Come out with us and have something to eat, then make yourselves some sandwiches and some fruit and get out of here. Frankly, Jim, I'll not stay, no matter how the meeting comes out."

Anderson had called to tell her he would see that she was not crucified by Miller.

All was quiet when Miller called the meeting to order at precisely two o'clock on Sunday afternoon.

Mr. Jenson was missing, it was the first day of the hunting season. No doubt Miller had hoped there would be more men who would not be able to forego the season.

Anderson, Kelly and Gunter were seated at a long table in front of the stage. Jack, Freda and Anne were in the small bar, listening, waiting.

"We're here to make judgment," Miller began in a pontifical manner, swelling with importance, "whether Anne Courtney is fit to manage this club . . ."

"Tom, aren't you overdoing this a bit?" Mr. Anderson broke. "We all know it's Sunday, but this pastoral posture of your opening is preposterous! This is not an inquisition."

"'Can you do better?" Miller smirked at Mr. Anderson.

"I most certainly could!"

". . . Since her coming here, she has shown little respect for members of the Board. Seldom, if ever, has she asked permission on how to proceed with business matters. For instance, she didn't seek Board input on the colors of these rooms and the entrance downstairs. Neither was there an opinion asked or request to plant shrubs."

"She left the club unattended while she was running around the state attending meetings that had nothing to do with the Yellowstone Country Club."

"She took prerogatives that exceeded her authority as hired help both in her hiring and expenditures!"

"I'd like to set the record straight," Mr. Anderson interjected. "I believe we all know in the year Miss Courtney has been with us, she has done an excellent job managing this club. Now, let me take these charges one by one."

"Apparently, some of you thought she had too much authority with too little surveillance. That is what it says here. Is that the word you want to keep, Tom?" Mr. Anderson asked.

"Why do you have to answer for her? Can't she speak for herself?" Miller turned to Anne. 'Well, Miss Manager?"

"She'll speak in due time," Mr. Anderson interrupted. "Number 2. An audit should be made and she should be held accountable for all expenditures since she began her stewardship. Mr. Kelly, would you like to answer that?" Mr. Anderson asked.

"She is the one who should be answering these charges." Mr. Miller insisted.

"Charges with no substance," Anne replied. "Please go on, gentlemen."

"All expenditures of this club are cleared through my office," Mr. Kelly began. "My name is on every check that goes out. The bank deposits are made by Miss Courtney and the daily income reports are turned into my office. My office does a running audit, not from distrust, but because the information is in my office every morning. I have never seen a cleaner or more efficient operation."

"Now you also speak of paint and shrubs, Mr. Miller. The club purchased the paint on approval of the house committee. They also chose the colors. The painting was done by our bartender, our manager and our maintenance man at no extra charge to the club."

"The shrubs were bought and paid for by Miss Courtney. They were planted by the same people who did the painting. As it was her money that paid for those shrubs, it was her prerogative to choose what plants and shrubs she wanted."

"Ladies and gentlemen, we found two jewels when this club was fortunate enough to get Anne Courtney and Jack Mahoney. To slander these two people in this manner is inexcusable," Mr. Kelly concluded.

"Thank you, Ken." Mr. Gunter continued. "There's the question of Jack's salary that should be addressed. This was taken up with the Board and it was decided Jack's salary was fair for the work he would be doing in assisting Miss Courtney. They were accustomed to working together and he could be of overall help in the club. Yours, Tom, was the only negative vote."

"As for the indecent show, we'll have to let the men attending decide how indecent it was, however, the golf committee had asked for a stag party. They got one. If Miss Courtney had tried to stop it, I'm afraid she would have had to answer to the Committee and possible to the entire Board."

"Now, let us come to the last and most unpleasant item on this list. Miss Courtney has been with us for one year. Mondays, which should normally be her day off, she is out here working; planning to make this a better club and working on programs that would encourage members to use the club. Two weeks ago, Miss Courtney was invited to Great Falls for the installation of a new president for the Montana business and Professional Women's Club, of which she was a past officer, a point we should have been proud of. Upon her return, very early Tuesday morning, she saw at a great distance the old Billings Club sign, flashing through the morning's first light. She hurried to the club, for the only switch to that sign was in the clubhouse. Mr. Miller, you insisted that sign be disconnected rather than taken down. You also assured the Board you would take care of it."

"She came to the club to find all lights on and all doors open. She turned off the sign and went upstairs. There, ladies and gentlemen, she found food and drink remains on all the tables and the bar. The entire club was in an "after the party" shambles."

"Anyone else would have called the sheriff first. I'm afraid I would have, but Miss Courtney held the interest of the club first. She called Jack to find out if he knew anything about the activities of a club that should have been closed all day Monday and was in proper order that evening, as attested by the maintenance man."

"Jack was as shocked as Anne had been. Then she called me . . ."

"Why didn't she call me. I'm just across the field?" Miller broke in.

"You made a remark, Tom, that Miss Courtney gave little respect to the Board. You're the only one who has complained of that. Perhaps, you showed such little respect for her. But to continue . . . I came out and was able to see, firsthand, the vandalism that had been done."

"Next on the scene was you, Mr. Miller, not at all surprised. Rather, you showed satisfaction at the carnage. Nor did you deny, when she charged you with that mess, that you were responsible. Now, you may have the floor."

"I'm not the one on trial here!" He shouted.

"Neither is Miss Courtney, Mr. Miller." Mr. Anderson told him.

"You can't blame me for anything. Sure, I saw that sign on. I wasn't coming over here in me middle of the night to see who was giving a party. Let her speak up. Let's hear what she has to say . . . go . . . go on, you've never been bashful before!" Miller yelled.

Anne was standing in the doorway, listening, waiting, shocked at the asinine rhetoric coming for this man. Suddenly a warm hand slipped into hers and pressed it. She turned around and Floyd Roberts gave her a reassuring smile and went into the dining room and found himself a seat.

". . . she allowed an indecent show on the premises of this clubhouse and then left the building in charge of her bartender!"

"That's not all." He waved a paper in his hand. 'What about these rumors of indiscretions in her relationship with her bartender? These rumors have to be clarified, for they are prohibited on page 8, paragraph 54 of her contract!"

Ken Kelly leaped to his feet. "Mr. Miller, what the hell are you doing? There is nothing, I repeat, nothing in the conduct of this lady to warrant your attack! I demand an apology!"

"An apology you will not get!" Miller smirked.

"Mr. Miller," Mr. Anderson took the floor, speaking softly and doodling with his pencil on his pad in front of him, "are you aware, that you have just placed this club in danger of a slander suit?"

"What . . . what . . . what do you mean?'

"Just what I said. This lady, because of your scurrilous remarks, has just cause to sue this club. The entire afternoon you have skirted on the edge of defamation. Now, before the membership of this club, unless they choose to perjure themselves, you have placed this club in a position, which will be impossible to defend. Unless this lady, this lady would be magnanimous enough not to choose to sue. For if she did, she would close this club.."

A startled silence fell over the room. Then a buzz of bewildered apprehension started.

"Is this true?" A voice from the middle of the room asked in disbelief?" "How much will it cost us?"

"I don't care. No woman has a right to manage a club!" Miller told them. "Let her speak for herself."

"Do you want to address this assembly, Miss Courtney?" Mr. Gunter asked. Anne came to the front of the room.

"Ladies and gentlemen, members of the Board, I'm not feeling very kindly at the moment. I don't feel I can be expected to when an attempt is made to tear my reputation to shreds, especially in my work which I consider a career, not a job."

"Get on with it get on with it . . ."

"Mr. Miller!" Mr. Gunter called to him angrily. "You wanted this meeting, now don't interrupt!"

"Thank you, Mr. Gunter. I came here a year ago. I went on duty two weeks ahead of time because Mr. Miller had gotten himself into a situation he didn't know how to get out of I came in to pull his chestnuts out of the fire. I have had to wonder since, if his extreme aversion for me—his reasons for maligning me this entire year-could be that he feels beholden to me in his mind."

"This club could not even afford to pay my salary. I agreed to work at half my usual salary because I thought it was a challenge, something I could get my teeth into."

"You made up for it on the percentage you insisted on!" Miller shouted.

Anne ignored him.

"In the year I have been here, I have taken a club with no income and no programs in what amounted to an abandoned building and built a successful club. I have nothing to apologize for, either in my management or personal conduct. I took responsibility for a club in an area where most members have never belonged to a private club and didn't even know there were obligations that go with membership. I look out in this room filled with members; or else you wouldn't be here. Most of you have never used this club. Why are you here today? Am I to assume you are here for a diversion? For the sport, as in ole England, to see a woman chastised by a buffoon?"

". . . and now, in answer to your questions, Mr. Miller and friends, I realize you cannot wait to be rid of me. You made that very dear on the first day I was here. You say I took prerogatives exceeding my authority. Never did I take upon myself a right that was not thrown into my lap because a chairman felt I had the experience to handle the responsibility."

"The money that was spent, was spent for the club. If you will recall, I advised you right from the beginning that to make a success of this club, everything had to be plowed back in for at least two years. We have done better than that. This club does not owe one dime, except for the real estate upon which it stands!"

"The indecent show? I had advice from the manager of the Elks Club. You see, I do ask advice. But I seek it from those who are capable of giving it. I have no other comments on that. Thanks to Mr. Gunter, the tempest in the teapot over that show has been adequately answered, as has most of these picayune issues."

"My bartender is a good, decent family man. He does what is required of him in this club and more, all for the good of the club. That includes staying for stag parties where it would have been embarrassing for members and their guests to have a woman privy to their entertainment."

"Now, let's go to the firing of that chef. The nomer, *chef,* does mean something in the food business. That very poor excuse you had for a cook should not be allowed in any kitchen and he certainly should not have been allowed to call himself a *chef.* He left six loins to spoil because he didn't know how to care for them! Had it not been for an exceptional butcher, they would have been unusable. The navy bean soup, which you complemented so extravagantly, and wanted it served to a banquet, had a mouse floating on top. Your chef took it by the tail, threw it out the door and had the audacity to say to me, 'There, good as new.' This, Mr. Miller, was your wonderful 'chef'!"

"Now, let us go to your last and final insult with which you have served me, page 8, paragraph 54 of my contract."

"I do believe, Mr. Miller, that membership should know of your insistence at a late night meeting, that if I were approved as manager of this club, there should be a morals clause. It was not required for the man you interviewed, only for the woman. Why, Mr. Miller? I ask, is your mind so sick . . ."

"Now, look here . . ."

"No, Mr. Miller. You wanted this meeting. You wanted this contemptible public hearing. What did you expect? An outcry for flogging? You want an explanation before these people. For what? To prove that I met with deception? It is I who have been wronged!"

Miller stood up and waved papers at Anne.

"It's time to stop this damn charade. These personal attacks that have no substance!" Bob Storm rose to his feet.

"She has overstepped herself . . ." Miller was not going to give up. He was going to have the last word.

"It sounds like personal attacks to me," Bob told him. "Everything that has been brought up here today should have been taken care of in a meeting of the Board and settled there. But since you have chosen to bring it out here and make a three-ring circus out of your jealousy and hatred, let me remind you that Anne Courtney has done a hell of a job here. She brought activity to this club and if she has another year, she might even get that golf course done. The revenue this club has made far exceeded what we expected. This lady has always acted with decorum. Whatever your personal feelings about a woman manager, let it go. For that is what is at the bottom of this, isn't it? It is a personal prejudice and has no place here."

"You speak well for her, Doctor. I didn't see you out here before she came." Miller retorted.

"That can be said of everyone here," Bob answered.

"There wasn't anything to come out for. I would think twice, Miller, before you slander me as you have slandered this woman."

This has gone far enough," Mr. Gunter rose to his feet.

Anne looked around the room again. Many members hung their heads uncomfortably. The Board was angry that they had been put through this. Anne stepped from the podium and left the room.

Freda and Jack followed her to the stairs.

Is there anything we can do, Boss Lady?" Jack inquired.

"Thanks, both of you. I think the best thing to do is stand by. If I lose, they'll want to talk to you. Make the best deal you can with them, Jack."

She went downstairs, got her coat and put it on. "Where are you going?" Jack asked, as he had followed her.

"I think I'll go for a walk up on the hill and think. She felt washed out. She had been stripped of her pride, her dignity, all that a person holds sacred.

Closing the door softly behind her, she braced herself against the autumn air and walked around the building. She went toward the path that led to the old sign. The air was fresh and clean. There had been an early fall of snow the night before and a covering of the white stuff laid lightly on the ground. She walked in the cleanness of it. She wanted to weep for the injustice that had been done her to have to go through that spectacle.

She was not naive. She understood that having walked into a man's world unprotected, except for the brash confidence she had in her ability, made her a target.

Now, this cruel blow. For in winning, she would lose. What had been said tainted her integrity. Once having her honor questioned, she could never like these people again.

She must've been on the side of the hill for sometime. She saw Bob coming toward her.

"You have to go back," he told her. "They've given you your vote of confidence. There are people in there who believe in you."

"I can't go back, Bob. All I can think of is those flimsy, outrageous things Miller said."

"There were a majority who didn't let you down. This is what you said you wanted."

"I know, Bob. Now, it's not enough."

"I proposed an alliterative, Anne. I mean it. I'll still run away with you," he smiled at her.

"Let me lick my wounds. I need to be alone awhile."

"I'll wait for you at the clubhouse."

He turned and left her. She watched him walk down the path. She knew he was walking out of her life.

"What's the matter with me?" She thought. "Have I put love so far out of my life that I can sit here and watch that man walk away?" Still, she would not go after him. At least there was feeling, or she could not have been so hurt over this thing that had just happened to her. There was feeling in her heart, in her soul. She could still be hurt. She could still feel disappointment pain then why not love? Oh God, she thought, what am I looking for? Do I want this rat race for the rest of my life? Do I want all this . . . this thankless existence?'

She guessed this was as good a time as any to take a good look at herself at her life. Here she was, just thirty-two years old and she already had these decisions to make. Her eyes filled with mist, but tears could not come.

She picked up a stick and began to move the sparse snow around. She saw someone coming up the hill. Had they sent someone else to bring her back? To face that room of people and thank them? Thank them for what?

Tears were still blurring her vision and she could not see who it was until he came nearer. Then she saw Floyd Roberts. He seldom came to the club, although he kept a membership. At both clubs for business reasons. It was like him, she thought, to know what was going on. She smiled up at him.

"Hello, Floyd."

"That was a pretty nasty display of ignorance in there this afternoon, Anne. I'm sorry it happened to you."

"We don't expect such things until they happen, do we?"

"Are you staying? They've given you your vote of confidence."

"I think it's best to move on. There will always be embarrassment now."

"Have you thought of another place?"

"No. I'll probably take a long vacation. I haven't had one since . . . since before the war."

"Why don't you take a run up to Helena? They need a manager at the Placer Hotel. I spoke to Fred Henry about you. Why don't you go up and talk to him?"

"Why have you appointed yourself my guardian angel, Floyd?"

"You were sixteen, such a delightful sixteen, when I first fell in love with you. Then you fell in love with Bill Courtney. I'm sorry for the way things turned out for you and him. I understand he's still in France, doing very well as a reporter . . . to me, Anne, you'll always be that happy, lovely young girl I used to know. So whenever I can help you . . ."

She rose and took his arm.

"Thanks, I'll go to Helena tomorrow."

"Good, I'll call Fred and tell him to expect you."

They walked down the path, friends, good friends, just as they had always been.

Anne took the trip to Helena. She talked to Fred Henry, the banker who owned the Placer Hotel. She carefully looked over the contract he offered her, so different from the last one.

She was to manage the hotel and bring it back to what it once was, the handsome hotel that had a history of high rollers, political shenanigans and home to the most expensive legislators in the country.

During the two-year contractual period, Anne would teach Dan, Mr. Henry's son-in-law, the hotel business. He had a business degree from Montana State.

If Anne felt Dan was ready for management before the two years expired, she would be paid off on her contract and she would turn the management over to Dan.

Anne returned to Billings, called Mr. Jenson, told him she was resigning and asked that her final check be sent to her. Mr. Jenson delivered the check with more than an adequate bonus. He asked her, "Are you planning to sue?"

"I'm not into suing, Mr. Jenson," Anne told him. "It wouldn't be good for my career. I hope you'll keep Freda and Jack. They will do a good job for you. As a matter of fact, you couldn't do better than those two."

"Is there anything I can do for you? A letter? Anything?" He asked.

"No, I don't need a letter. This," she pointed to the check, "is quite sufficient. If you really want to do something for me, when you announce my resignation, just say that I'm taking the management of the Placer Hotel in Helena."

'Then you have another place?" He asked.

"Yes, Mr. Jenson. I'll be in Helena."

"I'm glad you found something. I know you'll do well, just as you did here. If . . . oh, by the way, you know those damn kids, they've gone off and eloped."

PLACER HOTEL

The Placer Hotel was one of the country's most famous/infamous hotels, politically speaking. It was a name in Montana history and as Anne had a special liking for history, the Placer Hotel had a special attraction for her.

Anne also had a liking for that 'Old Helena', and for Last Chance Gulch, with it's freewheeling past. For the men who made Montana's history one of courage, audacity, and a heedless rush into plunder, this held a special fascination. Some of those men still walked along Last Chance Gulch, Helena's main street, with their memories.

Montana legislators, in years past, were paid ten dollars a day for their stay while the legislature was in session. Anaconda Copper Company, needing special legislation kept suites at the Placer for these elected officials who found envelopes of gratuities under their pillows.

It was the hey day of the Placer Hotel, which also had a gold mine in the basement and was now, in 1950, the site of the men's restroom.

In this lap of history, Anne was anxious to begin work. Richard, the young clerk, checked her into the hotel and assigned her to a suite on the fifth floor. Richard was a personable young man, conservatively dressed, and with a winning attitude that welcomed guests to the hotel. Dan came from the inner office, to the right of the registration desk to greet Anne.

"I'm glad you're here. There's lots that needs to be done. How soon can you take over?"

'Tomorrow morning, if that's agreeable with you."

Dan showed Anne the office before she went upstairs.

"I'll be sharing this with you. I hope you have no objection?"

"None at all."

Dan called Frank, the bellman, to take Anne to her suite.

"You're our new manager?" Frank asked.

"Yes, my name is Anne Courtney, And yours?"

"I'm Frank Peterson."

"I hope we'll work well together, Frank."

"I'm sure we will. There's a lot to be done and we heard you're someone who gets things done. That sounds good to us."

"Thank you, Frank, but sometimes getting things done hurts too."

"Good things usually do, I guess."

Anne unpacked, bathed, dressed and went down to the coffee shop. She decided to have an early supper and check out the coffee shop.

She made a note of the dishes, checked the menu and watched everything as she read the paper and lingered over her meal.

When she left the coffee shop she took the supper menu with her and asked Clara, the waitress, if there was a breakfast menu she could also take with her.

When Anne came down to breakfast early the next morning, Clara was on duty. "Seems to me you were on duty when I left here last evening," Anne said. "How many hours do you work?"

"I'm the headwaitress so I have to put in long hours," Clara said as she placed the coffee and ice in front of Anne. Anne had told her the night before that she used ice to cool her coffee.

Anne ate a sweet roll and drank her coffee before going into the office. Dan was already at this desk.

"Good morning, Dan," she said.

"Good morning. I guess you'll be pretty busy today. If you need anything, let me know."

"Right now, I'm looking around for a transcript," Anne replied.

"Transcript?" He asked.

"Yes. Yesterday and last night's occupancy record."

"All we have is the cash deposits from each department," he offered.

"I guess I'm at a loss. How do you know what your percentage of occupancy was for yesterday?" Anne asked.

"Beverly just gives me a list of the empties," Dan said.

"Sounds like whisky bottles to me. Do you depend on someone just handing you a list as a record of income?" Anne asked.

"Never paid any attention. Empty is empty," Dan replied.

"Sure is. You should know how many is what. I'll get some transcripts and show the night clerk how it works. That also needs to be checked against the housekeeper's record of 'empties'.

"I'd like to have a meeting of the department heads. We can have it in here. I want you to be privy to all that goes on. We can also watch the front desk from here," Anne said.

Dan called the department heads into the office. They each found chairs and sat down. They looked at Anne, wondering what they could expect with this new manager.

Anne looked at them and said, "My name is Anne Courtney. I'm your new manager. Please tell me your name and the department you're in charge of. First names will do for now." Since they were hesitant to start, she continued speaking to give them time to relax a little. "I know you haven't had a manager for awhile, so I'll tell you what I'll do. I'll take one department at a time, and we'll go over everything that needs to be done. The first thing I must concern myself with is the cash flow. The immediate cash flow always comes from the food and beverage. So Clara, we'll look into the food department first. Since the food and beverage must work together, we'll have to wait and see what we have to do about the food before we can take any action with the beverage. Now, your names and departments, please."

Anne pointed to Bill, a tall, well built Irishman. Bill was neatly dressed, well shaven and sported a clean haircut. There was warmth in his demeanor.

"Bill, bartender," he said.

"Clara, the headwaitress, another name for coffee shop manager, without the compensating pay," Clara said unhesitatingly. Clara was a frank, outspoken woman of about thirty-five. She could have been a model for the 'pioneer woman.' Her husband was Frank, the bellman, a sly Irishman, with a wonderful sense of humor.

Mrs. Hopkins, the housekeeper, introduced herself. Like most hotel housekeepers, she was an elderly lady almost grandmotherly in appearance and demeanor, until you got to know her.

She preferred gingham checked house dresses to a uniform and wore a voluminous white apron. Her gray hair was pulled back into a bun completing her grandmotherly appearance.

George, the engineer, was tall and lanky with kind eyes. He dressed in his engineer's uniform of blue and white striped overalls.

Richard, the afternoon clerk, introduced himself, as did Joseph the night clerk and Rite the switchboard operator.

Often times there are favored employees or those for whom the hotel feels a responsibility for one reason or another. Beverly, the morning clerk, fell into this category. She had been with the hotel for twenty-five years. She stood in the open doorway without entering.

A favored one never made trouble. Beverly was the exception.

Jake, the 'chef' was a former dude ranch cook. He was an uncouth, unwashed, chewing tobacco individual.

After introduction had been made Anne suggested anyone not feeling comfortable working for a woman, should resign at this point. No takers. She asked how their departments were faring. No one spoke up after all; no one had asked them before. Finally Mrs. Hopkins stood up, "I guess since you're going to be the new manager, I might as well come out with it. What are you going to do about all that worn out linen?"

"We'll look at it and see what condition it's in," Anne said. "If it can't be used, we'll replace it."

"And what about enough maids?" Mrs. Hopkins demanded.

"Surely you have extra maids on call, Mrs. Hopkins. I believe the normal practice is to have your regular crew and to have maids on call who are willing to work part-time," Anne said. "When the house is half empty as it is now," she continued, "you use your regular crew. When the house is full, you have a full contingent by calling in your reserve. So what is the problem, Mrs. Hopkins?" Anne asked.

"When do I have permission to call in my reserves?" Mrs. Hopkins persisted.

"There's a union in this town that I think determines the amount of rooms a maid can work. You use that as a rule of thumb. While we're on the subject of cleaning, the floors and the sideboards of the lobby are a disgrace," Anne said. "There is grime from dirty mops splashing the sideboard and the floors are streaked, for the same reason"

"The night janitor takes care of the lobby!" Mrs. Hopkins interrupted angrily.

"As housekeeper, Mrs. Hopkins, it is your duty to inspect the janitors' work as well as that of your maids," Anne replied.

"I don't have time for that!" Mrs. Hopkins yelled.

"Very well," Anne said. "We'll turn the housekeeping duties of the lobby, the stairs and all public areas over to George. George, we'll discuss this later and set up a department for you."

"Yes Ma'm," George said. "I think that would be the proper thing to do anyway."

"Mrs. Hopkins, I'll be going over your department with you no later than day after tomorrow," Anne said.

Mrs. Hopkins rose to leave and the others followed suit. Anne watched them go. Beverly had a cunning look on her face as though daring Anne to say anything to her. Jake wore a sneering grin. The others had friendly looks on their faces.

When Joseph rose to leave, Anne asked him to stay.

When everyone had left except Joseph and Dan, Anne picked up the pads of transcripts she had procured.

"Oh," Joseph said, you got some transcripts."

"Then you have done night auditing?" Anne asked.

"Sure. Gosh, I'm glad you got those. It sure beats guessing about charges to the rooms," Joseph said.

"Joe, would you mind teaching Dan how to do transcripts?" Anne asked.

"Hell no, be glad to," he said.

"What about you, Dan? You would like to learn the transcripts, wouldn't you?" Anne asked.

"Sure," Dan replied.

"Would you rather Joseph or I taught you?" Anne asked.

"Joe and I will get along just fine. But it's as you say, Anne; there's a hell of a lot of work to be done around here. From the sound of things I just heard, it's going to cost a lot of money, too. So where's the money coming from?"

"Dan, I've always believed any business should pay it's own way after three months. That's what we're going to do here," Anne replied.

"Good luck," he said with skepticism.

"May I have the profit and loss statements for the past three months?" Anne asked. "I'll have some coffee, then I'll be right back."

Anne sat at the end of the counter. Clara brought her some coffee.

"Now Clara, I had dinner in here last night. This morning, as you know, I had breakfast. I was served on cracked dishes. This alone is prohibited by the state health laws. I haven't seen anything that matches. This . . . silver, which I assume to be dude ranch tinware, I'm ashamed to ask guests to eat from."

"Our greatest cash flow comes from food and beverage. We're going to have to do something about this. So, Clara, are you capable of carrying out incomprehensible orders?"

"Boss Lady, you name it," Clara laughed. "You can depend on Frank, Bill and George, too."

"Thank you, Clara."

Anne sat awhile. Taking a pad and pencil, she listed what she had to work with. What did they have? What did they need? After having glanced at the profit and loss statements, she knew she couldn't depend on them for accuracy. She had seen how the bookkeeping was done. If that's what it could be called, an arbitrary list of occupancy.

How much revenue could she really expect when she didn't even know how the room charges were handled.

Dan had a degree in business. What was he doing with it? She mused. Apparently, he didn't have an interest in the hotel. He had an independent income, which did not make it conducive to any improvement of an aging hotel, no matter what the historical value. It was not long before Anne discovered he spent most of his time at the stock exchange and was doing very well.

Anne needed a budget. She could not depend on past income performance. She would have to make up a summary from the bank statements.

The standard of this hotel after her two-year tenure had to be the best! Not second or third in the state of Montana, but the best!

She sat at the end of the counter, thinking. "Where would she start"?

Clara came in with the newspaper. "Have you seen this?" She asked.

"I haven't had time to look at the paper, Clara," Anne replied.

"Well, you'd better look at this one . . ."

An announcement had been made to the press. "The Placer Hotel had Anne Courtney as manager. Dinners in the private dining rooms and the ballroom would be available"

"They say you make changes where ever you go."

Anne took the paper from Clara and read the item. Then she sat there and thought about it.

"Clara, is this a sample of the dishes I can expect to feed people from?"

"That's all we have. I wash the cups and saucers out here, or we'd run out before a meal is over."

"That's how I make changes, Clara. So something will have to be done, wouldn't you say?"

"What do we do first?" Clara grinned.

Before Anne had time to think, Daniel came into the coffee shop and sat down beside Anne, smiling.

"What do you think? We already have results. From this announcement, the Montana Stockmen want the ballroom for their Christmas dinner-dance. That's a hundred and fifty couples."

What could she say? Another November one!

"Did you take a menu, Dan?"

"They'll be out later to talk to you about that." He gulped his coffee.

"You'll have indigestion that way, Dan."

He didn't hear her, as he hurried from the coffee shop.

Clara came over to pour another cup for Anne.

"Well, Clara, looks as though we're going to make some changes before we're ready. You see how one can't always depend on a schedule. Circumstances interfere. So, I'll tell you what we'll do. As soon as breakfast is over tomorrow morning, I want you and the girls to pack every dish, glass and piece of . . . tin. I'll have boxes for you. I want everything out of here by nine thirty."

"What are we going to use for lunch and dinner tomorrow?" Clara asked.

"There won't be any lunch or dinner tomorrow." Anne laughed and started to leave.

"What will we do with these?" Clara called to her.

"Set them out in the alley and hope someone steals them," she replied.

Anne went to Dohrman's. She had determined the amount of dishes she needed immediately. She picked out an open stock pattern of crockery, glasses and silver. She told them they had to be delivered by four o'clock the next day.

She called on a steam cleaning firm and told them she wanted them at the hotel by nine thirty to steam clean the coffee shop and the kitchen. The kitchen was a firetrap of accumulated grease.

She told Jake she was closing the kitchen at nine thirty that night until two o'clock the next day.

"There's nothing wrong with my kitchen! I won't have it closed down!" He yelled at her.

"Good. Stay and have yourself a steam bath, you need it!" Anne quipped. "It's dirty, it's greasy. I can't touch a thing in here without having to wash my hands. Now I don't want an argument, Jake. Close her down and we may open for sandwiches for dinner. And get yourself cleaned up, Jake. You're filthy and have no place around food!"

"You go straight to hell!" He yelled.

Anne left without answering him.

The next day at five o'clock the coffee shop opened. They served sandwiches and pastries. At six o'clock, Mr. Henry came into the office where Anne was going over the bills from Dohrman's.

"How about coffee, Anne?" He asked.

"Happy to," she smiled and went with him into the coffee shop.

Clara served them coffee and Anne suggested Mr. Henry try a piece of apple pie.

Mr. Henry picked up his saucer, turned it over, read the hallmark and looked inquiringly at Anne.

"Nice, isn't it?" She asked. "Now these dishes look like the Placer Hotel should look, wouldn't you say?"

He looked her straight in the eye. She met his gaze eyeball to eyeball.

"Sure beats that old stuff doesn't it?" He grinned and set the cup and saucer down. "Did you get enough?" He asked.

"It's open stock. We can always get more as needed. With the Stockmen coming in at Christmas, and there will probably be many more parties in the private dining rooms, we can add as we go along," she said.

Bill came into the coffee shop, picked up crockery, glasses and silver. He looked them over and said, "Things can get done in a hurry after all, can't they? I never knew they could move this fast."

"Only when you're pushed in a corner," Anne told him.

"I notice Mr. H was over here in a hurry. Who do you suppose tipped him off so fast?" He asked.

"Probably Dohrman's, for a credit approval."

After the steam cleaning and the new dishes, cleaning the lobby went into a flurry. Anne had the stream cleaners back that night to clean the marble in the lobby and another company that would shampoo those glorious carpets which covered the center of the lobby where there were six seating arrangements. The couches and chairs were also cleaned.

The lobby was now sparkling clean.

That night she worked on new menus, 8x11 heavy stock. For breakfast the commonly ordered breakfast fare, including a space for specials in season, or something that could vary from one day to the next. She also hired Maggie as sous chef for insurance.

There were also new menus for lunch, with five daily specials boxed into the left-hand margin for each day, except Saturday and Sunday. The body of the menu contained the five regular items along with desserts, sandwiches and salads.

There was also a notice on each menu that prime rib sandwiches with salad would be served at noon in the bar. Anne had Bill hire a waitress to take care of this service . . . and she made another trip to Dohrman's for a portable hot serving cart.

At dinner time there was another menu, with five dinner items, dessert, sandwiches and salads, with a notice that steaks would be served in the bar.

Early the next morning she took these to the printer to be made up.

She would like to have done something about Jake, but since she had been moving rather fast, she thought the best thing to do was give him enough rope to hang himself She had pretty much taken the fangs out of his bite by taking the purchasing of food stuffs away from him and forcing him to cook what was on the menus.

Meanwhile, she busied herself with the housekeeping department.

She started the next day with Mrs. Hopkins. Word had gotten up here that Anne could be pretty ruthless as to how she wanted things done. When Mrs. Hopkins had complained of worn linens, Anne could see she was certainly justified in her complaints.

There may have been a dozen or two dozen sheets that were not patched. Mrs. Hopkins did the duties of a seamstress. After checking all the linens, which were in like condition, Anne said, "Just let me sit down and think, Mrs. Hopkins."

"Would you like some coffee," Mrs. Hopkins asked.

"I most certainly would appreciate some, thanks, Mrs. Hopkins."

Anne drank her coffee and thought. Could she go to the dry goods store and order five hundred sets of linen? This was beyond what she had done about the dishes; however, it was just as important, if not more. For this is what guests had to sleep on.

"I'll be right back, Mrs. Hopkins. I can see you have reason for complaint. I'll see what I can do about it."

She went to her room, got her coat and went across the street to the bank.

"Good morning, Mr. Henry."

"Good morning, Anne. I hear things are shaping up over there."

"Not exactly, Mr. Henry. That's what I've come to see you about. As you know, we have had quite a response from that news item. That means we have to take care of our guests or they'll be here once and they won't be back a second time."

"But I thought you had what you needed?"

"Not exactly. I hadn't gotten to the linens yet. Do you know that we have a dozen, maybe two dozen sheets and pillow cases that are fit to use?"

"Why . . . why wasn't I told?"

"You're being told now. I can have the spreads cleaned or washed as the case may be, but the linen, Mr. Henry, will have to be replaced. In going over the last three months laundry bills, I noticed the cost of sending laundry out. We could have our own laundry in the basement, at cost."

"What about additional employees?" He asked.

"We can move the linen room down there and they, along with George, can handle that, at most. For the satisfaction of the union, we can hire an extra woman, at no more than the cost of a maid, to act as laundress."

"What do you do, Anne, stay up all night working these things out?" He asked. "Do you have figures at your fingertips?"

"Just about . . ."

"You might as well go ahead and get what we need. Tell the folks over at Bradley's to call me for credit, o.k.?"

"Thanks, Mr. Henry." She rose and started out.

"By the way, Anne, you didn't ask about the dishes. Why are you asking about the linen?"

"I didn't think I could get away with the same strategy the second time," she told him. "You know, Mr. Henry, I think we should consider a gala New Years Eve . . ."

"Go right ahead, good for business."

It was the first of December, Anne had moved quite fast. She felt she had to. The food, beverage and housekeeping were in fairly good shape and getting better with practice. She still had to keep her eye on Jake, but she had to get to that front desk. It was a total disaster.

Beverly, the twenty year employee had so entrenched herself and her antiquated method of handling reservations it would require an act of God to change her from the ways that harkened back to the days when registration was not always required.

Time and again Anne had walked away from that desk, until Dan asked her why she was avoiding it.

"I'm keeping it 'till last, I know it's going to be a war zone," she told him.

"So you've gotten wise to our Beverly?"

"Is there something I should know?"

"You'll find out soon enough," he told her.

Anne saw trouble coming from both the kitchen and the front desk. As those things tend to happen, they would hit at the same time. She decided to forestall the kitchen problem, she knew what that was. She didn't know what to expect from Beverly.

Anne called Bill and Maggie into the office.

"Sit down, both of you. I smell trouble from two directions. I can only watch my back in one place. So, I'd like the two of you to take over the Stockmen's dinner dance. We'll be serving baron of beef."

"We'll set up two chopping blocks just outside the service kitchen, and Bill, if you'll get another man, you and he can carve the meat. Everything but the meat will be on the tables. The girls will serve that. We'll need two service bars and your man will also act as bartender after dinner . . ."

"What about Frank?"

"If he's free, fine. Remove the chopping blocks as soon as dinner is over. I've ordered an orchestra. Maggie, you keep alert in the kitchen."

It was time for the front desk!

The following morning Anne came downstairs ready for battle. She went to the front desk and told Beverly she would be working her shift with her.

"I don't need anyone working with me," Beverly said. "I'm not exactly new here, you know. I've been here twenty five years!"

"Good. Let's see how much you've learned in those twenty-five years. Where's the reservation book?"

"What reservation book?"

"The one you will use to block out your rooms as of today," Anne replied.

"Block out?" Anne asked incredulously.

"Yes, your reservations," Anne answered unflinchingly.

"I know where these people coming in are going to stay, " she answered Anne sarcastically.

"I don't," Anne said. Neither does anyone who might have to take the desk in an emergency!"

"That's none of your business! I'll take care of this desk!" Beverly screeched.

"I'm afraid that won't do, Beverly," Anne said calmly.

Anne went into the office and made up a reservation sheet. Then she went to the printer and had a hundred made up. When she came back she told Beverly, "Now, I'd like a list of all guests coming in today, tomorrow, and the next day. We'll start with today. I'll do the first sheet. That's today, and you do the rest."

"How do I know! . . ."

"You said you did."

"I don't have to take anything from you!"

"Just so we understand each other, Beverly, neither do I have to take anything from you. You may be a privileged employee, but I can send you home. Too sick to do your work, I believe. Or what other reason would you have for not doing it? You see, two can play this game. Now, where are your reservations?"

Beverly began to pull registration cards from the rack. Anne watched her, wondering what she was doing.

"What exactly are you doing?"

"You want these damned reservations, you're getting them!"

"Reservations, Beverly. Not registrations!" Anne corrected.

"That's what I'm getting!" She continued to pull cards from the room rack one after another, from behind the current registration and threw them at Anne.

"I don't believe this!" Anne said in amazement.

It was after lunch now and check out time. There was confusion for Beverly had angrily pulled too many cards and couldn't find some of those for the outgoing guests. Those she did find, she carried on long conversations while Anne waited. Beverly, aware of Anne's annoyance, stalled even longer.

Finally, Anne went to the rack and pulled all cards except current guests. Then she placed the sheets in a loose-leaf folder.

When Anne had entered all the known reservations, she turned to Beverly and said; "live listed your reservations here and I'll return after lunch to help you block out these rooms."

"I don't need your help. I've been here twenty five years!" Beverly cried.

"I want these rooms properly blocked, Beverly. I want every single reservation accounted for. If you can block out this board the way I want it, fine. If not, I will do it and you will stand by and watch."

"I'm sure I can get along without you," Beverly insisted. "I've been here for twenty five years."

"I'm not impressed with twenty five year employees. I think all employees should be fired every five years and hired back on merit. So now that we understand each, start blocking!" Anne ordered.

She didn't know where to begin. There was so much anger bottled up inside her, she could not think.

"Go ahead. Start blocking," Anne told her.

"How can I block with you standing here watching every move I make?" Beverly retorted.

"I have to stand here, Beverly. I can't trust you to do it right."

"We've gotten along without you so far . . ."

"Yes, I know. For twenty five years," Anne mimicked. "That's probably the reason you managed to lose at least four reservations last night. Or was it six? This morning we had six vacancies. Rooms are not like inventory. You should have learned that in twenty-five years. You can't sell a room tomorrow to make up for today's loss. That room revenue is gone."

"They didn't come in until late," Beverly said defensively.

"That's another thing. Since you were here behind this desk late last night, why didn't you help the night clerk find the reservation you had hidden and he couldn't find without tearing the board apart? What were you doing here last night?" Anne demanded.

"I had come down to see that everything was alright."

"Well that's my job now. So if you do this right the other clerks, or whomever has to take the desk in an emergency, will know where to put late-incoming guests and you can get your sleep," Anne admonished.

"Look here, those people had rooms!"

"But not at the Placer Hotel, because the board showed a full house. Their reservations could not be found. They were sent to another hotel. That is no way to pay the bills."

Beverly slammed her pencil on the desk and threw a telephone book in a corner. She started to pick up the reservation book but Anne took it before she could reach it.

Beverly angrily stomped into the coffee shop and Anne took the desk.

Carmen, the switchboard operator had been watching this battle of wills with interest. When Anne began to block the rooms, Carmen asked, "Miss Courtney, will you teach me how to do the board?"

"If you would like to learn the front desk, I don't see any reason why you shouldn't," Anne said. "Yes, I'll teach you."

Anne showed Carmen the procedure of checking guests in and out. She explained that the housekeeper had to be notified when a room became available. Carmen was a fast learner.

Anne waited for Beverly to return. When she had not returned in an hour, Anne left Carmen on the desk and went into the coffee shop. Beverly was seated at the counter, angrily smoking and drinking coffee.

"The rest of your shift is covered, Beverly. It will be covered for three days. Almost any ailment can run its course in three days. If not, I'm sure we can spare you until you're well enough to work," Anne said.

Anne left while Beverly was still sputtering for an answer. She went behind the desk and told Carmen, If you would like to work the desk for three days, you can call your relief. I'll be here if anything comes up and you need me. Anything you learn can be an advantage to you sometime or another."

It was time to start thinking about that New Year's Eve Gala. She was busy making up a menu. Just two or three items, she thought. Keep it simple, easy to serve and keep hot.

Dan came in and asked her what she was doing.

"Getting ready for the New Year's Eve party," she replied.

"You just never quit, do you? Don't forget we have the legislature coming in too."

"How could I forget?" She asked.

"You know, Anne, this transcript thing is really good. I've a better idea of the whole procedure around here. I've a whole new outlook of the accounting now. Do you suppose we'll have that front desk straightened out by the time the legislature comes in?" Dan asked.

"I don't know if we'll ever get it straightened out, Dan. The solution, of course, is to pension off our twenty five year employee."

"I'd have to agree with you. I can sure see where we've been losing money before we started using this," he said pointing to the transcript.

"Do I get a feeling you're developing a greater interest in this business?" She laughed at him.

"Yes," he said very seriously. "It's all beginning to make sense."

Beverly came back after three days and Anne was diverted from her New Year's Eve party. Beverly returned to her old ways.

Dan began to complain that all charges were not posted. Charges were not balancing out. Anne gave instructions to the bar and food department to make triplicates of all charges for Dan and Joseph. This worried her about what would happen when the legislature came in and charges were heavy.

New Years was a great success Maggie kept an eagle eye on Jake that he couldn't contaminate the food. There was dining in the ballroom, all the private dining rooms were engaged for private parties and the carpets in the lobby were rolled back for dancing. Bill had set up potable bars in the lobby and on the mezzanine. It was indeed a gala affair.

The next week the legislators were in and Montana's government was in session. They would be in Helena six months.

The Young Democrats were coming in February. Senator Mansfield would be coming from Washington to address their convention. The Young Democrats wanted fried chicken.

Maggie prepared the chicken for frying, cutting it up country style and placed it in the cooler' the night before.

The morning of the Young Democrats dinner, Anne started as usual making her rounds. First the housekeeping, checking to make sure there were enough linens as there was a great drain with both the legislature and the Young Democrats in at the same time.

She passed up the front desk as Dan was assisting Beverly and hoped all was in order.

She checked the bar where she never had to worry then the coffee shop and the kitchen.

She noticed Jake had two large pans of chicken sitting out on a worktable. Maggie had not yet come in.

"What are these chickens for, Jake?"

"For that dinner tonight. What did you think?"

"It isn't even noon, Jake. These chickens should be in the cooler until Maggie is ready for them."

"I'm taking care of them. I know what I'm doing."

"I'm afraid of that," she said as she felt the chickens. They felt warm.

"How long have these chickens been out of the cooler, Jake?"

"I had to have space in the cooler!"

"Jake, I swear to god, if there's anything the matter with these chickens, so help me . . ."

Anne went to the coffee shop and told Clara to call Maggie. "Tell her to get down here as fast as she can." All the time Anne was thinking, "there's time to get others but is there time to get enough."

She went back into the kitchen and felt the chickens again.

"I said I know what I am doing. You'd think I never cooked a chicken before!" Jake said.

"You're not cooking these chickens, Jake. Maggie is." Anne picked up a piece of chicken and smelled it. Then she picked several others and felt them for sliminess, the first signs of spoilage. Borderline, she thought, but she wasn't sure. It perturbed her that they were so warm and she called the dishwasher to wash the chickens thoroughly in soda water and place them in the refrigerator, instead of the walk-in.

"I haven't room for those damn chickens in my refrigerator!" Jake bellowed.

"Then make room," Anne told him and walked out.

After lunch she came back to have another look at the chickens. There was still time to get others in case the soda bath did not work. She opened the refrigerator and the stench rocked her back on her heels. She looked around at Jake. He was watching her. Maggie and the dishwasher came running over.

"My god, what has happened?" Maggie picked up a piece of slimy chicken and dropped it.

"What did you do to these chickens, Jake?" Anne demanded.

"I thought you were taking care of those little chickies," he turned and went behind the range. His sarcasm grated on her already raw nerves and Maggie asked, "What'll I do with this mess?"

"Get rid of it, Maggie, I'll call the poultry man for another order."

She marched over to Jake who was behind the range. He knew she would not go back there because of the hot grease in the french fryer.

"I want you to come out here and speak to me, Jake," Anne demanded.

"It'll have to wait until after dinner," he said. "I haven't got time now to chat with the ladies . . ."

Jake wasn't coming out and Anne wasn't going behind that range. Neither would she have him in the kitchen any longer. She went to the coffee shop and told Clara to hold up all orders. She had to get him out and she had no intentions of putting Maggie in jeopardy by sending her back there. Anne went back into the kitchen.

"How did you do it, Jake?" She asked him.

"Do what?" He asked innocently. "That chicken's your party. Let's see what you can do with it, BIG BOSS," he sneered.

Bill came into the coffee shop and Clara told him what was happening. Maggie was with Clara. "God, Bill," Maggie said. "We didn't expect him to spoil food . . . and he's behind that range. He might as well be behind a barricade. She won't send anyone after him because of the hot grease back there."

"I'll take care of that for her," Bill said. "He's a lousy cook anyway. We'll just have to smoke him out."

Bill went into the kitchen. "Where's my food, Jake. I ain't got all day," he said. Anne had gone into the coffee shop.

"That bitch thinks she's so damn smart, I showed her! "Jake bragged as he came to the coffee urn to fill his cup.

Bill drew himself some coffee from the huge urn in the kitchen. "Why is it that you can't get along with her?" He asked.

"No woman's got any business running a hotel!" Jake ranted. "Why you know what goes in hotels . . . what kind of woman would want to get messed up with anything like that? Unless she's a whore," Jake continued. He came over to the urn and drew a cup of coffee.

"You saying our boss is a whore?" Bill asked.

"Sure acts like one to me," Jake replied.

"Well, tell you what, Jake" Bill hauled off and knocked Jake out cold. Anne came running into the kitchen. Jake was prone on the floor and Bill was standing over him.

"What you want done with him, Boss Lady?" Bill grinned.

"Oh, my God," Anne said, flabbergasted. "Get him out back and lock the doors. Maggie, you'd better come and start dinner," Anne said.

A tall young man with a German accent followed Clara into the kitchen. "This is Ed, Anne. He's a chef and he'll help you," Bill told her.

"Thanks, Bill. Anytime I can return the favor, let me know." Anne patted his arm and sent Frank to pick up the chickens he had ordered.

Ed turned out to be a pretty good chef and Anne kept him on. The Young Democrats, not knowing how close they came to being poisoned, had a most delightful dinner. So did Senator Wheeler.

The bar was turning a fantastic profit, luncheons were standing room only and everyone was willing to share a table. Hot prime rib sandwiches were carved to individual specifications.

For the happy hour, there were hot d'oeuvres and in the evenings, there were steaks.

The coffee shop was also enjoying a new flux of business. Breakfast and lunch were solid and dinners, except in private rooms were early. Private dining was late.

Housekeeping was in good shape. A laundry had been installed and the linen room that had been on the fifth floor was moved to basement, next to the laundry. The furniture was good when it had been purchased and had stood up through the wear and tear of the years. Cleaning and polishing took care of that.

The only problem that was left was the front desk and the Montana Medical Association was due. Beverly could be most charming to the guests. She was about as rude as she could be to Anne. Anne ignored this and stood by to see that Beverly handled the reservations and registrations close to the proper manner.

When the doctors began to arrive, Beverly, to provoke Anne, leaned across the desk and whispered to incoming guests. Anne reprimanded her for such insensitive behavior, but Beverly excused herself by saying they were personal friends.

Anne advised her as long as they were guests in the hotel they would be treated as guests and her entertaining would have to be done on her own time, off the premises.

Anne stayed on the desk most of the day, leaving the desk only long enough to have lunch. As she was coming from the coffee shop, Anne saw Bob Storm at the desk. She was surprised at his being here, though she should have known for a medical convention, the chances were that he would attend. As she approached the desk, he asked Beverly, "Is Ms. Courtney here?"

"Oh, I suppose she's around here somewhere," Beverly answered sarcastically. He was appalled at her response.

"Bob! What are you doing here?" Anne called as she approached the desk.

"I'm speaker at this here convention, Ma'm," he smiled at her. Then turning to Beverly he said, "I'd like a room on the fifth floor. A northern exposure, please."

"Oh God," Anne thought, what ammunition he has unwittingly given Beverly! Anne turned away from the desk and Bob grabbed her arm.

"You're having dinner with me tonight, aren't you?"

"Why not? I do need to get away from here for awhile. How will seven o'clock be? I'll meet you down here."

"See you right here, at seven," he smiled at her.

They went to dinner at the Montana Club, where they spent the evening arguing. He wanted to know why she had left Billings without letting him know. "Our lives are too far apart to ever have a common ground," she said.

"Listen, Anne. We can make a life for ourselves anywhere," he persisted.

Anne knew she was giving up a lot. She also wondered if she could really be in love to give up so much for what was beginning to look like a very empty life.

Was fighting with people like Beverly, the Jakes, the Millers of this world really worth it? Anne looked at Bob Storm's offer. There was a strong physical attraction, but could she honestly say she loved him. Then she knew that no matter how thankless it seemed, work was best for her. When she could give up her work without hesitation, without a qualm, then and only then would she know she had the right man.

Bob Storm spoke at the convention the next day and was applauded on his view of treating the whole person in the coming age of specialization.

The next morning, they silently stood by the elevator holding hands. They both wanted to keep this moment as long as possible. He pressed her hand tightly as the elevator indicator squared at their floor. They stepped in, strangers. Fellow passengers. The elevator was crowded, giving them the opportunity for closeness a little while longer.

When the elevator slid to a stop in the lobby, Bob gave Anne's hand another squeeze. Their eyes met, caressed, "You know where to find me," he whispered to her. Then he spoke to an acquaintance and was lost in the surging crowd. He was out of her life.

Anne crossed the hall into the coffee shop. Clara put a cup of coffee with a glass of ice in front of her.

"I never saw anyone spoil good coffee the way you do," she scolded but Anne didn't hear her. She was too near tears. Sensing something was wrong, Clara said, "What you need is a good breakfast. You hardly ever eat! I don't know how you keep going the way you do without eating."

Anne looked out the window at the new fallen snow, which had piled high overnight. By noon, the whipped cream whiteness would be dirty slush and Anne wondered if that would be the way of her life. Clara broke into her thoughts again. "Here, eat this. It's one of those hot cinnamon rolls you like so well."

Anne choked on a bite of the roll and went to the office. She found Beverly struggling with reservations. There weren't very many for the house was still full except for those who were checking out that morning.

Dan was helping her and she left them alone. She checked the bar and the housekeeping. Then she checked the kitchen and made all the other usual rounds before going back to the front desk. If Beverly could work better with Dan, that would be good. He could show her why things had to be as they were to balance out with his transcript.

Dan had gone back to his office and Beverly was happily working away at the front desk. Anne went behind the desk and looked at what she had done. Beverly had gone back to her old way!

"Beverly," Anne patiently said to her, "this will just not do! I mean it! When I said this antiquated system has to go, that's what I meant"

"If you don't like it, you do it!" She told Anne and walked off the floor. Anne straightened the board and called Carmen to take the desk. "I'll do it, Anne," Dan said coming from the office. "I'll have to learn sometime," Anne knew when this convention was over she would have to do something about Beverly, as she was undermining all Anne's efforts. She found Beverly in the coffee shop and sent her home again for three days. Anne was tired. She checked all the departments, had a light dinner and went to bed. She was reading when thought she heard the sound of a key in her door. Her watch said midnight. She grabbed her robe and went to her living room. Jimmy, a new bellman, was standing in the doorway with a strange gentleman!

"Jimmy! What on earth is the meaning of this?" Anne asked.

"Golly . . . oh gosh . . . I . . . I didn't know, Miss Courtney. Beverly said you moved your room."

"I see. Step inside, both of you while we get this straightened out. I'm sorry, sir, to inconvenience you, but we can't wake up the entire hotel."

They stepped inside and Anne asked the man to be seated while she went to the phone.

"Kay, who is on the desk?"

"Joe is here," Kay said.

"Let me speak to him . . . Joe, have you been on the desk since your shift started?" Anne asked.

"Yes, Miss Courtney, that is almost. I just got back from having a bite to eat. I've been here all but about twenty minutes. ? Is anything wrong?" He asked.

"Who relieved you?"

"Beverly came in and said if I wanted to get a bite, she'd watch the desk for me."

"I see. Joe, my living room was mistakenly assigned to a guest. Do you have anything vacant on this floor for this gentleman?"

Joe gave Anne a room number which she relayed to Jimmy and told him to let the man in with his pass key and then bring his key up for him later.

"I'll take care of this matter tomorrow," she told Jimmy. Anne knew she could no longer wait until the convention was over to take care of this matter with Beverly.

The following morning, Anne came down and had her coffee. She did not speak to Beverly or go near the desk, as was her habit.

When the bank opened, she went over to talk to Mr. Henry. Anne was ushered into his office and he looked up in surprise.

"You're down bright and early," he said as he rose and shook hands with her. "I hear we have had a full house onto a week now."

"Yes, so full that Beverly thought she might double up, our guests last night, starting with me "

"Why, what do you mean?" He asked, startled.

Anne told him what had happened the night before.

"Mr. Henry, we really have to do something about Beverly. I realize she's been with you for twenty-five years, but in that twenty-five years, she has not learned one thing. She certainly does not have the interest of the hotel at heart to do what she did last night."

"The entire operation of that hotel was so antiquated that I wonder how you operated at all. Now everything is in good shape except the front office. Dan already knows more than Beverly and that little Mexican girl on the phones learned in three days! I have to reconstruct Beverly 's work every day."

Mr. Henry hung his head silently fiddling with his fraternity key.

"You can see by the balance sheets . . . in fact, in the deposits being made everyday here in this bank, that we're on the right track. We're making money."

"The front desk is a disgrace! If that is not straightened out, you can lose everything you're making through one department alone. If you turn away enough people and lose enough reservations people will find somewhere else to go, even the motels."

"Well, Anne, I have to admit you've done an excellent job for us. What do you propose we do?"

"What are you willing to do, Mr. Henry?" Anne asked rhetorically. "I believe the answer is simple. Are you willing to pension Beverly off? That's the logical solution. She's been with the company for twenty five years."

"Oh, Anne, I don't know. What would the poor woman do?"

"The poor woman would do her mischief elsewhere. She surely has family."

"But twenty five years," he mused.

"Twenty five years, hell. It's time she's pensioned off. When one doesn't keep up with the times"

"I don't know how I can do it," Mr. Henry said mopping his brow and seeming very uncomfortable.

"Would you keep an employee of your bank that did not keep up with new procedures?" She persisted.

"No. No, of course not, but that's different."

"How is it different, Mr. Henry?"

"Well . . . a . . . a . . . bank . . . is a . . . a business," he stuttered.

"What is the Placer Hotel? Pray tell, a plaything? A toy?" Anne was not about to give up. "That's not what I came here to manage. You've got a million-dollar plant going to hell because of one incompetent woman! What value is she to your business? When she sabotages me, she's also sabotaging you."

"Now maybe you can afford to play with this toy but my reputation alone in this business would be destroyed. I have no intention of allowing Beverly do that to me."

"Anne . . . Anne . . . What can I say? You don't understand."

"No, Mr. Henry, I don't understand." Anne looked at that troubled man and suddenly realized there had to be a reason for his tolerance of this woman. Anne asked, "Mr. Henry, does this woman mean something personal to you?"

"No. No, of course not," he said playing with some objects on his desk. She pushed on.

"Then why do you hesitate to do what you know is best for the hotel. I need to know the interrelationship, which exists here. I am not, nor do I intend to pass judgment, but I have to know."

"A man does things when he's young, Anne."

"You allowed her to hold a club over your head for twenty five years!" Anne said incredulously.

"I . . . I . . . I . . . I don't know what to do," he said.

"Mr. Henry, twenty five years is a long time. Too long to be threatened like this. Times, attitudes have changed. While I can't see that in Montana there was ever the bigoted attitudes that are prevalent in other parts of the country, I wonder how you could've gotten yourself in such a fix!"

"A man does foolish things when he's young," he repeated.

'That's true. Everyone does foolish things when they're young. But they don't allow someone to hold the threat of a scandal over their heads for twenty-five years. Your first mistake was to allow her leverage. You're making a greater mistake in allowing it to continue."

"But there's my family."

"As you said, Mr. Henry," Anne said softly, "a man makes mistakes when he's young. Do you have another woman at home who doesn't want to understand? Another one who delights in holding a club over you head? Or one who carries a grudge for twenty five years?"

He didn't answer Anne. She looked at that beaten man with pity and walked to the window, which overlooked Last Chance Gulch, the busy main street. Standing there, she thought about his revelation. Then she went back and sat down in front of the desk.

"Mr. Henry, was she of age? Was she a willing partner . . . to this drastic deed?"

"I thought so," he said. "My God, she was twenty-two and I certainly thought she was willing. It wasn't a one-night stand. It went on for some time."

"Then was she pregnant at any time?"

"No. Not that I know of and I'm sure she would have used that against me had she been."

"Well then, now is your chance to break free of this blackmail. I don't give a damn what you did with a willing woman who was old enough to know her mind. I'm sure as hell not going to work under the shadow of your guilt. Guilt that has been manufactured by a conniving woman. So, blame it on me. Blame it on business. Now, Mr. Henry! Now is your chance to rid yourself of this threat which probably everyone in town knows about anyway, else why would you put up with her?"

"So I'm going over there and I'm going to get rid of that woman by pensioning her off. I would advise you to get out of town for a few days. When you return, the smoke will have cleared. The heat will be off and you should be able to handle it from there."

Anne turned to leave.

"Wait. Wait I'll go with you. I might as well face it."

"You're making a mistake. It would be better if you let me do it and let tempers cool."

"No. It's my responsibility."

If ever a man looked as though he was going to face a firing squad, this man did.

They walked back to the hotel together. Anne asked Beverly to come into the office. Mr. Henry seated himself at Dan's desk. Anne closed the door.

"Beverly, after last night I decided it is no use trying to work with you. You have held a favored position here that I could have worked with. You have abused that position. While I was willing to overlook a lot, after last night, I can no longer do that. You're inefficient stubborn to change and a troublemaker. I have, therefore, asked Mr. Henry, who has your welfare at heart to pension off your twenty-five years of service."

Beverly turned on him.

"You . . . You have allowed her to pension me off. You son-of-a-bitch. Your pervert! You fucking bastard! You think you've found a way to fire me! You just wait till I get through with you. You'll wish you've never been born."

"Beverly!" Anne snapped. "How dare you speak in such a vulgar manner!"

"You want to know what kind of man he is, Miss Know-it-all?"

"I'm much more shocked at the kind of woman you are, Beverly. The wickedness I see in you far exceeds any immorality he might have been guilty of. It's time to put twenty-five years of hate behind you! You were old enough to understand what you were getting into and that's no excuse for twenty-five years of blackmail. Blackmail, Beverly!"

White-faced and trembling, Mr. Henry said, "Let me talk to Beverly alone, Anne. Leave us, please."

Anne was shaken with anger and frustration. What kind of Pandora's box had she opened? The brutal vituperous expressions coming from Beverly could only make Anne feel shame for her. Anne went for a walk.

When Anne returned, Beverly had gone and Frank told her Mr. Henry wanted to see her in the office.

Mr. Henry was still sitting at Dan's desk. He had her contract in front of him.

"Sit down, Anne," he said. "Do you think Dan is ready to take over?"

"He has shown a greater interest in the operation lately. Surely he's ready as far as the front office is concerned. I had hoped to have m ore time with him in food and beverage," she said.

"I see. What happened this morning was bound to happen sooner or later. I want you to know I don't blame you for anything. You've been with us for several months now and you've done a marvelous job. I'd like nothing better than for you to stay. The problems are too great. I had hoped for just a little while there, that I would be out from under that . . . you call it guilt. I call it my burden. Whatever it is, I can't fight it."

He handed Anne a check for the entire length of her contract. She looked at Mr. Henry and said, "I can take this and lay in the sun for a year or two. It's a tidy little sum. But what about you? I'm sorry that I was instrumental in bringing things to this point but you can still cut yourself free of this."

"Anne, you're the new kind of woman. The pathfinder for women of the future who will compete with men but also take responsibility for your actions. I hope nothing ever happens to change you."

"Thank you. I know one thing, Mr. Henry, I would not let anyone blackmail me. You say I would take the responsibility for my actions. Yes, I would, but it would be head on, right at the start. No club over my head."

He put his head in his hands, a broken, tortured man. Anne went around the desk, patted him on the shoulder and said, "Heaven bless you, Mr. Henry. Good-bye."

Anne walked out of the office and Dan went in. She went toward the elevators and met Bill coming from the bar.

"Is it true you're leaving, Anne?"

"I'm afraid so, Bill."

"The first time in I don't know how long this hotel has been run right since the old days. Now What?"

"Cheer up, Bill. Some good should come out of this."

Frank interrupted their conversation with a message that Dan wanted to see Bill in the office.

Mr. Mahon, a businessman in the city was with Frank. "Let's have some coffee, Anne," he suggested. After they were settled with their coffee, Mr. Mahon said, "I hear you're leaving, Anne? What's going on here this morning?"

"Just a little reshuffle in management. Happens all the time," she said.

"I don't understand it. Why just last night at the Montana Club, Fred was telling me how lucky they were to have you."

"Sometimes there are conditions one can't work with, Mr. Mahon. Dan will be the manager now, which was in the plans anyway."

All of a sudden there was shouting from the lobby. Anne and Mr. Mahon jumped up and ran out to see what the trouble was. There was another explosion of voices with Bill's the loudest. ". . . Like hell you will! I work my tail off for what I make. I'll be damned if you cut my wages!"

"That's the way it has be," Dan was telling him.

"Then you can take this job and stick it . . ." Bill came over to where Anne, Frank and Mr. Mahon were standing. He was in a rage.

"What's the matter, Bill?" Mr. Mahon asked.

"They've got an adding machine for a manager again. That's what ruined this hotel in the first place. You know what he's doing?" Bill asked, looking at Anne.

"I heard it all the way in the coffee shop."

"Cuts, straight across the board. All we've worked for in the past few months, wiped out!"

"I'm sorry, Bill," Anne told him.

"What will you do now, Bill," Mahon asked.

"Hell, I suppose I'll get a job somewhere."

"Need money for a place of your own? "

"What?" Bill asked.

"You heard me. I've got that little building down the street. It's not very big, but . . ." he shrugged.

"You mean it?" Bill laughed.

"What do you think, Anne" Mahon asked her.

"You couldn't back a better man." She told him.

They shook hands, both of them beaming.

Frank came from the office and said to Clara, "Honey, we're leaving. This is no place for us anymore."

"Need a job, Frank?" Bill asked and Mahon nodded.

"You damn right. What am I doing?" Frank asked.

Bill told him of Mahon's offer to back him in a bar.

"Always wanted to be a bartender," Frank laughed.

"What will you be doing, Anne?" Bill asked her.

'What am I going to do?' Anne asked herself. 'Did it matter?' She had plenty of money in her pocket and somewhere, out there, was a hotel, just waiting for her to make it pay. Another hotel that only a woman manager would consider.

"Look for another hotel to manage," she said aloud. She smiled and they all went into the bar for a farewell drink.

EN ROUTE

Anne's long awaited vacation never materialized.

First she went to Denver, where for the past eight years Bekins had stored her furniture. Her nomad lifestyle did not lend itself to having furniture. Everything had to fit into trunks or bags. Everything except her books, that is. She started with one box, then two, then three boxes, then hinges attached to plywood for the front so that they could be shipped wherever she went. These would be the only pieces of furniture she would have. She sold everything else.

After taking care of personal business, Anne called at the Cosmopolitan Hotel. The same faces she had left behind eight years ago greeted her. They were still doing the same jobs. She knew she had done the right thing moving on. She would have died of boredom had she stayed. Old friends welcomed her back as though she had never been gone.

Nothing was mentioned of her invasion into management. Only Mr. LaChance and Mr. Beatty discussed it with her. How it had gone for her and whether she would continue with it.

A meeting of the Hotel Greeters told her plainly what her position was in the hotel business. She could attend auxiliary meetings of this august group, but as a woman, she could not attend the general meetings. Anne resigned.

In Montana they had been glad of her membership. But of course, in Montana, the membership was limited and they were glad to have anyone

Mr. Beatty asked Anne what her plans were.

"I haven't any, Mr. Beatty. I do feel I need a vacation."

"Albuquerque needs a front desk clerk for about six weeks. That would give you a couple of weeks off. They need you there the first of March"

"That sounds like it might be interesting, temporarily," Anne agreed.

Mr. LaChance came into the coffee shop where they were chatting and asked to join them.

"Anne can take that turn in Albuquerque, Jean. She's just interested in a temporary spot right now and that would fit right in with her plans."

"Sounds good. But you know, Anne, things are changing in this business. NCR is making a lot of things obsolete. Why don't you stay a couple of weeks up here? NCR will teach you the machines, then you can go down there and get some practical experience."

Anne took the course NCR was offering, by courtesy of the Cosmopolitan Hotel. To say it was making hotel accounting obsolete was putting it mildly. It would never be the same. Anne was pleased that she had the opportunity to learn the new machines before she was faced with using them, for these new machines opened up a whole New World.

In March, Anne went to Albuquerque.

Six weeks later, they needed someone in El Paso, Texas.

Anne went to El Paso.

"Western needs a food manager in Salt Lake, Anne." Mr. Nelson told her when her time at the Hilton in El Paso was nearing its end.

Anne went to Salt Lake.

Anne soon realized being a food manager, or any kind of department manager, was not for her. She had to think about finding a hotel.

Mr. Davis called Seattle, home of Western. He told them he had a woman, well qualified for management, who was looking for a hotel to manage.

"Right now we need a reservation desk, someone that is willing to learn the new telex that is being installed in all hotels and networking the industry," Mr. Davis was told.

For the purpose of learning this new telex, Anne accepted the assignment.

In Seattle, after learning the workings of the telex, Anne made it very clear her goal was to manage a hotel.

But Western was not hiring women managers. They would like to keep her on, they said. "We do have something, that is, if you don't mind going to San Francisco. We're looking at an experimental program there."

Anne went to San Francisco. She reported to Mr. Dahl, auditor at the Sir Francis Drake Hotel. She was put in charge of coordinating services in all Western Hotels, to standardize rooms and prices according to the location of the rooms. Nothing came of the program.

Next she was charged with standardizing all menus. They wanted the same menu in Boise, Butte, Denver and San Francisco on the same day.

When that project was finished, they sent her to Honolulu to work as a night auditor.

When Anne returned to San Francisco from Hawaii, Mr. Dahl called her into his office.

"Anne, how long are you going from pillar to post around here?" He asked.

"Mr. Dahl, you know what I want. I keep looking . . ." She began.

"You're not going anywhere with Western Hotels," he said. I spoke to a friend who has an accounting firm. He needs an auditor. Now there you would have a chance. He admires women with gumption and is willing to give someone like you a break. I want you to go see him."

Auditor-at-large for one of the largest and most prestigious accounting firms in the country! Anne was excited.

The pure variety of the job was most intriguing. Just two or three weeks on a job and then off to another. One could make a career out of a position like this, with the bonus of living in San Francisco. What more could she want!

Grocery stores, electrical engineering firms, construction companies, restaurants, plumbing supply houses, and best of all, hotels!

Anne couldn't help wonder why people could not see that their problems were poor management. Her job was to clean up after a relative or a trusted employee brought the company to near bankruptcy.

It was not long before she became involved in reorganization loans. After an audit, the company arranged these loans on the basis of the audit.

Finally, a project in her own specialty! A hotel. No, a whole chain of hotels!

The lady who owned them inherited them from her husband. They had been managed by her brother, a good manager, except he had been called to a 'little war'.

The lady took over. Her husband had built the Sir Francis Drake, which Mr. Hilton had purchased for what she considered a give-away price.

The brother, Victor, came home from that "little war' and found the chain in shambles. He called in the accounting firm since the hotels were a blink away from bankruptcy.

Mr. Howard sent for Anne.

"We have something that's just what you've been waiting for."

"A hotel?" She asked excitedly.

"A chain of hotels. It isn't a management position. It's an audit to start with. Who knows where you can take it if you want to take the chance? They want a loan. Now, Anne we've had this account for some time. Management is very bad. The only reason we've kept this account was to see if the brother came back from the war. He's back now and wants our help. He doesn't have trouble with women in executive positions, but his sister does. And she owns the hotels. So walk softly."

Out of the four hotels in Northern California, Victor chose the Marysville Hotel as the starter hotel for reorganization. His sister, Mrs. Newsome, had only agreed to a woman auditor because it was their last chance to get a loan. She had exhausted all other possibilities.

Victor went to South Carolina where there were two other hotels. Anne went to Marysville!

MARYSVILLE HOTEL

Anne Courtney came into the Marysville Hotel late on a Sunday evening. She was to audit the books and determine if and what kind of loan would be feasible to rescue this hotel from bankruptcy.

She registered and told the desk clerk, Roy, that she was the auditor from San Francisco. "I believe you have a room reserved for me."

"Yes, Miss Courtney. I've put you right next to the accounting office," he smiled at her.

"Thank you. That should be very convenient. Is your manager here?"

"No Ma'm, he takes weekends off."

"Then I'll see him in the morning. Will you let him know I've arrived?"

Yes, Ma'm"

The following morning Anne came down to breakfast. Bill Meyer; the accountant found her in the coffee shop and sat down to have breakfast with her. They chatted some about the work ahead, although Bill's conversation leaned more to what fun could be had in Marysville than on the state of business. Mr. Ryder, the manager, had not yet made his appearance.

They finished breakfast then they went to the accounting office on the second floor.

"If you could bring me the books, Mr. Meyer, I can get started here," Anne said.

"Oh, call me Bill. We're very casual up here."

"O.K. Bill, I'd like to have the journal, the payroll ledger, the accounts receivable and the accounts payable."

He left and brought back a box, a 24x13 carton.

"What is this?" She asked as he set it on her desk.

"What you asked for," he said.

"Where do you keep it?"

"In my room," he replied.

One entire side of the office was solid with built-in files. "What do you keep in these?" Anne asked pointing to the row of files.

"Oh, the junk that's in there has been here since year one. I've never been through that stuff."

"Where are the ledgers and the journal? This just looks like a lot of bills," she said as she casually perused the contents of the carton.

"What ledger?"

"You did say you were an accountant, didn't you?" Anne asked.

"Hell, no. That's what Jim likes to call it. He says it sounds better. I'm a bookkeeper."

Anne could only sit there and look at him in shock. She couldn't believe what she was hearing. Even a bookkeeper would know about a ledger.

"You know what a check register is?" She asked.

"Oh, you mean the check book. Jim has that."

"No, I don't mean a check book. I mean a register of accounts paid. Get it!"

"Oh golly, I don't know if I can. You see, Jim . . ."

"God damn it, I said get it!"

He left and she began going through the carton. Bill upon bill emerged and none of them appeared to have been paid. Just about the time she came to the bottom of the carton-a hundred and thirty bills later-the door opened and Bill came bearing two drinks in his hands.

"Refreshment time." He said cheerily.

"Where's the check register?" She asked

"Jim keeps it in the office downstairs and he isn't here yet."

"I'd like to have it, please." Anne persisted.

The door opened and Jim came in carrying three hi-balls. "Hope you like scotch," he grinned at Anne with his *haw to charm women grin*.

Anne got up from the desk and knocked the drinks out of both of their hands.

"How!" She demanded and war was declared, "could you allow any place to get so out of hand and in such a mess as this hotel is!"

"What do you mean?" Jim asked as he watched the drinks soak into the carpet.

"Don't you know anything about accounting?" She asked.

"Why should I? I got Bill here for that."

"Perhaps you should have a manual you can refer to on the duties of a manager! One of your responsibilities is to see that the bookkeeping is done. If you can't, or if you don't know what to do, you've no business being a manager! You could at least let the company know you needed someone to do the books and put your playmate here on another job. There is no reasonable excuse for this situation! At this point, this hotel is in jeopardy of closing!"

"Now you look here. I won't have some woman coming up and raising hell."

"Sure, blame it on a woman! Blame your inadequacies on me. You have only yourself to blame for this mess and I very much fear someone else will have to clean it up!"

"I'm here because of the people up her like me. I understand them. Don't think you can come up here and high-handedly push me out!"

"I didn't come up here to push you out. I came here to get your chestnuts out of the fire. To save your ass if I can! Though why they would want to keep either of you is more than I can figure out. How long did it take you to get into this mess? You know you could get away with a lot of incompetence if the books were in order!"

"You know I don't have to put up with you!"

"Oh yes you do! Are you not aware, Mr. Ryder, that your company has asked my company to arrange a loan on the result of this audit? How the hell do you expect to get a loan when this the way you handle your accounting? There are bills here a hundred and eighty days in arrears!"

The man had the audacity to grin at Anne and say; "You take everything too seriously. Now that was good whiskey you spilled and that's serious."

"It wasn't spilled, Mr. Ryder. I'd hate to have you imply it was an accident! Now get the hell out of here, both of you, and get me what I need to reconstruct a set of books! I want the check register. I want the checkbook. And I want the journal. What's more and please remember this, I do my drinking on my own time."

The next day, Mrs. Newsome came up from San Francisco. Since Anne had never seen the lady or her brother, she did not know what to expect. Anne was standing by the front desk conferring with Roy, the clerk, when a woman, swathed in black walked ever so slowly into the lobby. She walked as though she was in a processional. Anne's first thoughts were that here was a widow, just coming from a funeral.

"Oh that poor woman," she said to Roy, "isn't there someone to help her?"

"That, Miss Courtney, is our boss making her entrance. Please bow." He turned to the room rack.

"I was not aware she was a recent widow."

"Yes," Roy said sadly, "it's just been twenty years now."

Mrs. Newsome came to the desk. "Roy. Clarice." She nodded to the clerk and the telephone operator.

"I understand we have a woman here going over my books. Kindly tell her I would like a word with her."

"I'm Anne Courtney, Mrs. Newsome. I didn't know we were expecting you today." Anne smiled at her.

"When I come, I come unannounced." She drew herself up to her entire five feet five. "I do not approve of women in business, Miss Courtney."

'That's unfortunate, Mrs. Newsome, as you'll be seeing more and more of us in the future and my company felt I was the person for this job. I don't believe it was specified male or female," Anne told her. 'What was this character!' Anne thought to herself.

'Then you will do your work as quickly as you can. I won't have anyone disrupting my staff "

"Your staff needs shaking up, Mrs. Newsome. Now if you want to talk business, I will be in the accounting office!"

Anne turned and went to the elevator.

"Miss Courtney? Finish as soon as possible," Mrs. Newsome purred.

Anne did not see Mrs. Newsome again until breakfast. She came into the coffee shop, still heavily draped in black. This morning she was dripping with assorted rosaries and a black prayer book. She came to Anne's table.

"I'm going to Mass now, to have a talk with God. He will advise me on what to do about a woman who puts home and children in second place."

"It's much further down the line than that Mrs. Newsome," Anne smiled at her.

When Mrs. Newsome returned from Mass, she came into the office. "I've had my talk with Him. I'm to be more patient. However, He did say that you must let Clarice go."

"I'm not here, Mrs. Newsome, to hire or fire any of your employees. If you're unhappy with Clarice, I'd suggest you speak with Mr. Ryder."

She left the office and returned to San Francisco. Clarice was still working.

A week later Mrs. Newsome came back. She rushed into Anne's office. "My deeear," she dragged, "I must apologize. I didn't know. It's because you worked for that Beast!"

"What? . . . What Beast?" Anne was stunned.

"Conrad Hilton! Oh, that I should soil my lips with his name!"

"Mrs. Newsome, I have no idea what you're talking about! I once worked for the Hilton Hotels. That was a long time ago. I found Mr. Hilton a very fine gentleman."

"I will forgive you for that! How is the work going . . . my deeear?"

"The work is going slowly, Mrs. Newsome, because I have had

to reconstruct the books, find missing invoices and non-existent requisitions."

"But . . . but . . . Miss Courtney, I need money!"

"It's going to take sometime to straighten this out and I'm not sure you'll have any money left."

"Don't say that! Never say that! You're just being unkind because you worked for that Beast!"

"Mrs. Newsome, I'll try my best to save your hotel for you. Since you can't say anything civil about Mr. Hilton, would you please not mention him to me at all?"

"Miss Courtney, the only reason I agreed to take you unto my bosom is that I was told you could make my hotel pay! I need money, Miss Courtney. I need money. I must have money for my cottage in Carmel, my office and penthouse in San Francisco and my home in San Jose! I do not want a woman running my business, so get on with your work."

"The reason you agreed to my staying here after your last little jaunt up here is because your back is to the wall, Mrs. Newsome. I can get you out of this mess without costing you a fortune, which is what it would cost you if a man were doing the same job I'm doing. When I'm through, you will have money for your various establishments. I might even be able to save your hotels. But next time; please try to share a little with the hen that lays the golden egg. These places do have to be repaired and supplied to keep operating."

"You're being very unkind, my dear. It's that Beast. It's all his fault."

"Please, Mrs. Newsome, will you just go to your suite and leave me to my work? The sooner I can get through with this, the sooner you will have your money. If you had thought about having better management and managers, instead of handsome men, you would not have gotten into this mess!" Anne was out of patience with this woman who looked upon her own sex as complete idiots.

"Just tell me when I'll have some money coming in."

"Money has been coming in right along, Mrs. Newsome. The bills have not been paid. So, you tell me, where is the money going?"

"Are you suggesting . . . Are you daring to imply that I . . . I . . . ."

"Perhaps I should enlighten you to what we look for when we audit. We want to know if there's money coming in and where it is going. You take yours off the top, Mrs. Newsome. You have a playboy manager and bookkeeper who are both alcoholics."

"I cannot allow you to speak to me like this." She started to cry. Anne thought her tears were affected and she continued.

"Then who is going to talk to you like this? Someone has to."

"You're cruel . . . cruel. I thought it was because of the Beast. But now . . . now . . ."

"I'm not being cruel and I've asked you not to talk to me about Mr. Hilton. He engendered respect and loyalty from his employees. I have not seen that here."

Other than Mass time, Anne did not see much of Mrs. Newsome that week. Each morning while Anne was at breakfast, Mrs. Newsome could come downstairs draped in her black and with her many rosaries dripping from her dark gloved hands, she would look into the coffee shop to see if Anne was there. Then she would stop by her table and say "I'm going to have a talk with the Lord, my Father, now. He helps me make all my decisions."

After Mass, she would come to the accounting office to ominously inform Anne, "God has told me He would have a decision for me in a few days." The she would solemnly leave and go to her suite.

It was a month before Victor, Mrs. Newsome's brother returned from his trip to South Carolina. He came to the accounting office to see how things were going. Anne related to him the state of affairs. She recapped for him her findings to date.

Among the items she listed was a column, which showed the amount of money his sister had been draining from the bank accounts.

"What's this?" He asked pointing to Mrs. Newsome's draw column.

"I believe that is the moneys thought to be necessary to operate various establishments in San Francisco and Carmel," she said.

He looked at Anne in disbelief while Anne focused her attention on a hunting print on the wall.

"Do you think you can clean this up?" He asked.

"I understand you need a loan. If you were to pull yourself out of this, you will have moneys coming through this little hotel that can pay for everything you need. If you would just plug up the leaks in this sinking ship, you wouldn't need a loan and you'd come out in good shape. Control, Mr. Snyder, is what you need here."

"It can't be allowed to happen again!" He said.

"These places don't run by themselves," Anne said.

"What do you need to finish this up?" He asked Anne.

"A little more cooperation from the front office."

"Who's giving you a bad time?" He asked.

She told him there was no cooperation since she had knocked the drinks out of Bill's and Jim's hands.

"Which one is worth keeping?" He asked'

"Neither." She told him. "If it comes to push or shove, Jim is popular with the people in town and the guests."

"Will you stay until we find another accountant?" He asked.

"Believe me, I won't be through here before you find someone else. Where have you been that you couldn't see what was going on?"

"I've been in Korea." He snapped at her.

"You've come back none too soon." She said nonplused.

"I guess it must have started going bad two or three months ago. That was when I started moving around preparing to discharge."

"This started long before three or four months ago. You have accounts payable six months overdue. Mrs. Newsome was advised of the condition. The company was ready to drop the account when you asked for an audit via cable from Tokyo. What are you? Clairvoyant?"

"They were going to drop us without letting me know?" He asked angrily, ignoring her last question.

"You were, until today, an absentee general manager. Mrs. Newsome did not complain."

"They should have let me know!" He persisted.

"Hotel operation is a day by day business. One can't wait for Mr. Absentee to come home and take care of business. Nonetheless, here you are and we know what the problems are. This is what I'd like to do. I've had a chance to look over the other properties. Urban blight is moving in on Stockton and Oakland. The best thing to do is to sell them now. Santa Cruz is worth keeping, but you'll have to spend money on it. Major refurbishing inside and out, Mr. Synder . . ."

"Call me Victor."

"All right, Victor. This hotel can carry the load for itself and the others if need be—that is if you decide to keep Stockton and Oakland."

"I can hardly believe we 're looking at bankruptcy!" Victor interrupted, dazed.

'The income is here, Victor. All you need to do is plug up the holes," Anne said reassuringly. "I'm almost finished, so if you will keep your sister out of my hair, we can get on with it. She may feel Mr. Hilton is a Beast and I don't know what their problems are, but I want nothing to do with it. Neither do I want to listen." Anne stopped to pick up the phone.

It was Mrs. Newsome. "My deeear, have you been divorced?" She asked Anne.

"Yes, Mrs. Newsome. I have been divorced. Anything else?"

Anne looked at Victor for help. "I had a talk with God this morning," Mrs. Newsome continued. "I cannot have a divorced woman working for me." Anne handed Victor the phone.

"What's the trouble, Sis?" He asked. There was a long waiting period, then Victor said, "I'll be right up, and Sis, don't call this room again. The lady is working. There's a great deal to be done and it doesn't help matters to be calling here. I don't care." He said in response to something she said. Then, "Look, we're dependent on her report for the loan we need."

Victor hung up the phone and left the office.

A few days, Victor fired Bill. It seemed that as long as Anne was there, Victor was in no hurry to hire an accountant. Jim Ryder had an even greater dislike of Anne.

Victor and Anne went to the bank for new signature cards. Victor's signature was now required on checks along with Ryder's. Mrs. Newsome was no longer a signator.

As Anne and Victor were leaving the bank, Victor stopped, suddenly turned back and said, "I think I'd better take out some insurance in case something happens. Anne, you are bonded, aren't you?" He asked.

"Of course," Anne replied.

"Good. We'll just put your signature on this account," he said.

"In case we should need it," he told the banker, "we'll just set up a card in Mrs. Courtney's name."

Victor took Mrs. Newsome back to San Francisco, while Anne started to work bailing the hotel out of its financial debacle. Then she notified the firm that she had decided to stay with the hotel until they found a new accountant.

Anne did the banking and kept close tabs on everything. She was somewhat surprised that checks were not cashed but was too busy with other matters to worry. She was amazed at the amount of money that little hotel was generating every month, when it all went through the books. Mrs. Newsome no longer had check writing privileges. Anne wrote and signed checks, made up a stamped addressed envelope, clipped the checks to the outside so Ryder could sign them and his secretary could mail them.

Anne had written letters to the creditors advising them of the reorganization and asking for their patience, and assuring them all outstanding accounts would be paid in full.

There was a diversion from the auditing business. Two basketball teams were staying in the hotel. During a pillow fight, one boy had a heart attack and died. No one was aware of his heart condition.

As Mr. Ryder did not live in the hotel, Anne was called to take care of the matter. She called the police. The incident distressed her deeply.

She had intended to look into the cause of merchant checks not being cashed by those who had claimed to be hard-pressed.

The utilities and telephone canceled checks were in, as were the payroll checks. No other canceled checks were in.

In getting the hotel on a paying basis, Anne paid the food accounts off first. They had to be her first priority. Two months had gone by since Anne had sent letters out to creditors.

She had received a call from two or three and she told them the checks were in the mail. Six weeks went by and there was an increase in calls. Mrs. Newsome called one night. She needed money to buy cradles for unwed mothers.

The following day she called again. She needed money for the Poor Clares, a charity she supported. She had to make compensation for hiring a divorced woman! She said. "My God, what next," she wondered.

On Monday morning Anne came into the office to find the bread man waiting for her.

"We must have cash or there will be no more deliveries," he told her.

"This is unheard of," Anne said. "Those checks have been sent out. Our account with you is current. Why don't you people cash your checks?"

"I'm sorry, but I can't leave anymore bread until your bill is paid in full."

"But your bill is paid!" She told him.

"I'm sorry, Ma'm, but the boss said, no money, no bread."

Anne couldn't believe this. She looked at the check register. There were entries to the Bread Company.

Then as though a light went on, she said, "Come with me." She started for Ryder's office. She didn't want to believe what it seemed she was forced to believe.

She opened the door to Ryder's office. He was sitting at his desk, feet on top, discussing cloud formations with his secretary.

"Mr. Ryder! Where are the checks I gave you to sign and mail?" Anne asked.

He looked at Anne with a malicious grin on his face. Then he slowly took his feet off the desk and opened the middle drawer.

"You mean these damn things are checks?"

Inside the drawer were the checks, just as she had given them to him, still unsigned.

"That's pretty obvious, Mr. Ryder" she kicked his chair out of the way. As it bounced off the wall she gathered the checks and started to leave. At the door she turned back and said, "For your information, Mr. Ryder, I don't need your signature on these checks. I left the space open to save face for you with your employees and the townspeople. Since you cannot appreciate the gesture, I suggest you call San Francisco and resign. Because as soon as I get these checks out I will call San Francisco and you can bet on this, you won't be here long!"

She gave the bread man his checks and he left the bread for that day. She put the rest of the checks in the mail. Then she headed upstairs and called Victor.

"He just resigned," Victor greeted her. "Looks like you have a hotel to run."

"Victor, I'm sure I'll never be happy here. Get yourself someone else."

"Ah, come on, Anne. Consider it a challenge," he laughed.

"Temporarily, Victor. Only temporarily." Anne knew that with Mrs. Newsome, it would only be temporary.

As was Anne's habit, she held a meeting of the department heads. The chef, Walter, was one of those favored persons every hotel seemed to have. The bar manager was a very able young man though somewhat lacking in the personality department. Anne would have liked a more outgoing bar man. His wife sat at the end of the bar every night, something Anne had little tolerance for since it discouraged women from coming into the bar. The housekeeper, suffering from the malady of all housekeepers, had no replacement of linens and had to do mending upon mending. She became acrimonious. The engineer/maintenance man was a fine gentleman, going out of his way to help whenever he could.

Business in the food department was good, which was surprising for the food was not at all up to standard.

She asked that inventories be turned in from all departments. The hotel was well on its way to being out of debt but still had to operate on a tight budget.

Mrs. Newsome cut back her weekly visits to once a month. She continued her church going routine, dripping in black and rosaries. Each morning after she returned from Mass, she would find Anne and as sorrowful as Our Lady, she would say, "Anne, I've had a talk with God. He said you would have to fire Leona, or Jane, or Maria, or Ardith."

"I'm sorry, Mrs. Newsome. I'll have to have a talk with Him myself and see if we can't have a better understanding. I'm sure He knows Ardith, Jane, Maria or Leona have families to support. I'm sure he'll understand."

"He was quite adamant!"

"I'll have a talk with him, Mrs. Newsome."

Then Victor would come up and take her back to San Francisco.

The next time Mrs. Newsome came up, she would look around and say to Anne, "I thought I told you to fire that girl, Anne?"

"I believe you said God was unhappy with her. I talked to Him and explained how things were. He quite understands that she should have another chance."

Then, she would go to Mass and someone else was in hot water.

Victor hoped to make Mrs. Newsome's eldest son general manager of the chain and sent him to Anne for training in hotel management. He was young, handsome and intelligent. But when he became acquainted with the ranchers and stockmen of the area, hotel management flew out of the window for him. He found kinship with the men of the earth and field. After that he could never happy cooped up in a hotel. He wanted the lifestyle, he confided to Anne, of these men who made things grow and raised stock. He was a joy to have around as his mind was starved for the exploration of ideas and he would talk far into the night of metaphysics, gods and devils, ethics and the lack thereof

Anne was satisfied with the general operation of the hotel. The little hotel was out of debt. Anne worked out a financial plan to get the others out of debt, but she preferred to stay at the Marysville Hotel. She was not yet satisfied with the food operation. Generally, she would tackle this department first but in Marysville, she had been obliged to put that on hold. Now she was ready.

She was not happy with the kitchen or the quality of food that was being served. Walter would never make a good chef, though he was a nice personable man. She did not question Victor about keeping Walter on staff. She just decided to make the best of it, there was a very fine young Chinese man, Kim, would make an excellent chef. She would find other work for Walter and leave Kim to do the cooking.

The dining room, which had not been in use, was remodeled and opened. The bar was remodeled into a motif of the hunting area around Marysville. The coffee shop was done over. The kitchen was clean and well set up. After one month of managing the hotel, Anne offered to help Walter with the inventory. This would give them a chance to talk. Walter welcomed the help since he planned to get away for the weekend. Anne found to her amazement the well-kept storerooms and records Walter kept. This gave her an idea.

"You know, Walter, I think we could use an executive chef here. I don't know how you have time to keep everything so orderly with all the work you have to do in the kitchen. How do you do it alone?"

"Well, Anne, a man has to do what he as to do. But as for executive chef well, I'm afraid it would cost too much."

"Not if you wouldn't mind waiting about a month for your raise. Maybe not even that long. I'll talk to Victor. Kim could do the kitchen and you would be much greater help to me that way."

"Me? But Anne, I wouldn't know what to do."

"I'll teach you. You're doing much of it now. You would consider being executive chef wouldn't you?" Anne held her breath, waiting for his answer.

"Do you really think Victor would go for it?"

"Of course he will. He thinks a lot of you."

"Well, if you think"

"That's sealed then. You can start turning things over to Kim. I'll instruct you. You're already doing it and just don't know it. We'll refine the making of menus a little."

No sooner said than done. Victor, realizing what Anne was doing, just laughed and told her to go ahead.

Management seemed to have its devious side.

Anne made sure announcements were sent out to all the trade papers and journals. She made Kim chef and the food improved. It was not long before the Marysville Hotel had a reputation for good dining.

San Francisco also found Anne an accountant a chartered accountant from Great Briton. Anne was reminded of the time she had been sent to the south area of San Francisco during her auditing period with the firm. She was to audit a restaurant supply house. The records were kept in Chinese, audit proof they thought. They weren't. She reconstructed a duplicate set of books. She set up a duplicate set again. For she could not decipher Mr. Treacher's writing.

Anne was in the office going over these books when Walter came to the open door.

"I'd like to talk to you in private, Anne."

"Certainly, Walter. Come in and close the door." She put her books aside. "What can I do for you? You are happy in your job, aren't you?" She asked.

"Anne, I have something to tell you."

"What's wrong, Walter? It can't be as bad as you look." She smiled at him.

"I'm sorry . . . after all you've done for me . . . you understand, don't you?"

"Understand what, Walter?"

"When a man has an opportunity to better himself . . . and I have to think of my family."

"I think a person should always look to better themselves, Walter. But what is this?"

'Well, I hate to do this to you, but I've had an offer from the Elk's Club in San Francisco to be chef there."

Anne's hands were folded on the desk. She looked at them as she counted to ten. She sighed and counted to ten again. "Yes. Yes, Walter. I do understand." She knew that sigh meant to him, "What on earth will you do without me?" While to Anne, it meant, "Thank God this expense is off my back." It was worth it from the standpoint of improved food and revenues.

She sighed again. "When do they want you?"

"The first . . ."

"You'll have to tell Victor. I couldn't. But I wouldn't feel right holding you back and I'm sure he wouldn't either. I suppose the money's better"

"Double, Anne." He was wringing his hands. Anne sighed. Then decided she had better not overdo this.

"My family . . . I have to think of my family . . ."

"Of course you do, Walter." Anne rose from her desk and pushed the phone to Walter. "Call Victor," she told him and left the office.

Victor was happy that Anne did not ask for another executive chef. He had seen through her ploy.

It had been another year. In that year the hotel was out of debt, without taking out a loan. The hotels in Stockton, Oakland and Santa Cruz were also free of debt. Mrs. Newsome had gone on salary instead of a draw and that was a great savings in itself.

Victor was making the rounds of hotels in South Carolina when Mrs. Newsome came to Marysville. She had had her talk with God. Her hotels were debt-free and refurbished. The Marysville Hotel had made that possible, but now God had told her she could no longer tolerate having a divorced woman in her company.

Anne returned to San Francisco. She had done a good job, one she could be proud of. It was time to move on.

It was Anne's birthday and a friend took her to dinner and dancing at the Fairmont Hotel.

At a table next to them sat Walter with a group of men.

"Anne! Anne! What are you doing in San Francisco?" Walter jumped up and shook hands with her and Sam.

"You two know each other?" She asked.

"Yes, Sam and I have been acquainted for a while," Walter told her.

"Well, Sam is trying to convince that I should go into the Merchant Marine. What do you think of that?" Anne asked.

"It might be a good idea. Are you still in Marysville?"

"No. I believe Mrs. Newsome is in charge until Victor gets back from South Carolina."

"You're with the President Lines, aren't you Sam?" Walter asked, pulling up a chair.

"Yes. Madre'd on the Wilson."

"That would be something different for you, wouldn't it Anne? Is that what you'd like to do?"

"I don't know, Walter. I don't know what I want to do right now."

"Well, if you make up your mind that you do want to go . . ." He took a card from his billfold. "I'm with Matson, now. Go see this woman," he wrote a name on the back of another card, "at the Marine Cooks and Stewards Union. You'll be turned down. Then you go back down to the lobby. There's a phone there. Call me and wait. The Monterey is sailing on Sunday. If you want on it, you'll be on board. See you."

Walter left the table and went back to his friends. Anne didn't know what to think.

The next morning she went to see Mr. Dahl at the Sir Francis Drake. She told him of Walter's offer.

"Anne, hotel management is changing. It's being taken over by the corporations. Even in your Montana, things are not the same. Western is going in there. I don't think the changes will be to your liking anymore than it is to mine. We're of the old school where managers managed. Hotel management is going to be by memo from Boston, New York and Memphis. It isn't management anymore. It's whipping boy. Yes, even women can be managers now. They're cheaper to hire. They can be had for a clerk's pay. I think going to sea for awhile might be a good idea, Anne. You can see something of the world and when you're ready, you can buy or lease a small hotel of your own."

The following Sunday, at eleven A.M., Anne sailed on the S.S. Monterey . . .